Cub Creek

A Virginia Country Roads Novel

Cub Creek

by

Grace Greene

A Virginia Country Roads Novel

Kersey Creek Books
P.O. Box 6054
Ashland, VA 23005

Cub Creek
Copyright © 2014 Grace Greene
All rights reserved.

Virginia Country Roads (series name)
Copyright © 2014 Grace Greene
All rights reserved.

Cover Design by Grace Greene

Trade Paperback Release: March 2014
ISBN-13: 978-0-9884714-4-3
ISBN-10: 0988471442
Digital Release: April 2014
ISBN-13: 978-0-9884714-5-0

DEDICATION

Cub Creek is dedicated to those who don't fit in, who follow their own path despite the doubts of others and even in the face of their own fears because they must, because it is their path, and who sometimes fall into self-doubt and get lost.

When in that valley where the shadows are deepest, it is the memory of the light on the other side, and faith that the light will be there, that keeps them moving forward.

Cub Creek is dedicated to those who may need encouragement and to those who encourage—those who hold the light.

The waters of Cub Creek, like people, run deep. There's always more happening below than what we see on the surface.

ACKNOWLEDGEMENT

My love and sincere appreciation to my husband, family and friends for their encouragement and support.

A special thank you to my mom who always believed in me, and believed I could do anything I set my mind to.

From Wikipedia: Synesthesia is a neurological phenomenon in which stimulation of one sensory or cognitive pathway leads to automatic, involuntary experiences in a second sensory or cognitive pathway. [March 2014]

Books by Grace Greene

Emerald Isle Novels

BEACH RENTAL
Emerald Isle #1
BEACH WINDS
Emerald Isle #2

Virginia Country Roads Novels

KINCAID'S HOPE
A STRANGER IN WYNNEDOWER
CUB CREEK

CUB CREEK

In the heart of Virginia, where the forests hide secrets and the creeks run strong and deep ~

Libbie Havens doesn't need anyone. When she chances upon the secluded house on Cub Creek she buys it. She'll prove to her cousin Liz, and other doubters, that she can rise above her past and live happily and successfully on her own terms.

Libbie has emotional problems born of a troubled childhood. Raised by a grandmother she could never please, Libbie is more comfortable *not* being comfortable with people. She knows she's different from most. She has special gifts, or curses, but are they real? Or are they products of her history and dysfunction?

At Cub Creek Libbie makes friends and attracts the romantic interest of two local men, Dan Wheeler and Jim Mitchell. Relationships with her cousin and other family members improve dramatically and Libbie experiences true happiness—until tragedy occurs.

Having lost the good things gained at Cub Creek, Libbie must find a way to overcome her troubles, to finally rise above them and seize control of her life and future, or risk losing everything, including herself.

CUB CREEK

Chapter One

One wrong turn and Libbie was lost.

The narrow country road dipped and curved through mile after mile of roadside forest, but if she kept driving south through Louisa County, she'd run into Interstate 64 eventually. She was traveling to Charlottesville to visit her cousin Liz and, given her mood today, eventually was soon enough.

The trees were closely-packed, but their branches were bare. Only the hollies and evergreens had color. As she rounded a sharp bend the vista opened and a horse farm came into view.

Clean white fences stretched across the pastures. A huge barn, faded red and picture-perfect, graced the crest of the hill. Before her foot hit the brake, Libbie was already grabbing her camera.

The shoulder was narrow and the ditch was deep. She angled the car across the oncoming lane to the far side. The tires hit the wide, grassy verge with a short, heart-jolting skid. When her car stopped, the bumper was kissing the black metal of a For Sale sign—now a tilted For Sale sign.

A close call, but no harm was done. Libbie held her breath, then slowly released it.

The lawn sloped upward to a two-storied white house.

She lowered the car window a few inches.

The air was cool, but very mild for February. She closed her eyes and breathed in the sharp, clean smell of pine tags and damp earth.

Tall trees framed the wide yard and continued around

behind the house. The house was old, but its lines were straight and true. Add that gorgeous view from across the road and this was a win-win for whoever lived here—if anyone did.

No porch furniture. No personal objects in the yard. Was it vacant? A car was parked at the top of the driveway with a sign on the driver's side door.

Libbie opened her door. Below, the tires had gouged the soft earth and mangled the turf. When she looked up a thin man with white hair was standing on the porch.

He descended the steps and strode down the hill.

The ruined grass was an indictment. She exited the car and stood, tense and waiting.

His eyes settled on the car. It was dinged and dented and nothing special, then on her person, again nothing special. She brushed at her blouse wishing the wrinkles away. When she reached up to tuck her long, unruly hair back behind her ears she realized she was still holding the camera.

"Ma'am, you okay?" The man squinted and the crow's feet around his eyes deepened.

She gestured at the damage. "I didn't realize the ground was so wet. I think the sign's okay."

"Had to stop fast, did you?"

"The horse farm caught my attention." She shrugged. "I wanted to get a shot."

"Fancy equipment. You a photographer?"

After a brief hesitation, Libbie nodded, then said, "Sorry about your grass."

"Not my grass. The property went on the market today. I'm the Realtor."

His expression and tone were friendly. Obviously, he wasn't angry. Relieved, she relaxed.

"It's a nice-looking house. It has…presence."

"Presence and fifteen acres of woods. It's a wonder the owner didn't sell the timber before listing the house and land."

"Did he move away?"

"No, he lives out west. He inherited the house and property when his mother passed." He shook his head. "Mrs. Carson would never have sold the timber, but her son's a different equation."

"I see." But she didn't. He spoke about these people as if she should know them, as if she should care about them. Libbie clutched her camera, feeling stiff again and glad to have somewhere to put her hands.

The man continued, "Properties like this usually get a contract before the sign goes up. This one'll go fast, probably to someone who'll turn it into a subdivision."

A subdivision. The thick woods, the stately house and the blessed privacy—it could be devastated in an instant. Once gone, you could never get it back. She knew that personally. Anxiety slapped her across the face.

"How much?"

"Ma'am?"

"What's the asking price?"

He pulled a paper flyer from a tube attached to the sign and handed it to her.

An argument was raging full force in her head. She tried to shut it down by ignoring it.

"Can I see inside?"

He took a quick glance back over his shoulder. "Can't stay long. I promised my wife and grandkids I wouldn't be late." He extended his hand and they shook. "Name's Sam Graham."

"I'm Libbie Havens."

"Aren't you chilly, Ms. Havens?" Mr. Graham was

wearing a light jacket.

"My sweater's in the car." She put the camera on the back floorboard, grabbed her sweater and put it around her shoulders as they walked up the slope.

The trees on either side stretched around the property like a barrier to the world.

She wanted it.

No, you don't want it. You live in the city and always have. Why would you want an old house out here in the woods?

"It's old," she said, as she followed him up the two steps to the porch.

He nodded. "It is, but well-maintained. Been in the same family since it was built." He paused to unlock the box on the doorknob. "Can't say that about much, can you?" He opened the door. "Old-fashioned, but solid."

He swept his arm in a gallant gesture. "After you."

Just beyond the threshold Libbie paused and placed her hand flat against the bare wall.

She held her breath and waited. A sense of wellness and a gentle flush of peach and gold, softly warm, flashed from her hand to her head. The sensation and colors might only exist in her imagination, as some insisted, but they reassured her nonetheless. She walked on into the foyer.

He asked, "Are you okay?"

Had he noticed what she'd done? She smiled to cover her awkwardness. "I'm fine."

"Yes ma'am. In fact, you look happy."

Oddly enough, she felt happy.

The city, with its constant noise and crowds, confused her, but it had never occurred to her that the solution was to live in the middle of nowhere.

Crazy or not, she found herself actually examining the

interior of the house.

The foyer or hallway ran directly back, past the stairs on the right. On either side of the entry way were large, square rooms with many windows. Lots of light and no unexpected shadows in the corners. The wood floors had scarring and uneven wear. The walls were grim, begging for fresh paint and wallpaper stripping. Fireplaces anchored each end.

Mr. Graham continued speaking as she went ahead to the kitchen. It was old but usable with white porcelain appliances and faded linoleum.

She looked in the fridge and rubbed at a spot on the stovetop where the enamel had worn through.

They walked into the dining room and then through the French doors to a screened porch with green wicker furniture.

He checked his watch and frowned. "Are you seriously interested in buying this property?"

"I think I am."

"Do you have a Realtor?"

Libbie shrugged. "I didn't know I was in the market."

"If you're serious about this, put down a deposit. A check will do. That'll hold it while you look into financing."

"Financing won't be a problem."

He eyed the scuffed and stained sneakers, her non-designer jeans, the wrinkled shirt and the hair that curled and fought to do its own thing. She saw the spark in his eyes when he decided where to pigeon-hole her—eccentric. She didn't mind. That was kinder than most.

When it came to people in general and some in particular, Libbie didn't like them any better than they liked her. But eccentric? That she could do, and with style.

"Ms. Havens, I don't usually suggest this. Put down that deposit. When I get another offer, you can either walk away or pull the trigger."

A day or two to think it through? Already, the internal pressure was easing off.

"Take some time to discuss it with your people. Do you have family? Husband and kids?"

"No." That wasn't quite true. "A cousin. I'm close to my cousin and her family."

Mr. Graham lowered his voice. "Not to dissuade you, but I'm pretty sure you're a city gal and it's mighty...well, lonesome, out here on your own, especially at night."

He waved his hands as if dismissing the words he'd just uttered. "Not my place to say, of course, but I have a wife and daughters. I'd ask them to think about it twice, too."

"I appreciate your concern. I'm a solitary person. I'm fine alone."

"Mind if I ask what brought you here?"

"I was going to Charlottesville. I took a wrong turn."

"Humph. Well, I'd call that coincidence. Or providence."

"Maybe fate." She stopped. "What's this area called?"

"You're on Cub Creek Loop at the old Carson place."

He pointed toward the house and then down the road. An old concrete bridge was half-hidden by the curve.

"It runs through the property and under the bridges at both ends of the Loop. Cub Creek. Watch out. It doesn't look all that impressive, but the water's deep and it runs fast."

He jingled his keys. "I've got the paperwork in the car. If you've got a check, then we have a deal. At least, a temporary one."

****

He left. Libbie stayed. She wanted to see the place alone.

She stared at the road because she knew that when she turned around she'd see nothing special, just an old house with a patchy lawn. The flaws would be obvious.

This was a big decision—a huge, potentially life-altering decision—but no worries. She'd walk away from this as she did from every commitment. She did, however, like to know what she was walking away from.

It looked even better. The house sat atop that slope like a crown. The white clapboards, brushed by the late afternoon light, wore a sheen of burnished gold.

What would Liz say?

Libbie snapped a few photos of the house, the yard and the view across the street, then she slung the camera strap over her shoulder and walked around back.

The kitchen door was locked, but not the screened porch door. The hook on the inside wasn't secured. She settled for a sit-down on the porch swing. The swing's back was curved. She rested her head against it. The narrow, tight-fitting boards overhead were painted light green. The porch floor was gray and the wicker furniture was dark green.

Serene.

Unseen birds chirped. A squirrel ran across the yard, then paused by an oak tree to nibble on a tiny something.

Peaceful. Idyllic.

She tried to empty her mind, to leave it open to sounds, smells, emotions—whatever might tell her if anything negative lingered here.

She waited, growing more relaxed. Her breathing slowed.

Crack.

It snapped directly behind her. A branch? A stick? She jumped. The swing swayed wildly. She struggled for balance.

"Ma'am?"

Had she dozed off? Apparently. The noise may have come from behind her, but the voice came from the other side. A man, some sort of cop judging by his uniform, was standing a few yards away. Further back stood another man, not in uniform, but the details were softened by the screen between them.

"Officer?"

"Deputy." He touched his brimmed hat. "I saw the car. Everything okay?"

"Yes, fine. You startled me. I'm taking a look at the place. It's for sale." That sounded foolish. He already knew, of course.

"Yes, ma'am. We try to keep an eye on vacant houses."

Her arms prickled. Libbie rubbed her hands along her sleeves.

Had she truly heard that noise? That snapping sound? She resisted turning and instead focused on dealing with the men in front of her.

"We'll be moving on. Will you be staying long?"

"No, I'm leaving soon."

He touched his hat. "Have a good day."

The other man nodded. They walked away, turning the corner of the house. As soon as they were out of sight, she spun around to stare at the woods nearest the porch.

There was nothing to see and nothing to explain the noise. The trees and undergrowth were winter-lean. Some natural noise must have gotten caught up in a snippet of dream while she napped.

She checked the time on her phone. Too late now to make Liz's house by suppertime. Liz would be annoyed, but she'd get over it.

Her brain was full of things to consider, but her anxiety had abated along with the contrary voices in her head.

Liz usually meant well, but they were very different people and sometimes her opinions weren't what Libbie viewed as supportive or encouraging.

Libbie wanted to think this decision through on her own.

****

The spell of the house on Cub Creek lessened with distance, allowing common sense to regain the upper hand. By the time she neared home, she regretted her impulsiveness, but Mr. Graham was a true gentleman. He would return her deposit.

The whole episode did make her think seriously about moving on. Whether to Cub Creek or elsewhere, the need to move away from here had become clear.

Her neighbor's over-large pickup truck was parked smack on the line between their assigned spots leaving her little space between it and the SUV on the other side, forcing her to squeeze her car in and then squeeze her body out. Typical thoughtlessness and arrogance. By morning, her car would have fresh dents on both sides.

She'd left the exterior light burning by the door, and there were other lights, including street lights, and her house key was in hand and ready. She slipped inside, locked the door and dropped her bags on the chair with relief. She poured a soda, grabbed a few oatmeal raisin cookies and plopped down on her flowered, overstuffed sofa to call Liz.

Her cousin answered on the first ring. "I thought you were coming to see us. The kids were disappointed."

Liz's voice was steady and low. Gentle. That's how Libbie knew she was angry. Libbie closed her eyes and slumped back against the sofa. She kicked off her shoes and pulled the rose-colored sofa throw down over her legs.

"I took a wrong turn and got lost. Besides, I told you I might come by. Might."

"That's true, but..."

"Maybe you'll visit me soon instead. It's been ages."

Liz sighed. "You never invite us."

17

"You're always busy with the kids or your friends."

"Not too busy for you."

Seemed better to let that line of conversation die before she said something rude. She changed the direction. "I may have some big news soon."

Liz's one word response was sharp. "What?"

"Nothing I can share yet."

A loud bang from next door—likely the Duncan's front door slamming—rattled the picture frames on their common wall.

Liz asked, "What was that?"

"Guess who."

"Not those people next door again?"

"None other." Libbie sat up straighter and began disarranging the blanket. "He works the night shift and leaves about now. He's probably unhappy about how I parked."

Sure enough, someone started banging on her door.

"I hear that. That's awful."

"I'd better go."

"Don't overreact, Libbie. You always do and then regret it after."

"Talk to you later, Liz." She hung up and opened the door. "Bruce?"

"You did it again. You blocked me in. I told you I'm going to get you towed."

"You can't have me towed. My car is within the lines, unlike your truck."

"I can't get in my truck. You're making me late for work."

"Your truck takes up too much space. Not my problem—except you make it my problem by parking on the line."

"You still have space on the other side."

"Needed for me to exit my car. Seriously, Bruce, either get a smaller vehicle, one you can manage, or climb in through that stupid little window in the back." She eyed his belly deliberately. "Either way, quit bothering me."

Libbie tried to close the door.

He stopped the door with his thick hand. "Move the car so I can get into my truck."

"Have your buddy on the other side move his. Now, get your hand off the door."

Bruce's face turned purple and seemed to be swelling. She remembered the phone still in her hand. She stepped back and put the phone to her ear.

"Liz? You still there?" No answer, of course. "I'm having a problem with the man next door and he's getting–"

Bruce grabbed the door knob and pulled it closed.

Libbie didn't expect to hear more from him this evening. She put the phone down a little saddened by the victory. Bruce left, yes, but why hadn't she simply moved her car so he could get into his truck the way he wanted to? A moment of her time would fix a problem she hadn't caused but had to deal with because of rude and inconsiderate people. At least, it would fix it for the moment. But she wouldn't do that because bullies were bullies. If they got away with it once, there'd be no end.

She turned in a big circle taking in the living room and dining area of her townhouse. After five years she hadn't finished hanging pictures, including the photo collections. She'd purchased no knick-knacks nor put up any curtains. Why? Because she didn't need more crap. She already had a bucketful from neighbors who weren't neighborly in a townhouse that was uninspired.

In a city crammed with people and traffic, she was alone. Couldn't even manage to get along with people on the job, time and again. So, no job. But where was the incentive? She didn't need the money and the jobs were a bore.

Upshot? If she was going to be alone, then why not do it her way and on her own terms?

She remembered the golden glow of the house on Cub Creek.

They'd say she'd lost it again. Her mind, that is.

****

The internal struggle followed her to bed. She spent a restless night at the mercy of thoughts, both eager and anxious, chasing around in her head, shrill and beyond control. She rose early, in truth giving up on sleep, and was glad to see morning. She was in the kitchen with a cup of coffee when the cell phone rang.

She knew it was him before she answered it. That's how fate worked.

Mr. Graham said, "Sorry to bother you so soon. A developer called with a substantial offer first thing this morning and wasn't happy an offer was already standing." He chuckled. "Upped his offer, in fact. Have you thought about it? Decided what to do?"

"I've thought about little else."

He cleared his throat. "No need to feel badly about rescinding the offer."

Percussion noises reverberated through the shared kitchen wall. Clanging and banging pots and pans was Mrs. Duncan's morning ritual. Presumably she was cooking, but who could tell?

They'll say you're crazy.

If living as she chose showed she was crazy, then they were right and they were invited not to share it with her. Her crazy life.

"No, sir. I'll move forward with the purchase."

Chapter Two

A sudden cold snap—but the air was fresh and bracing and proved the furnace worked well. The house had passed inspection. She held the keys. Front door, French doors and back door. Each had a knob lock and a deadbolt.

Liz was coming. Libbie saw the house through Liz's eyes. Scarred floor. Dingy paint. Faded and stained wallpaper. What did she, Libbie, see? Numerous windows, nature all around and a picturesque horse farm across the road.

The moving van would empty her townhouse in the morning and deliver the furniture and boxes here the next day. She didn't think she had a lot of stuff, but boxing it up had taught her otherwise. Most of it was junk and she would've tossed it, but then she'd have to buy more junk to replace it. The exception was the old desk and armoire. They weighed a ton and were antiques with more than sentimental value. They would grace the study.

Liz's midnight blue Benz pulled up the driveway. She let it idle for a minute before cutting off the engine and getting out. Through the window, Libbie saw her staring at the house. She knew Liz was asking herself if this could possibly, in a million unlikely years, be the place.

With the palm of her hand against the window glass, Liz eased the car door closed, but her eyes kept moving, taking in the house, the woods. Libbie shrugged her shoulders to ease the taut pinch growing in the back of her neck.

By the time Liz reached the porch, Libbie was waiting there to greet her, glad of the fresh cool air against her cheeks.

Liz asked, "You're kidding, right?"

"You cut your hair."

Liz tilted her head. The blunt ends of her straight cut brushed her jawline. "You bought a house."

"True."

"It's huge."

Libbie shrugged. "Looks bigger from the outside."

"What are you thinking?"

"Where are the kids? I thought they were coming, too."

"Fine. Have it your way. Audrey has a sleepover and Adam has soccer practice."

"Oh."

"I'm sorry you're disappointed, but we were too, when you never arrived."

"That was more than a month ago."

Liz climbed the steps. "Yes. It was the last time we saw... Rather, it was the most recent time we *didn't* see you. One more no-show."

"Not fair. You know I love to visit you, Josh and the kids." Libbie opened the door and stood aside. "I like your new cut. Maybe I should get this mop of mine trimmed." She gathered her long curly hair into a twist and held it behind her head.

Liz fixed her brown eyes on Libbie's. "Up to you."

Until now, they'd kept the banter light despite the emotion behind the words, but at this rate, it wouldn't last.

"Let me show you around. Consider this, I'm almost two hours closer to you. We can visit more often."

Liz turned away and spoke, but it was more like a low grunt, except Liz would never grunt. She said, "I'd like to ask you something. You won't get angry? Promise?"

Cautious, she answered, "Okay."

"Have you seen Dr. Raymond recently?"

"Barry Raymond? Why?" She shook her head.

"Anyone else? You know…someone you can talk to?"

Libbie crossed her arms and stared through her cousin, not wanting to see her, wishing she'd kept her words to herself.

"The past is the past. Let it go, Liz."

"I worry about you. If you blame me for anything, blame me for that."

"I'm fine. I wish you'd trust me. Let's drop it, okay?"

"Deal."

They looked at each other in shared relief. Libbie knew her cousin didn't enjoy the tension either. She shook it off and waved at the next room.

"My living room. Over there on the other side of the front door will be my study. Behind it is the dining room." She moved forward. "The kitchen is that way."

Liz was underwhelmed. "Ancient appliances, but that hardly matters. It's not like you'll be cooking."

"I'll cook. I'll learn. How hard can it be?"

Her eyebrows arched and she laughed. "I want to see that."

"Better to see than eat, I imagine." Libbie smiled. "At least for a while, but you underestimate me."

"On the contrary, you are capable of doing anything you set your mind to. That's part of your problem. You're too smart."

Part of her problem? Libbie knew what she considered to be the other part of her problem…

"But you don't have any common sense," Liz added.

And that wasn't it.

Liz had been staring out the kitchen window. Now she

23

moved into the dining room to stand in front of the multiple windows along the side wall.

"These windows are nice. Unexpected." She did a three-sixty in the middle of the room. "This is a nasty shade of gray or brown or whatever it is."

"Needs cosmetic work, but the house is sound. It has lots of potential." She waved her hand toward the ugly walls. "In fact, I have some fun ideas as to–"

"What about your job? You can't commute from here."

Liz's question hung in the air between them. Libbie tried to answer in a casual kind of way. "Oh, no worries there. I'll be telecommuting. Working remotely."

"Really?"

Doubt was in Liz's voice and its shadow was in her eyes, but she moved on anyway, heading to the front door.

Libbie followed. "Are you leaving already?"

Liz paused in the doorway. "I have to pick Josh up at the airport."

"What do you think?" She waved her arms around.

"Honestly, I don't know. Maybe if I'd ever heard you, even once, express the least interest in country living..."

She quashed her own misgivings. "I'm sorry you feel that way."

"Well, no matter what, one thing you can count on is me. I'll be rooting for you." With a smile that was more business-like than chummy, Liz tossed her head and turned away. Again, as if by appointment, her perfectly cut hair framed her cheek and brushed her jaw.

Liz. Perfect Liz. She stepped lightly down to the sidewalk. Perky Liz.

She loved her cousin and maybe envied her a little too, but perky? No, thanks.

Liz waved through the car window and backed onto the

lawn, then turned and drove down to the road crunching gravel under her tires as she went.

Libbie stayed a while longer determined to erase the doubts Liz had expressed, her own doubts, and any negativity from the premises. She wasn't stupid. She knew she might end up regretting this decision.

Take a chance, Libbie.

And she was. As she left the daylight was fading and the sunset had a hint of lavender and red as it bloomed above the horse farm and splashed some of its color across the front of her house.

Her house. She tried to imagine how it would look with her furnishings filling it.

She was ready for a change and this was a big one.

****

A neighbor was standing on the sidewalk watching as Libbie pulled into her parking space. Not Bruce this time but his wife who was not exactly his better half. Had he stationed her there to monitor the parking? No. Their pooch was nearby pooping in Libbie's grass.

Libbie waved and smiled broadly. Tomorrow morning the For Sale sign would go up on this little patch of lawn.

They'd be glad to see her gone, but that worked both ways. Maybe they could have a neighborhood celebration in the parking lot and she'd be the absentee guest of honor.

****

Mr. Graham arrived while the men were unloading the truck.

"Welcome to the county, Ms. Havens." He held out a large blue magnet with lettering on it. "This has all of the important numbers. County business numbers, emergency numbers, sheriff's office and so on."

"For my fridge."

"Yes, ma'am."

"Makes the move-in feel official."

"Ms. Havens, I hope you don't mind me saying, but I think you'll do well here. You remind me so much of Alice Carson."

"In what way?"

"Well, not in appearance, of course. She was ninety-two. It's something in your manner, in the way you express yourself." He added, "There was no woman more respected in this county than Mrs. Carson."

Mr. Graham did a bit of a head-bow, shook her hand, and left with this last sentence, "Call me if I can be of assistance."

Pretty silly, but she put that magnet on the old fridge. It felt official. That might've been the nicest welcome she'd ever received anywhere.

****

Boxes, furniture, and odds and ends were scattered throughout the rooms.

The sofa was pushed back against the double front windows on the living room side. Libbie found the rose-colored throw and arranged it neatly across the back. It was a spot of colorful tidiness in the midst of chaos. She'd personally transported her photo collection. It took a lot of trips back and forth from the car to the house to bring them inside. She placed the frames around the living room, leaning them against empty areas of wall.

The afternoon was well along before she thought about the uncovered windows.

After dark, with the lights on, anyone passing by would have prime seating for "The Libbie Show."

She owned no curtains because she'd only used blinds at the townhouse. Here, there was nothing to work with except leftover, misshapen hardware ground into the top corners of the window trim.

She dug through boxes seeking sheets, anything she could hang over the windows before the sun set. She found a lightweight blanket and stood on the back of the sofa trying to snag it onto the remaining hardware.

A board creaked on the porch.

Balanced with one foot on the cushion, the other on the sofa back, she held her breath and listened. Something was brushing against the house.

Carefully, she stepped down and back. Thin glass was between her and…what? Her heart pounded, ramping up as a louder creak sounded. She looked around for a weapon.

Someone knocked on the door.

The knob turned. The door, which she'd neglected to lock, opened. A voice called out, "Libbie? You there?"

"Liz?" She gasped.

Audrey clunked in behind her wearing small suede boots. An orange sleeping bag overflowed her arms and trailed along the floor. Liz set an overnight bag on the floor.

"I hope you don't mind us crashing your first night in the house?"

Audrey pushed her fine brown, almost red, hair out of her face and added, "It's a pajama party, Aunt Libbie. Adam has soccer practice, so it's just us girls."

"So it appears." Libbie felt like she was grinning all over.

Audrey continued up the stairs. Libbie turned to Liz, letting her delight show on her face.

Liz smiled. "I hope you don't mind."

"I'm glad to see you. Both of you."

She held up a bulging paper bag. "I've got groceries."

"Excellent. I don't have much in the way of food. Meal-type food, I mean."

Liz laughed. "Do you ever?" She headed to the kitchen.

Libbie followed her. "We could go out to eat. Not sure what's around here. Just moved in, you know."

"Ha, ha." Liz stuck her head in the fridge and then re-emerged. "You have maple syrup. I have eggs, bread and milk. Why don't I whip up some French toast?"

Libbie leaned against the doorway and hooked her thumbs in her jeans pockets.

"French toast. Not to be picky, but is that meal appropriately balanced?"

"Fresh fruit too. Strawberries and blueberries. Antioxidants. The milk is skim."

Libbie threw up her hands. "Okay. I give up. You win. I'd love French toast."

"But not yet. What can I help you with first?"

"I was trying to find sheets to cover the windows."

Liz walked back through the living room. Her shoe caught the corner of one of the framed photos.

"Oops." She pushed it back into place. "No harm done but… Are there more of these?"

"My photo collection? Sure. Ever-growing. Did I tell you about the ones I took over at Great Falls Park?"

"More roads and rails?"

She asked in such a way that Libbie wanted to deny it, but couldn't. "A few more."

"Well, different people enjoy different things." Liz sighed and moved forward into the study, done with the subject of the photographs.

She couldn't blame Liz for not being interested in the photos. It just wasn't her thing.

"Were you able to locate those sheets for the windows? You'd have to tape them up or tack them somehow." Liz turned slowly in a circle. "I have an idea."

They unpacked several of the quicker boxes and emptied others by dumping the pots, pans and utensils on the kitchen table, then cut the cardboard boxes into panels slightly wider than the window openings. They wedged them in against the glass. Liz inspected the results and brushed her hands together as in "job well done."

She said, "Not pretty, but they do the job. We'll have supper and then take care of the windows upstairs. Tomorrow we'll find a more permanent solution. I drove Josh's SUV. We've got plenty of room for some serious shopping."

Liz cooked while Libbie sorted through the kitchen stuff they'd piled on the table. They chatted. Amazing what other warm bodies could do to make a house feel homier. The atmosphere had lightened. Even the bulbs in the lamps and overhead fixtures seemed brighter.

"I'll fetch Audrey."

The front door was cracked open. She was on the porch sitting on the steps, wrapped in the rose throw—the one thing Libbie had actually taken the time to arrange.

"What are you doing outside?"

"Looking at the stars. They're bigger here."

"You mean they're brighter out in the country?"

"Yes, ma'am." She added, "Mommy didn't tell me you had a dog. I want a dog, but Mommy says no. A cat would be good too. Like maybe a kitten, you know?"

"A dog?"

"Yes, your dog."

"I don't have a dog."

"Oh."

How could one two-letter word sound so sad?

"I've never had a dog. Doesn't mean you'll never have one. Come inside. Supper's ready."

Audrey walked past, the fringe of Libbie's rose throw trailing along the porch floor. She bit her lip and held it. She wouldn't tell Audrey to put it back where it belonged. She was thirty-two. Was she already an old woman set in her ways? Shame on her. Audrey was here for a night. She could deal with it.

****

Audrey planned to sleep on the floor in her sleeping bag. Libbie had one bed but it was a big one with a luxury mattress and before long Audrey had climbed over the footboard and curled up between Libbie and her mom.

Moonlight filtered in over the top of the cardboard panel which was about a foot too short in coverage. Libbie liked the moonlight. It drained Alice Carson's faded flowered wallpaper of the little color it still had. It tried to lighten the darkest corners of the room, as if teasing their secrets from them. There were precious few secrets left in her. Her life had been on display in personal and dreadful ways for too long.

The whistle of a distant train broke the night's silence. The locomotive and boxcars were breezing through some sleepy crossing, running the same route over and over, yet each trip was new with the potential for new events. Where was it going? It was kind of cool to hear a train in the night given her predilection for such photos.

She rolled over and saw Audrey staring at her.

"Aunt Libbie, are you awake?" she whispered.

Liz didn't stir. Her light, regular breathing continued.

Libbie pushed up onto her elbow.

"What's wrong?"

"I have to go to the bathroom."

"Do you need me to take you?"

"Do you mind?"

"Nope." A trip to the bathroom was preferable to

possible alternatives.

She got out of bed and Audrey followed. She tucked her small hand into Libbie's.

The upstairs rooms were nearly empty and there was no carpeting. With the help of the moon they traversed the night landscape inside the old Carson place. She flipped on the bathroom light and Audrey disappeared inside while Libbie waited in the hallway.

No longer the old Carson place. Her place now. A niece in the bathroom surely sealed the deal. She smiled in the dark. The townhouse was the only dwelling she'd ever considered home, by her own choice, and it had been okay for a while, but almost anywhere was more welcoming than where she'd grown up.

Libbie's Place? The Havens place. Havens' Homestead? Havens' Home? She envisioned one of those signs hung at the entrance to rural driveways.

The toilet flushed and she heard the sound of tap water running in the sink, then the door opened. Mission accomplished, they walked softly back to the bed.

"Goodnight, Aunt Libbie," she said, as she settled down under the covers.

"Goodnight. Wake me if you need me."

Audrey gave a sleepy nod, then went into dreamland, just that easily. No one could sleep as soundly as a tired child. The sleep of the innocent?

If innocence was the key to a good night's sleep then it was a wonder she, Libbie, ever slept at all. Or ever would. Because sooner or later, everyone had to pay for what they'd done, mistake or otherwise.

Chapter Three

After leaving the home improvement store, they stopped at a small diner for lunch.

Audrey pushed the salt shaker across the table and said, "You aren't my real aunt, Aunt Libbie."

Liz was still in the ladies' room.

"It's called a courtesy title. I'm actually your cousin."

"You're Mommy's cousin."

"First cousin. You and I are first cousins once-removed." Simple and accurate. She thought that would end it.

After a prolonged stare with her mouth hanging slightly open, she asked, "What about Adam?"

"That's enough, Audrey." Liz was back, taking her place in the booth next to her daughter. "You already know the answer. Finish your meal, please."

Audrey pushed the salad around her plate. "Mommy said you were like sisters."

"When we were young."

"Because your mommy and daddy died."

"Audrey, eat the rest of that salad and we'll go." She folded the paper napkin into quarters and pushed it under the edge of the plate.

Liz and Libbie were cousins. Their fathers were brothers. Twins, in fact, who married on the same day and had their first and, as it turned out, their only children, daughters, within a week of each other. Libbie was the elder by a handful of days.

She looked at Liz, but Liz had arranged her face into a neutral expression. Libbie knew they wouldn't be discussing the relationship of their younger days.

They carried the purchases home. Two room-sized rugs were rolled and tied to the top of the SUV. It was going to be a bear to get them down and into the house. Libbie liked the wood floors, scars and all. She wouldn't have bothered to buy rugs if Liz hadn't insisted. But that's where she drew the line. When Liz tried to pull her into the drapery department, Libbie refused. She'd made enough decisions for one day.

Liz and she were moving boxes aside to make room for the rugs when a man spoke from the open doorway.

"You ladies need a hand?"

Libbie jumped, startled, and turned toward the voice.

The deputy.

He gestured at the SUV. "Need a hand with the rugs?"

Liz's voice rang out with a lilting tone. "Are you offering?"

"Yes, ma'am."

She walked over, smiling, and held out her hand. "Hi, I'm Liz Parker. I'm Libbie's cousin. I'm helping her get settled in."

He nodded toward Libbie. "Yes, we met a while ago. I'm Deputy Wheeler." He looked directly at her. "You're the lady who was on the screened porch, right?"

"Yes, you were checking on the house. Is that what brings you here today?" If her words or tone sounded rude, she couldn't help it. He was wearing a uniform and his car had those flashing lights on top, not currently flashing, but replete with the ability to make her feel instantly guilty. Besides, the house was no longer vacant—it was hers—and didn't need to be watched by the local police force.

"What about your friend?" Libbie asked.

"My friend?" He seemed genuinely puzzled.

"The man who was with you that day?"

"Oh." He nodded. "Jim Mitchell. He was interested in the property. Didn't know you'd already made an offer."

"I see."

"Not a problem. He has plenty to keep him busy." He reached up and removed his hat. "Today I'm checking to make sure everything's going well. Sam Graham told me you're new to the area. It's lonely out here. Wanted to make sure you were doing okay. No problems or anything."

Liz shot a look at Libbie, then turned back to the officer.

"We'd love a hand with the rugs."

Before she'd ended the sentence, Liz was already outside and crossing the yard to the vehicle. The deputy's car was parked down near the road. He waved toward the vehicle and another officer, younger, walked up to join them.

So many uniforms. Libbie had a problem with authority figures. These men seemed reasonable, almost friendly, but you could never tell what people would do. And people with power could be especially tricky. Sometimes even treacherous.

Deputy Wheeler caught her eye as he and the other officer untied the twine securing the rugs. She thought he appeared stern, but then he smiled at Liz and his dark brown eyes twinkled.

Better that he smile at her like that than at you. No complications needed, thank you.

Too true. She tried to achieve an expression of friendly reserve as she held the door open for the men. They maneuvered the first heavy roll of carpet into the hallway and then into the living room.

"Here, ma'am?"

"Yes, that's good."

They set the rug on the living room floor and did a quick glance around the room. The place was a mess. Boxes were stacked and scattered. Stuff was piled around. The dirty paint and wallpaper contributed to the air of disorder. She was glad her photo collection was turned to face the wall.

When they returned with the second rug, she asked them to set it on the study floor. Liz had disappeared, so she walked both officers back to their cruiser.

"Thank you again. I appreciate your assistance."

"Yes, ma'am. Deputy Smith and I are glad to help."

The younger man nodded. "Yes, ma'am."

She watched them drive off. "Thank goodness they're gone."

Behind her, Liz spoke. "He's cute."

"Cute? Which one?"

"Deputy Wheeler, of course."

Libbie turned to face her. "You're married, and to an excellent man, may I add?"

Liz laughed and put her arm through Libbie's. "I wasn't noticing for myself. Handsome and friendly. Useful too, and no wedding band. Seriously, your little piece of the country might have possibilities."

"No, you don't. Don't even think about it."

"Of course not." She threw her arm around Libbie's shoulders and laughed again.

****

Gone, Liz and Audrey both.

Libbie emptied boxes, straightened the linen closet and cabinets as she went, and by evening most of the boxes were flattened and stacked. The pictures still leaned against the walls, but were now turned outward so she could see them— her railroad track and road photos. Her Get-Out-Of-Town

Collection.

She still hadn't found her hammer or the plastic bag of picture hanging hardware she'd brought from the townhouse.

As the afternoon waned, she put the cardboard panels back into the windows, but left the front windows for last so that she could enjoy the view. The pink was fading to dark gray. As she leaned across the sofa with the cardboard panel in her hands, something dark and swift, barely glimpsed, raced across the front porch. She lost her footing and stumbled backward, barely missing the coffee table.

What on earth?

Shy or scared? Certainly wild. Too big to be a possum and too small to be a bear. Did they have wolves in Louisa County?

All she could find was a broom. Not a great weapon.

Libbie opened the front door. No creatures on the porch. No porch rails, so an animal could've slipped off into, or over, the bushes and escaped without difficulty.

Bracing herself against the corner column, she leaned beyond the end of the porch. In the back yard the thick trees edged up to the yard creating a prematurely deep night. Nothing would be seen there that didn't want to be seen.

Turning around, she saw something else. Across the front yard along the tree line, in an area where the shadows seemed especially dark, a figure stood. A person. In less time than it took to blink, it disappeared. He, she, or it, had slipped back into the blacker night of the forest, that's if she'd actually seen anyone. If.

She checked the locks again, then turned on the TV to shut out the quiet. Whatever had been on the porch was obviously afraid of her, and the other? Probably nothing more than lint on her eyelash.

Liz called soon after. "You doing okay?"

"Sure," Libbie said. "I enjoyed you and Audrey being here. Thanks for staying over and for the help and stuff."

"Call me if you need me."

"Thanks, Liz. Give the kids and Josh my love."

She stayed up late in solitary celebration of living alone in the middle of nowhere. By choice, no less.

Finally she gave up listening for noises, checked the locks for the twentieth time, set the alarm and went upstairs while it was still beeping. Alarms were a fact of life, like locks on doors, dishwashers, Internet and air conditioning, and she'd had it installed before moving in. The things that couldn't be seen worried her more than thoughts of intruders or Mother Nature. If a tree was going to fall on you, then it would fall. The best course was to avoid loitering under ailing trees in a wind storm.

She crawled into bed with her cell phone and kept it near at hand, just in case.

After that, she was aware of nothing more until morning.

****

The sun streamed in over the top of the cardboard panel. She woke gently and stretched, rested and relaxed. Through that same open space between the cardboard and the top of the window, a wide slice of deep blue sky was visible.

Welcome home.

Welcome to her home on Cub Creek.

Cub Creek.

She pushed up and leaned back against the pillows and headboard. She could see it clear as day as if it was already in place down by the road.

Her sign would say "Cub Creek" and it would be simple and elegant, hanging from a post by a chain. The links wouldn't be shiny, but burnished and understated. Everyone who drove past would know this was a special place.

Throwing the covers aside, she sprang from bed feeling energized. She hit the shower singing her favorite top ten while the great, old-fashioned water pressure blasted her like a massaging sauna.

Down in the kitchen, Libbie scrambled an egg and made toast with cherry preserves, then rounded it off with a glass of juice and her morning vitamins. She washed up the dishes and wiped the counter and table, humming. Finished, she picked up the trash bag to carry it out.

Something had already been in the trash cans.

Knocked over. Lids off and in the dirt.

The garbage was strewn on the ground. Scraps of torn paper, shards of a broken vase, crumpled napkins sticky with syrup mixed with fragments of eggshells, and more. The hungry creature, maybe last night's porch visitor, hadn't found much, but Libbie had learned a lesson. Next time these lids would be on tight. Real tight.

Now what? No one else was going to clean up the mess.

A rake would be handy.

There were tools in the garage. Unlike the house that had been totally emptied, the garage was full of bent, dusty boxes and rusty tools. No one had bothered to take anything or even to steal them. All junk. As for the garage itself, the paint was peeling on the drop door and rot was rampant around the bottom edges of the building.

The garage door key was in the house, but she didn't need it because the knob on the side door turned. She could've sworn she'd locked it.

She stared into the unlit interior. The dark, old dirt smell assaulted her nose, forcing the memory of Grandmother's basement to surface in her brain.

Not a happy memory, but not far off the mark, at least the first time Libbie was there.

When they were six, while the adults were visiting upstairs, Liz and she had sneaked down the narrow stairs. Surely it was some fairy tale or other that had given the basement special appeal, like maybe a story about a dungeon or magical tunnel or such. Libbie no longer remembered what inspired them. It hadn't been Liz's fault, she remembered that much. It had been her own idea.

The whispering and giggling gave them away. A maid found them, ushered them up the stairs and escorted them directly to Grandmother. Grandmother probably didn't care about the basement adventure, but their actions interrupted her chat with Uncle Phil. Her eyes turned cold and her lips disappeared as she pressed them together.

Libbie knew that the longer it took for words to make it past those thin lips, the worse it would be.

They were in big trouble.

As Grandmother opened her mouth to speak, Uncle Phil jumped in. He laughed, appearing unaware of his mother's ire, and led them back into the basement, talking about how he and his brother, Libbie's dad, had played there when they were kids. Uncle Phil's voice came back to her...*Where'd those pirates go? I'm sure I remember a monster or two hiding down here.* He waved his arms around. *Looks like they're all gone.*

The girls were wide-eyed. Libbie wanted to see those pirates. *Are you sure, Uncle Phil? Will they come back?*

Her cousin Liz cried. Uncle Phil winked at Libbie, but picked up his daughter and hugged her. He distracted her by pointing out the old coal chute. The ground there was black and the area was hemmed in by half-walls on either side, creating dense shadows. The exterior opening to the chute had been sealed off many decades before and the coal heaps were long gone. There was little else in the basement, just unwanted cast-offs not worth the cost of paying someone to haul them to the dump.

It was Liz's last visit to Grandmother's basement, but not Libbie's and she didn't need this garage to remind her. She closed the door. Anything in there could stay where it was.

She scraped up the garbage with her bare hands. The hard gray dirt offered up no paw prints or other clues.

Before leaving the house, she made a list, checked it twice, and tucked it into her pocket. She had stuff to buy, including bungee cords with hooks.

****

She drove in the other direction today, away from Charlottesville and toward Mineral, with her destination the town of Louisa.

In town, old shops with antiques, used books and thrift items lined the road. Around the corner were newer, less quaint stores and restaurants. A large cemetery was on the right side near the train tracks. She pulled into an open-air old-style mall and found the hardware store.

For the large portrait of her ancestress, she might need a Molly bolt, but for the photo collections in their lightweight aluminum frames, simple picture hanging brackets and nails should work.

Libbie selected a bunch of paint chips. A neutral color in the living room would play well with the framed photos, but she wanted something bright in the kitchen. When it came to color choices for the rest of the house she was open to ideas. For now, a couple of gallons of Adobe Tan would get her started, along with brushes, painter's tape and spackling.

A tall man with dark hair caught her eye. He was standing at the counter waiting his turn. His eyes were on her and even from across the room, his gaze drew her attention.

He nodded. She offered a small, quick smile to be polite, but then moved around the end cap to another aisle, suddenly shy and not wanting to seem like she was offering encouragement.

Stupid to get so worked up over a man's glance. Probably hadn't even been looking at her, but at someone beyond her.

While a store clerk mixed the paint she peeked back at the counter. The man was gone.

Libbie toted her purchases to the car. Ready for lunch, still she bypassed restaurants as she drove out of Louisa not wanting to sit alone in a room full of loud, chatty people.

In Mineral, she bought groceries. Across the street, in a small shopping center, she ordered barbecue and hush puppies to go.

The aroma filled the car, and alone made the trip worthwhile.

Her nose was full of the smell of barbecue as she pulled into the driveway. She walked straight up to the front door, key out.

The front door wasn't latched.

Libbie blinked and looked again. Definitely not latched.

She stood on the porch, bag of barbecue in one hand, a bag of painting supplies hung over her arm, and keys in the other hand, dumbfounded. The narrow, vertical line between door and jamb revealed no clues.

She hadn't set the alarm—she often didn't during the day—but she'd locked the door, no question.

Paralyzed by indecision, her shoes glued to the porch floor, she stood. She should ask the police to check the premises before she entered. She looked around. No help in sight.

She had her cell phone, of course, but to ask for help

from strangers? Especially strangers in uniform? She knew better.

This was a world in which one's own family couldn't be trusted most of the time.

Old locks can be tricky. You're worked up over nothing.

She'd been careless with locking up. Probably hadn't pulled the door all the way closed, that's all. Lightly, she pushed the door. It swung open a few inches more.

"Hello? Anyone here?"

No answer. The smell of barbecue wafted up and teased her nose. She stepped carefully through the door and into the foyer.

No one. Relief made her grin until she saw the woman slumped on the sofa looking withered and dead.

Chapter Four

The old woman listed slightly to the left, her fly-away white hair all out of place and her mouth hanging open. The rose throw was across her legs.

She snored.

The container of spackling slipped from the bag and hit the floor with a solid thud.

The woman's eyelids fluttered open. "Alice? Alice?"

Speechless, Libbie knelt to pick up the dropped spackling and saw the dog at the woman's feet. Gray. Short-haired. A large dog with weepy-looking eyes, so immobile he almost begged not to be seen. He fastened those sad eyes on her, but didn't make a sound.

There appeared to be no actual danger here, but this old lady and her dog had inconvenience scrawled all over them in big, bold letters.

"Alice?" She piped up again. "Where's Alice?"

Libbie spoke slowly, carefully. "Alice Carson used to live here."

The old woman pinned Libbie with her faded eyes. "Where's Alice?"

"Alice is gone."

"Gone? Gone? I can see that, can't I?" she rasped, sharp-tongued.

"I mean she's dead. She died. A few months ago."

The woman sank back against the sofa and closed her eyes. She clasped her fingers together over her face and moaned. As Libbie moved toward her, the dog rose to its feet. He made a wide arc around her and ran out through the door she'd left open.

Not only was the old woman distraught, but Libbie had let her dog escape.

She took a deep breath and tried again. "I'm sorry you found out this way."

What would she do if the woman collapsed? She looked collapsed already, deflated, wrinkle upon papery wrinkle covering thin bones.

"Can I get you something to drink?"

"I knew," she whispered. She lowered her head, shaking it slowly back and forth. "How could I not know? I forgot, that's all."

"Water? Or iced tea? Instant coffee?"

The woman didn't respond.

Libbie said, "I'll be back with a glass of water." She started for the kitchen.

"That must be Big Billy's Barbecue. I'd know that smell anywhere."

Libbie stopped mid-stride. Was the woman merely commenting or was she asking to share lunch? She saw her faded pink blouse and the bony wrists sticking out of her sleeves, and pity beat her.

"Would you like lunch?" Libbie said the words, but without invitation in her voice.

"Did you get hush puppies?"

"Yes." But only a couple.

"Rolls?"

"No."

"Oh."

She felt substandard offering the barbecue without Big Billy's rolls—an abject failure—a state with which she was well-acquainted from her years with Grandmother.

"I already have bread. I can eat just so much before it goes stale."

"Well, then." The woman seemed resigned. "No matter. A bite to eat would be welcome."

Libbie hung her jacket over the back of a chair and got plates out of the cabinet.

The woman's name was Joyce. The barbecue went further than Libbie expected, but she didn't like giving up the hush puppy. During lunch, Joyce explained she lived nearby and had walked over.

"Alice and I, we were great friends for many years. I forget sometimes she's passed because she still lives in here." She tapped her forehead. "I started walking this morning and decided I must be going to visit Alice."

"Where do you live? How far away?" She stared at the cane and her thin limbs.

"Up the road a piece. A nice walk in good weather."

"It's cold out there. Lucky for you I neglected to lock the door."

"Lucky for me I knew where the key was hid." She chuckled, more lively now. "Alice has hid that key in the same spot for forty years. Maybe more."

That sat her back in her chair. "Where's the key now?"

"I hid it again, of course, as soon as I unlocked the door. Wouldn't want to lose Alice's key. Cain't hardly get keys like that made anymore."

Libbie asked, "Where is the key hidden?"

"Where?" Joyce stared at the crumbs on her plate and shook her head slowly. "I don't recall."

Should she believe her? Her claim seemed too outrageous not to be sincere. The clock on the kitchen wall ticked, ticked, ticked as the afternoon slipped away.

Joyce sipped from her glass and smacked her lips. "Alice always had the sweetest water I ever tasted."

"Is that so?" The water seemed ordinary to Libbie. Was well water sweeter than city water?

"You can freeze bread."

Libbie glanced up at the wall clock. She'd been sidetracked. Now they were done. Freeze bread, indeed.

"It was nice to meet you, Joyce. You'll have to come back and visit another time." She didn't mean it, of course. She was giving Joyce a polite cue to leave, which the woman ignored.

Joyce's shoulders were stooped and her hands trembled.

"I'll drive you home."

She shook her head and said, "I can walk back as I came."

"No, I insist." Libbie's heart sank as she saw her afternoon slipping away. Joyce hadn't asked about her pet, so she had to volunteer the info.

"Your dog ran outside. Will he come back when he sees you leaving?"

"I don't have a dog. No dog for me. Too much work. Not allowed at the Home anyway."

Libbie shook her head. "There was a dog with you. I saw him."

"Oh, that was Alice's dog, Max. She loved that dog. Likely, he recognized me."

"Alice's dog? Alice has been dea—gone for a while."

"Guess he's been scrounging for food where he could and sleeping in the woods."

"Poor dog. I'll call the animal warden and see if they can lure him out and take him away to…to where he can get proper care."

"You mean Max?" She squinted at Libbie as if she

hadn't heard right.

"Yes. Alice's dog."

She pursed her lips then said, "I reckon he's your dog now. What did you say your name was?"

"Libbie. Short for Elizabeth."

"Libbie's dog, then. I'm pretty sure the dog comes with the house."

We'll see about that.

Joyce had left her coat on the sofa. Libbie retrieved it, helped her into it and put the cane in her hand. When they were settled in the car, Joyce pointed them north on Cub Creek Loop, then south when they reached the main road. Soon after they turned onto a private, paved road leading to Ethel's Home for Adults. It sat back a distance from the main road.

These country roads weren't designed for pedestrians.

The Home had been enlarged and elongated, like several brick ranchers lined up in a row, and converted to an assisted-living adult home. Libbie drove up the asphalt drive and maneuvered around several vehicles, one of which was a sheriff's cruiser, to get Joyce closer to the house.

"Looks like some kind of doings is going on here." Joyce pointed at the vehicles as she eased out of the car.

Libbie hadn't planned to get out. She'd intended to drop Joyce off at the curb and go back to her own life, but the front door of the house blew open and a large woman dressed in flowered scrubs flew down the ramp.

"Mizinman, mizinman." She rolled the syllables together as if they were one word.

Was she saying "Ms. Inman" or "Ms. Zinman"? She was a large person, but she moved quickly, fluidly.

"Well, hey there, Agnes." Joyce waved a thin hand and turned to close the car door.

"Where've you been? We called the sheriff and all. You walk off into those woods again and again and I don't know what all could 'a happened. You cain't go off like that, Mizinman."

"I went to visit Alice." She gestured in Libbie's direction.

Libbie shook her head *no*, but was distracted by the sheriff coming out onto the front porch.

Agnes insisted, "You cain't go off like that." She eyed Libbie accusingly, adding, "She isn't supposed to go anywhere without notifying the supervisor. Mizhuges has to authorize her to go off the premises."

"For your information, I'm not—"

Agnes ignored her. She didn't care who Libbie was or wasn't. She held Joyce by the arm and ushered her up the ramp. Agnes' hustle was in direct contrast to Joyce's creeping walk. They couldn't fit side by side. Agnes followed with a rocking gait, appearing to herd Joyce up the ramp. They stopped to exchange words with the officer. He nodded and patted Joyce on the arm.

The man in the sheriff's hat walked down the ramp and he was heading her way.

He was broad-shouldered and walked with a purposeful stride. Libbie couldn't read his intent from this distance, but she knew him. He wasn't the sheriff. He was the nice, helpful, house-watching, rug-toting deputy.

She felt stuck, but why? She'd done nothing wrong. In fact, she was the one who'd been inconvenienced.

"Ms. Inman had everyone worried." He spoke the words in a measured tone. "Folks were out searching. Agnes said Joyce Inman was visiting you. I thought you didn't know anyone around here?"

"I don't and, correction, Joyce told Agnes she was

visiting Alice."

"That so?" He shook his head. "I guess she surprised you." As his serious demeanor dropped away, his eyes became a gentler, warmer shade of brown and the corners of his lips turned up.

He had a pleasant face when he smiled. It was a mere piece of a smile and she was disturbed that her own lips tried to mirror the curve of his. She spoke more sternly to cover her weakness.

"Yes, she did surprise me. I fed her and drove her back. That wasn't an easy walk. Walking along that road must be dangerous."

Deputy Wheeler nodded. "Yes, ma'am. She probably took the path through the woods. You might not know about that. She's been walking that path for years, but it's still a long way. You should encourage her not to walk there anymore. If something happened no one would know, not 'til too late."

"What? You think she'll come again?"

"She's been walking that path to visit Alice Carson for a lot of years. If she can get past the supervisor, she'll probably be taking it to visit you." He nodded his head. "Excuse me, I need to let people know that Ms. Inman is back home, safe and sound."

Libbie drove away, thoroughly annoyed. The best part of the afternoon was shot and there was potential for future, unannounced visits.

What about the dog? Alice's dog.

Surely he'd found another home and had showed up at the house today because of Joyce. He wouldn't be back now that Joyce was gone.

For the next few hours, she spackled, sanded and cleaned up the dust, then washed her hands at the kitchen sink. She stared through the kitchen window at the woods.

Where was Joyce's path? She'd been walking it for years, the deputy had said.

When Libbie left the old folks' home after dropping Joyce off, she'd driven north, then turned onto Cub Creek Loop, passed a brick rancher on the left, a couple of overgrown dirt roads, the Pettus farm and then her driveway. Going by the road it had to be a mile or two.

How did the path run? Was it a straight shot? Or winding and twisted?

Her back yard wasn't a gateway from which uninvited, unwelcome visitors could emerge at will. It made her feel like someone was parking on her line again.

As Libbie stared, the woods darkened. The trees stood out in sharp relief as if someone had tweaked the contrast. She walked out to the back stoop. The sky was blue. No clouds were in sight. A trick of the light or a visualization of her own apprehension? Usually it meant there was something she needed to know about, but these things revealed themselves in their own good time so it did no good to worry over it.

She pulled her attention away from the woods and went back to start painting.

Amazing was the comfort to be found in a paint brush and a can of Adobe Tan. Dr. Raymond might've called it therapy. Libbie knew better. Like therapy, painting walls was merely an exercise in disguising flaws.

Chapter Five

Come Monday she'd been living in the house for a week. The grass on the front lawn was looking ragged. Twigs and pine cones had fallen and a smattering of old, dead leaves had blown in from the woods. Libbie didn't know what to do except cut it, and it needed more. With the weather warming, the yard was soon going to need a lot more.

She turned away from the window. Staring at the yard wasn't getting anything done and she had plenty yet to do inside the house.

A short time later she heard noises out front, the sound of gravel under tires and footfalls on the porch, but no knock. She returned to the front window. A white pickup truck was already backing down the driveway and to the road. It shifted quickly into drive, then sped out of sight.

She found a bright green flyer stuck in the storm door. Mitchell's Lawn and Landscaping. It was a listing of their services. Whoa. Talk about timing and coincidence.

It was early, but she dialed the phone number and left a message. Until she owned a lawn mower and knew how to use it, she needed help with the acreage.

Acreage. Now that sounded grand, didn't it?

She was determined to finish the living room and the last task was to hang the Get-Out-Of-Town Collection. The computer was on and the speakers were hooked up. She worked while Playlist #3 streamed Adele's "Someone Like You." She hung the rail group six across, four down on the largest expanse of wall, alternating the grayscale photos with the color ones.

On the exterior wall where the fireplace broke the blank surface, she hung the road group in pairs from ceiling to floor. She integrated the interstate photos with what she called the lonely road photos.

As Uncle Kracker hit the chorus to "Smile" she passed through the foyer and spun in her socks twirling on the bare wood floor.

Why? Because she felt like it. Why not?

The third wall, the one between the living room and kitchen, was reserved for her next collection: Fences. She was going to start with the horse farm across the street. Taking those photos would be a lot tamer than hugging the side rails of overpasses while trying to get the depth of field correct for the train tracks, or dodging semis for photos of the interstate highways.

Libbie taped paint chips to the walls of the study. These walls were her blank slate. She could make of them what she would. The same should've been true of the townhouse, but it hadn't. Here, she felt freedom. Unrestrained freedom.

She danced back into the foyer. She felt like she could handle anything.

After a late lunch, she picked up her camera, checked the battery level and chose a zoom lens. Her sneakers were on her feet in a flash. She donned a quilted vest to keep her arms free and she was ready for the expedition across the road.

Not a soul drove by as she stood, perched on the edge of the worn pavement. Where should she jump? The ditch on this side of the road was wide and deep. She needed a safe landing place. On the far side of the ditch, the briars, weeds and shrubby growth filled the twenty feet or so between the ditch and the cleared ground. A tricky crossing, but taking a photo from here wasn't worth the effort of pushing the button because of the angle and growth.

She could drive up Cub Creek Loop to the farm road. There was bound to be a house on the far side of the hill. She could knock on their door.

Or not. The fences were here in front of her. Was a little vegetation going to stop her?

Libbie tugged on the camera strap to double-check that it was secure around her neck. She put one hand on the camera to further secure it against her body and kept one arm free for balance as she bent her knees, focusing on the other side of the ditch, ready to go. A horn sounded. She twisted toward the sound and saw a large truck rounding the curve.

Already past the point of no return, she tumbled over, straight off the side of the road. Most of her missed the ditch, but the sticker bushes caught her. She didn't land on her camera and that was the most important thing.

As she righted herself, plucking at stickers snagged in her clothing and one in her flesh, she saw the truck had stopped. A heavy door slammed. There was a sign on the passenger side door. Mitchell's Lawn and Landscaping.

"Ma'am?"

In direct proportion to her disarray, this man was perfectly put together from his creased slacks to his crisp cotton shirt. His dark hair was arranged just so and even from the disadvantage of her current position, Libbie saw that his hazel eyes and perfect complexion might have been worth killing for. Standing awkwardly, she brushed at the dirt on her shirt and jeans and sighed in frustration.

"Are you okay?" He sacrificed his polished loafers by stepping gingerly but confidently down the slope. He tested his footing and extended his hand.

To her. Libbie.

His fingernails were better cared for than hers.

He offered, "Take my hand?"

It was him. The man who'd come to the house with the deputy. The man who'd been thinking of buying the property. That's why he'd seemed a bit familiar in the hardware store.

Wet muck was seeping through her sneakers. She stretched forward and placed her hand in his. With a strong, secure grip, he said, "Ready? On three. One, two, three, now." He pulled and she jumped. With two big steps he was back up on the road and she went with him. She was flailing, but he grabbed her arms and steadied her.

His shoes were a mess and he now had a smear of blood on his arm and dirt on his shirt, all courtesy of her, yet his attention stayed on her and she was impressed.

"You must be Ms. Havens." He smiled clear to his hazel eyes and slowly released his grip. "Steady?"

"I am. You're Mitchell's Lawn and Landscaping?" Libbie pushed her hair back from her cheek and found a long blade of grass plastered to her skin. "You're unexpected."

He laughed. "And you're agile. I'm Jim Mitchell." He nodded at the camera. "Are you a photographer? Trying to get the best angle for a photograph of your new home?"

As he spoke, he was effortlessly escorting her across the road.

"I'll pull the truck into the driveway. You should go wash up those scratches. Take your time. I'll wait on the porch."

Neat, attractive and a gentleman.

As she jogged up the lawn and ducked into the house, he maneuvered the truck and trailer back then forward again to hit the driveway at the correct angle.

She put the camera on the desk and ran back to the

bathroom. She had sticks and bits of weeds in her hair, and mud on her cheek. Her shirt sleeves looked like she'd taken a big cat on in a fight and lost. She rolled the sleeves up grateful they'd acted as a first line of defense. She splashed water on her face and dabbed at the scratches on her arm. She shook her hair, but she didn't want to take too much time because he might get the mistaken idea that she was primping for him. She was not a primper by any stretch of the imagination. Not perky and definitely not a primper.

The adhesive bandages were in the corner cabinet. She grabbed one and, on impulse, took it out to the porch.

"Can you give me a hand?"

Libbie leaned against a column and he carefully placed the bandage on her arm.

"Thank you."

"Least I can do since you had to dive for your life. I guess it was the honk."

"No harm done."

He raised an eyebrow and touched her arm. "Not exactly. Are you sure you're okay? Maybe you fell harder than you think? Did you twist anything?"

"I'm fine."

"I got your message about lawn care. Actually, I was out this way when the nursery forwarded the message so it made sense to stop by. I would've called, but you didn't leave a number. What did you have in mind?"

"For the yard? Nothing fancy. Basic weed killing and grass trimming. Maybe some mulch."

"I'll write you up an estimate and suggest a few things for you to consider. The size of the property runs up the price, but we have equipment over on this side of the county, so that'll help price-wise. Should I call you with the estimate or drop it off? Your preference."

"Either is fine."

"What's your number?"

Libbie recited her cell number, suddenly feeling stiff and awkward. She crossed her arms, uncrossed them, and then didn't know what to do with her hands. She settled for hooking her thumbs in her pockets. He was watching and no doubt realizing what an idiot she was.

He put the pen in his notebook. "I'll contact you soon."

"Sounds good. By the way, did I see you the other day? At the hardware store?"

"Yes, ma'am. Didn't think you'd noticed."

"Well, I was pretty focused on those paint chips."

"If you need the names of reliable painters, let me know."

Without another word, he walked down the steps, but as he got into the truck, he waved. It felt like a gift.

Silly girl, what about those complications you want to avoid?

There was that to consider, of course, but he was nice and it was all business anyway. He was going to cut her grass. She wondered how she felt about it being *her* grass?

He hadn't mentioned coming out here that day with the deputy—the day that changed the direction of her life. The sudden realization of the hope she had placed in that change was stunning and sobering.

She sank down onto the porch planks, placing her feet on the steps below.

How badly had Jim Mitchell wanted this property for himself? The timber, maybe? Did he already have a subdivision planned as Mr. Graham had suggested?

The scratches burned. The small ones were also chiming in. She needed to wash them properly and smear ointment on them, including the one Jim had bandaged.

Jim. Mr. Mitchell. Whatever.

Interesting hazel eyes.

****

Liz called early the next morning and wanted to bring lunch to share.

Libbie surveyed the interior with a critical eye. The furnishings were sparse, but the living room walls were freshly painted. Unfortunately, the newly painted walls highlighted the need to paint the foyer and other rooms, but this room looked and smelled fresh. Like fresh paint anyway.

She straightened a picture or two and picked up a speck from the area rug. In the kitchen she put out plates and glasses. Libbie was folding the napkins when she heard a car in the gravel drive and went to the front door.

Liz carried white bags from a Chinese restaurant, one of their favorites near where she lived in Charlottesville.

"We'll have to warm it up in the microwave anyway, so why don't you show me around first? I want to see what you've done."

Libbie gave her the tour. Liz liked the paint job, but was dismayed by the cardboard panels that showed no signs of being replaced by something classier—which would be almost anything. She seemed preoccupied. Libbie tried to be amusing.

"I'm considering covering the cardboard with flowered contact paper." She said it flippantly, but her attempt at humor fell flat. She gave up trying to cajole Liz into a better mood. "I like the windows uncovered during the day. I don't want to cover them with curtains."

"It's your house. Do as you like, but I think you're going to get tired of cardboard."

Liz ran her fingers along the glossy top of the desk and looked around at the bookcase and the portrait on the wall.

Her gaze flitted here and there, then settled back on the desk as if fascinated by the fine grain of the wood. She drew her finger along the fretwork edge and said, "Libbie, I have to ask you something. Please don't take offense or shut me down. I want you to talk to me. Okay?"

Libbie felt a chill and the stirring of claustrophobia. "So?" Her breath felt short. "What?" She stiffened her stance and crossed her arms. "I'm listening."

"You quit your job, didn't you?"

She tried to think of a satisfactory response.

"I called your work place yesterday. They didn't want to tell me anything, but after I called several times someone finally told me you no longer worked there."

Libbie felt the gulf widening. They were always on the brink of falling back into the estrangement of their teen years. It was like baggage—no, like a big steamer trunk—and they carried it around between them. Liz should be more careful of tipping the balance. Couldn't she feel the change in the air?

Apparently Liz did feel a chill because she crossed her arms. Her face paled and her lips pressed together. Libbie stared at her and she stared back. Anger helped Libbie find her words.

"Why were you checking up on me?"

"What? No! I called to talk to you about coming over here today. I wasn't checking up on you. Why would I?"

"Then why did you call there? I'd already told you I'd be working remotely—*which means not in the office*." She pointed at her. "You have my cell phone number."

Liz's bottom lip pressed up briefly in a pout. She shook her head and said, "Are you? Working, I mean? Remotely or otherwise?"

"No, and you knew it at the time we discussed it. I could

see it in your eyes, so don't pretend to be shocked. You called my employer wanting to verify it, like a game of gotcha'."

Liz sighed. "Wait, that's not what we need to talk about. It's not what I meant to say." She unfolded her arms and gestured at the room.

"Look at this! No one stood in your way when you wanted this furniture. No one dared to challenge you..."

Liz stopped for a deep breath, then continued with a calmer voice. "Maybe I was wrong to urge you to move into that townhouse. I admit that. I just thought... But now you buy this house in the middle of nowhere, and you set this room up like some kind of memorial to...to what? To Grandmother's house? With Grandmother's furniture?"

"Grandfather's. Nothing of Grandmother's."

Liz ignored her, pointing at the furnishings. "Here's the desk. There's the armoire. And what about that portrait? We don't even know who that woman is and yet she's on your wall."

"She's grandfather's mother."

Liz looked askance and asked sharply. "Do you actually know that? No, you don't."

"I believe it."

"You believe."

"Suit yourself, then. Don't believe that's Grandfather's mother. Forget the portrait. Just believe in me, Liz. Just that."

Liz closed her eyes. When she opened them, she said, "I'm sorry. I shouldn't have said what I did and not in that way." She held up her hands, as if in surrender. "I care about you. You know that. Are you going to hide here like you used to hide in Grandfather's study? Are you going to become a hermit? Will I come here one day and find you–" She broke off abruptly, pressing one hand to her cheek. With a deep breath, she resumed. "When you had a job I knew you'd be going out every day. I knew you'd be around other people."

Liz was sincere, Libbie didn't doubt that, but her concern was misplaced. This wasn't Grandmother's house and Libbie was no longer the little girl who grew up unloved. She was fine now. She was fine alone. Often, she was *better* alone.

"I enjoy solitude. You aren't like me and you don't understand. You've always been good with people. For pity's sake, you even like them. But I'm not you and I'm okay with that, with being me." That wasn't precisely true, but she badly needed it to be true.

"Libbie, I'm not being critical, but concerned. Josh said what you said, that you prefer solitude. That any problems you had were in the past, the long ago past, and I shouldn't worry. But we're family, and friends too. That gives me certain rights whether you like it or not." She stopped for a deep breath. "I won't worry, and I won't bother you about it as long as you promise me you won't be isolated. That if you feel lonely or if you are alone too much, you'll call me. And don't get so angry when I ask questions." She waited for a reaction before continuing, "And don't think you can intimidate me by looking like Clint Eastwood."

Libbie was confused. "Okay, I'm no beauty queen, but really?"

"You know what I mean. I'm talking about your 'make my day' look. Like in *Dirty Harry*?"

Libbie shook her head in disbelief. They'd been on the verge of something terrible, something awful, and Liz made a corny joke about an old movie. She didn't feel like laughing.

She said, "I need some lunch."

"Me too." Liz took a long, clearly audible breath. "And Libbie?"

"What?"

"Things are shaping up around here. You've made nice progress. Are you truly okay?"

"Yes," she said, and meant it. She wasn't a lost, lonely kid anymore. She was an adult.

When they were fourteen, when Liz's friends were her friends and no one was Libbie's, not even Uncle Phil could overcome the gulf circumstances put between them. Liz was peppy and perky. Happy. Successful. Aunt Margaret made certain she wore the right clothing and had the best haircuts. Pink pompoms hung from the dresser mirror in her bedroom. Her ambition was to make the junior varsity cheer squad.

Liz was vivid and colorful. Libbie was strictly grey tone. She couldn't compete with Liz's new friends. They visited a couple of times that year and then everyone let it go, if not by official mutual consent, then something very much like that. Libbie had never spoken of it and didn't intend to now. Some hurts were better left unexposed.

They ate lunch and when they were done, she put the dirty forks in the sink. The paper plates went into the trash can. They'd shared a reasonable meal together, but it was a relief when Liz said it was time to go.

"I'm glad you came. Don't worry about me. I'm doing fine."

Liz measured her with her gaze. "I think Josh is right and you are, too. You are fine. Still, I wish you weren't so alone here."

"To avoid being alone isn't a great reason to have a job. Think about it. It would be wrong to take a job someone else needs more than I."

"Fine. I give up." Liz laughed. "But one day you're going to run out of projects and then what will you do?" She punctuated the sentence by wagging her finger.

"When that happens you'll get to say you told me so."

Libbie watched her get into the car. She waved as her cousin drove away and spoke softly to the dust clouds left behind.

"Watch out, Liz. One of these days, you're going to have to admit you're wrong and I'm right. I can manage my own life and do it my way and do it well."

She leaned against a column and watched a squirrel run down a tree headfirst. He paused to peer at her before moving on. All was peaceful and birds sang in nearby trees. A bit of a breeze brushed her cheek.

Over by the tree line she saw the dog. Alice's dog. Doubtless that was the creature she'd glimpsed running from the porch. Audrey must've seen him too, and thought he was hers. Joyce said he came with the house.

If she moved would he run away?

Did dogs understand about death?

He was leggy, grayish and she could see his ribs, so whatever breed he was, he'd been living rough.

"Hey, boy," Libbie called out in a soft tone. He made no move either way.

Slowly she moved away from the column and went into the house. She didn't have dog food or a stew bone to toss him. What else did dogs eat? She figured steak was a good bet. She took a steak from the freezer and heated up the frying pan. He probably preferred it rare.

He wasn't in sight when she carried the paper plate outside, but she was willing to bet he wasn't far. She stood holding the plate aloft and encouraging the aroma to swirl through the air.

Libbie spoke gently to the nearby woods as she put the plate in the grass, "Well, Max. It's yours. Eat it or the possums or raccoons will get it."

The idea of the condemned man's final meal popped into her head, and it was fairly apropos. She was pretty sure she'd find the number for the county's animal control division on Mr. Graham's refrigerator magnet.

Chapter Six

Another amazingly restful night of sleep—the city noises that surrounded her all her life must have put her more on edge than she'd realized. The shenanigans with her old neighbors hadn't helped either. Or those jobs she'd tried to hold down. But now that was all in the half-forgotten past. Libbie awoke glad to greet the day and remembered Max.

After her shower, and with a cup of coffee in hand, she went to the end of the porch and scanned the lawn. The steak was gone. The plate was halfway to the woods.

"Max?" She called out trying to put a loving, welcoming tone in her voice.

No answer.

Plate in hand, she walked back to the trash can. She hadn't spent much time in the back yard. Talk about something needing a fresh start... The back yard was mostly dirt, hard-packed and too tough for grass.

Farther back, by the garage, was the old oak. The tree was huge and twisted, but appeared healthy. The garage was rotting.

She unhooked the bungee cord on the first can and dropped the plate inside.

The phone rang, vibrating in her jacket pocket. She fumbled the lid and the bungee cord as she grabbed the phone and still managed to answer it despite the juggling.

"Libbie? That you?"

Aunt Margaret. *Groan.*

"Libbie? I know you're there. Answer me."

"How did you get this number?"

"From Liz, of course. How are you? Well, I hope?"

"What do you want?"

"Have it your way." Margaret dropped all pretense of civility. "Liz told me you moved closer to her. I'm concerned for my daughter."

If she opened her mouth to speak, she might explode.

Margaret continued, "I don't want Liz to be hurt. Or the children."

"Hurt?" Libbie's voice rose higher as each word was spoken. "Why on earth would I hurt them?"

"I never said you'd do it on purpose. You attract tragedy. Look at your track record, at your history. Think about the people who've been close to you. Where are they now? How many of them are still alive?"

"Don't call back." With shaking hands, she carefully hit 'end.'

The nature of the conversation wasn't new, but she'd never get used to it.

Goodbye, Aunt Margaret. Good riddance.

Libbie wished she could call animal control on her.

In the end, she didn't. Not for Margaret or Max. She put it off. Her mood had tanked and she didn't want to talk to anyone.

Aunt Margaret. When Libbie's parents died, everyone thought she would live with Aunt Margaret and Uncle Phil. She was his only brother's only child, plus the little girls were like sisters. When she didn't, when her grandmother took her in, people said Libbie would be a comfort to her. None of it was true. The truth was that Aunt Margaret refused her and Uncle Phil allowed it. Aunt Margaret never shared her reasons with Libbie, but then, at the time, she was five and didn't understand the game.

Encounters with Aunt Margaret, even by phone, left her in an unsettled mood. She sat on the swing in the screened porch and slowly rocked.

She laid her head back and allowed the soothing air to touch her face. She tried to clear her mind, to see the good and to shake the gloom.

The surface of the screening rippled with the breeze. A bird sang. Its call was echoed back from nearby trees.

Liz would say she was staying in the house too much. Maybe she had a point.

Libbie rubbed her hands over her face and decided to get up and move on with the day. The air had a chill to it this morning. She needed another cup of coffee. The chain links squeaked as she rose from the swing. She wished she'd left the French doors unlocked. Not even the kitchen door was open. She had to walk around front to get inside the house.

He was on the porch. He was stretched out with his nose on his paws. For an instant, she thought he was waiting for her, but he was waiting for Alice. Probably always would be. He was no better than she—or she was no better than he. Always thinking she was moving forward, but one short phone call from a mean-spirited woman could put her instantly back in an emotional pit. Never better.

"Well, boy? Max?"

He raised his head. He looked disappointed.

"Are you going to run away again?"

The muscles moved in his torso, mostly bunching in his hindquarters, as if thinking he should leave, but he didn't.

"I'll get you some water. If you stay to drink it, I'll buy some dog food." If she was going to call animal control, it would be hardhearted to leave him thirsty and hungry before he was lured out and carted off.

Lured out and carted off. She didn't like the sound of that even if it was for his own good.

As she walked up the steps, Max stayed in place. She went inside, found an old bowl and filled it with water. She carried it carefully to avoid dripping. When she stepped back out to the porch, she stopped abruptly and the water sloshed over her fingers.

"Ma'am? Ms. Havens?"

"Deputy." His cruiser was in the driveway. She hadn't heard him drive up.

He saw the bowl and the now empty porch, but he didn't ask. Instead, he said, "I understand you had a mishap a couple of days ago?"

A mishap? "You mean the fall?"

"Yes, ma'am. You fell into the ditch, I heard. You weren't hurt?"

Libbie wracked her brain trying to figure out his angle. Why would he care? Had she broken a law? Reckless falling? Was Jim Mitchell worried she might sue?

"I'm fine. A couple of scratches, that's all."

He nodded toward the horse farm. "I understand you were trying to get onto the property across the street?"

She bristled. "Is there a problem with that? I suppose that's against the law?"

"Well," he scratched the back of his neck. "Technically, it is trespassing. They have the property posted, but that's mostly meant for hunters and to protect the horses, of course. Can't have anyone damaging the fences."

He seemed sincere. She tried pull back her antagonism.

"I assure you I'm not a horse rustler."

"No, ma'am. Never thought you were. I did think you were trying to take some photos. Jim mentioned the camera. Sam Graham said you liked the view, that you're a photographer, so I thought you might want to meet the owners. They're good people. I'm sure they won't mind if you take some pictures."

The idea of meeting new people voluntarily, stymied her. It brought out the worst of her discomfort with, maybe fear of, people and the potential of people for ugliness.

"I can drive you over." He gestured toward the horse farm. "I know they're home this morning."

"You mean just go over there?"

"Yes."

"I'm not dressed for meeting people." She pulled at her shirt and gestured at her jeans. The water sloshed over the lip of the bowl again, drenching her fingers. She set it down on the porch.

He removed his hat. "You look fine. We aren't dressy out in the country."

She could see in his face that he meant it. His brown eyes and the intense gaze grabbed her.

"Okay. Let me get my house key."

"Yes, ma'am."

She paused. First, the rugs, now this. She said, "If you're going to be doing favors for me, I think you should call me Libbie." She went in to fetch her key.

Outside again, she repeated, "It feels wrong to drop in on these people uninvited."

He opened the passenger side door of his cruiser. Thankfully it was the passenger side and not the back with that awful one-piece plastic seat. She'd come close to occupying one of those before and once was more than sufficient.

"Ann and Allan Pettus. Out here people drop by."

"Still…"

"Plus I mentioned I might bring you over."

She tried to shape her response instead of blurting it out. "Deputy–"

He interrupted. "If I'm going to call you Libbie, then I think you should call me Dan."

Deflated. Disarmed. Was he flirting? His expression never changed, so she decided he wasn't.

She sat back for the ride. Truth was she was apprehensive about meeting neighbors, but not as nervous as she would've been if she'd had time to think about it, so she was also grateful.

The turnoff was a short distance down the road. The roadside mailbox looked like a miniature horse stall. A flag hung below it stating, "Pettus Horse Farm."

The dirt road climbed the hill, the same hill she saw every day from her front windows. As they crested the rise, the house and stables were laid out before them.

Ann Pettus was in front of the nearest barn talking to a teenage girl with long blonde hair. Ann yelled back into the building and her husband, Allan, came out to meet Dan. Dan made the introductions quickly and simply. The girl was their daughter, Faith.

Ann and Allan were polite. Both had known Alice Carson well and expressed their sadness at her death. Their welcome seemed genuine. Ann offered to show her the stables. Libbie followed her into the darkened building. She was a petite woman with a mass of brown, curly hair pulled back into a ponytail.

The floor of the stable was hard-packed dirt and littered with pieces of straw. Libbie stepped carefully, not trusting the toilet habits of horses. Some of the horses greeted them, others kept to the back corners of their stalls. Ann introduced her to the two newest arrivals, true babies, stabled with their mothers. Faith was now in one of the stalls brushing a tall horse.

Ann explained, "Mercury is a performer. Faith rides him in shows. Most of the horses here are boarders. We exercise and train them."

The blond duo of Faith and Mercury made a striking picture. "Your daughter is a beautiful girl." The horses were nickering along stable row, watching our passing.

They walked back into the sunshine. Ann asked, "Do you have children? Husband?"

"No, it's just me."

Ann harrumphed. "Well, it was good to meet you, Libbie. Come back over here and visit when you can. If you'd like riding lessons, I'm happy to offer my services."

"I'd like to take photos of your fences."

"My fences? You photograph fences?" She looked doubtful.

"Yes. I have an interest in lines and shapes. I did a series with train tracks, for instance. Your fences caught my imagination."

"Oh, I got it. You mean like those fancy coffee table books? The ones with the big, gorgeous photos?"

A little spark flared in Libbie's chest. "Yes, like that."

"Well, you're certainly welcome. Stay on the outside of the fences, out of the pastures. Only the stable hands are allowed in with the horses. Don't want them to be startled and get hurt, or you either."

"Of course. I understand."

"Sometimes they'll act all friendly and come up along the fence to greet you, but they have big teeth and more than one horse has gotten an attitude and used them."

"They bite?"

"Knock on the door and I'll take you wherever you want to go on the farm. Let's get you familiar with the place before you wander too much. I hope you understand."

"I do."

Ann and Allen were friendly, but busy. Dan opened the car door for her. She turned back to wave and caught unguarded speculation on Ann's face. Oh, dear.

Was there a girlfriend who'd be annoyed with Dan if gossip started flying?

He climbed into the vehicle and started the engine.

"Thank you. It was nice to meet them."

"No problem. Glad it worked out. It's a good idea to know your neighbors. You never know when you might need a helping hand."

When they returned to the house Max was back on the porch. The deputy exited the car. Max didn't stir more than to lift his head as he awaited Dan's touch, a rough rub between the ears and a scratch under his chin. When Dan pulled his hand back, Max dropped his head back onto his paws.

"He's missing Alice." she said. "I've heard dogs can get depressed when they lose the person they're closest to."

Dan nodded. "I didn't know he was still in the area. We watched for him for a while, but no one saw him." He glanced at the trees, surveyed the road, then settled his gaze back on Max. "Been living in the woods, I guess, on whatever he could find, competing with the coyotes."

Libbie was aghast. "You're serious? Coyotes?"

"Pretty common out here these days, especially if you leave food outside. You have to be careful about that."

Now guilt. Aghast and guilty. What a freaking crazy combination of emotions. No wonder Dan misread her face.

"I'll send an animal control officer out here."

She'd considered doing that herself, but something had shifted.

"Why? He's doing okay."

He frowned. "No, he's not. There are coyotes in these woods and the occasional black bear wanders through. Wild dogs too. If he survives and doesn't get hit by a car or shot by a hunter, he's one more potential spreader of rabies."

"Hunters? Rabies? You make the woods sound awful." They did appear different now. Less pastoral. Shadowy. More treacherous.

"It's nature. Nothing's all good or bad, including nature."

She considered. "Don't call them yet, okay? I'm not sure how this will work out, but he's been out here this long, let's give him a little more time."

"You thinking of adopting him?"

"I don't know. I've never owned a dog or a pet of any kind." Why was she telling him this? "Maybe it's up to Max, anyway. He might not want to be my dog."

"If you, or he, decide it's not a match, let me know. He'll get a home without much trouble. He's a fine dog. A Weimaraner."

At some point he'd put his hat back on. He tipped the brim and spoke as he turned away. "Yes, ma'am. Let me know how it works out."

****

Libbie heard those coyotes in the night. She thought she saw them skulking in the dark at the edge of the woods. One of them stood upright in the moonlight, like the shadowed figure she'd seen before—someone who could not possibly be confused with other varmints. Finally she acknowledged some of it, maybe most of it, was a product of her brain stem working overtime, hyper-alert to danger.

It was Dan's fault for planting scary ideas into her head. She was uneasy that evening. She checked the locks on the doors and the latches on the windows.

Dark and cold—the day's warmth had fled with the sun. She wandered from room to room, anxious, unable to settle. The windows were all covered, but she paced through the house like an obsessed sentry.

Libbie felt a presence outside and the pressure of eyes staring at the house.

Unable to bear the rising tension, she strode to the front door and opened it wide. She stood there boldly, her feet planted on the threshold, staring into the moon-bright night.

Something moved in the periphery of the shadows. She held her ground. It slipped up to the foot of the steps, sat back on its haunches and uttered a short bark.

"Okay, Max." Libbie stepped back, pushing the door wider. "Come in."

He bounded up the steps, doggie smell and all.

"Tomorrow you're going to the vet and the groomers. I won't take no for an answer."

He sat at her feet. A quiver raced up his body and he barked again, almost no more than a huff, and then raced up the stairs to the bedroom.

It would've been cute except for the rank odor. Suddenly it occurred to her that he might have jumped up on the bed. She took the stairs two steps at a time.

No, he wasn't on the bed. He reclined politely on the floor a few feet away.

Alice must've had a bed for him over there near the window.

There was a blanket in the closet. She shrugged. Easily replaced. She tossed it onto the floor.

"Here you go, Max. Sleep tight." He kept those sad eyes on her, but didn't follow her back down the stairs. Funny, but she thought he would. Apparently he wasn't all that hungry, just in search of a home. Or content being home.

Maybe it was having a dog in the house, or maybe it was because he was no longer staring holes through the exterior walls, but her uneasiness slipped away.

****

The next morning Libbie located a vet in Mineral who agreed to see Max that same day. She was relieved. Dogs, especially big dogs, didn't belong in the house. At the least, they needed to be clean and free of fleas, ticks and other tiny vermin.

She dressed, put on her shoes, picked up her purse and keys, then realized Max would have to agree to come along.

"Are you going to be a problem?" She opened the door. "Come on, boy."

He moved reluctantly out to the porch. She shut the door and walked to the car as if she expected him to follow, and he did. She opened the door to the back seat.

"Get in, Max."

Nope. He stared at her, then trotted away disappearing around the back end of the car. Great. She'd never catch him now, woods or no woods.

But, no, he'd stopped on the far side and was waiting politely, staring at the front passenger side door.

"You're kidding, right? You expect to ride up front?"

Woof.

Well, it solved the problem, if not in the way she'd expected.

As they traveled to Mineral, Libbie considered how she'd get him from the car to the waiting room. He didn't have a collar and she didn't have a leash. As they approached the vet's office, he became agitated. A high anxious whine filled the car. He moved back and forth checking the windows, ending up with one foot and leg in her lap.

What had she been thinking? Her inexperience with animals was showing. The vet and his staff could figure it out.

"Sit, Max." He did, but barely. "Stay. I'll be back."

He looked at her in disbelief and woofed.

She pushed open the glass door and walked into the vet's office. The receptionist smiled.

"I'm Libbie Havens." She gestured toward the car. "I don't have a leash for my dog."

A man in a white coat walked up while she was speaking. He held the door for a woman toting a cat carrier.

"Bye, Martha."

"Thanks, Doc."

Libbie stood aside to let the woman exit.

Smiling, he asked, "Ms. Havens?"

"Yes. I brought that dog I called about. I don't have a leash. Should I try to bring him in?"

"Let me see." He opened the door for her, then followed her outside.

The receptionist came to stand in the doorway, curious.

Max pressed his nose to the glass. The vet pulled the handle.

Libbie said, "Watch out, he's not on a leash."

The door opened. Max jumped out—and up into the vet's arms. Max stood on his hind legs with his front legs over the man's arms and licked his face as if his cheeks were smeared with ice cream.

"Hey, Max. Good to see you!" The vet nodded to the receptionist standing in the open doorway. He stepped back from Max and Max obediently dropped to all fours.

"Let's go in, boy."

Max did.

Was Max smiling? All Libbie could see for sure was his

stubby tail wagging as he headed for the exam room.

****

When they left, Max was still chipper, but now he wore a shiny new collar and leash and he didn't seem to mind one little bit. He was riding high from the whole experience. Libbie shook her head, amazed. Max had, in fact, been almost transported with joy during the bath the vet tech volunteered to give him.

"He's one of our favorite buddies," the girl had said leading him into the back.

It had been like a big "Max is back" party. Libbie was almost jealous.

The vet, Dr. Walker, followed them to the sidewalk.

"You said he just showed up on the porch? I'm glad, and I'm glad you're willing to keep him on. He's a fine dog. Someone else would be happy to adopt him, but he knows where home is."

Clearly Max understood he was being praised. He sat and waited for more.

"I don't have experience with animals. Pets, that is."

"Any questions, you just give us a call, Libbie. Max is a lucky dog."

****

Liz called Friday morning. She asked if Adam and Audrey could visit for the weekend.

Her breath stopped. The walls closed in around her and squeezed.

"Are you still there? Don't feel obligated. We can make other arrangements. Josh is up in DC and I'd like to join him for the weekend. There's something playing at the Kennedy Center and he has free tickets, but I can get a sitter or Mother will come. Josh suggested I ask you. He thought it would be a good chance for the kids to spend time with you."

Libbie's reaction was total panic. Two children who visited for a couple of hours with their mom was an entirely different proposition from two children who became the responsibility of a woman who has never had a child in her care, ever, in her entire life. Liz was a loving, conscientious mother. If Liz was willing to entrust her two precious babes to Libbie Havens, then clearly, Liz had lost her mind.

"Libbie? Are you there? It's okay if you'd rather not. I waited until the kids had gone to school before calling you. We can say you already have commitments for this weekend. I told Josh you might be uncomfortable. Libbie?"

Maybe Liz didn't want her to take the children, after all. Maybe Liz wanted her to say no. She could say she'd asked, but Aunt Libbie said, "No way." But Liz wouldn't say that. That was the voice of Libbie's own panic.

She forced the words out in a rush. "Sure. No problem." She was saying "yes" and her heart had gone from pounding to sinking.

"Libbie? Are you sure? Do you need some time to think about it?"

"No, it's okay." Maybe it was okay. She could survive one weekend. Would the kids also survive? They would be so bored. What did she have to offer a pair of ten-year-olds? Her palms began to perspire. Breathe slowly, she told herself.

"I'll be two hours away. I'll keep my cell phone with me and you'll be able to reach me anytime, day or night."

"Sure."

"I'll drop them off on my way north and pick them up Sunday afternoon coming back. Don't worry about food. I'll bring what they like to eat. We'll keep it simple. Do you have room in your freezer?"

"I don't have enough pillows." What had she agreed to? Two nights. Three days and two nights.

"I'll bring pillows, an air mattress for Adam, and extra blankets."

They would arrive late afternoon.

She stepped out onto the porch. The cool air soothed her. She closed her eyes and did a slow, controlled breathe in, breathe out.

Max was stretched out in a patch of sun near the edge of the porch. He lifted his head when the floorboards squeaked and asked a question with his eyes.

"Sorry to disturb you, Max, but we have guests coming."

****

Adam and Audrey were twins. They had the same reddish-brown hair and freckles, but very different personalities.

He carried the air mattress, pillows and blankets upstairs. The spare bedrooms were unfurnished. Libbie invited him to choose either or he could camp on her bedroom floor. Audrey dragged her purple backpack up the stairs to Libbie's room without asking. No sleeping bag this time.

Liz was almost breathless and had a quizzical look on her face. Did she think Libbie might change her mind? Or maybe she, herself, was reconsidering. She gave a quick rundown of the groceries, frozen, canned and fresh, as she efficiently put them in the appropriate repositories, but Libbie didn't pay much attention. Food was food. They made multi-vitamins for a reason.

"Liz. It's okay." She waved in surrender. "Go. Say 'hello' to Josh for me, and the two of you have a great time."

"Are you sure, Libbie?" Her brown eyes were almost tearful in their earnestness. "I hope I'm not imposing." She stuck her cell phone number, written on a sticky note, under a refrigerator magnet she also brought with her. The magnet had the poison control center number.

Liz sailed into the living room and grabbed the kids, kissing them. "You two be good for Aunt Libbie. If you aren't, I'll know! Adam, be a help to her and watch out for your sister. Audrey, you mind Aunt Libbie. Promise me."

She turned and said, "Well, they're in your hands now."

Then she was gone.

Chapter Seven

Audrey and Libbie waved goodbye to Liz from the front porch. When they went back inside, she found Adam hovering around her desk.

"Can I turn your computer on? Do you have games?"

"No, my computer has no games and is not a toy."

"I can download some."

"My computer is off-limits."

"Sure. Whatever." His face showed his disappointment. "Can I go out and look around?"

"Stay near the house. Don't go out of sight."

He nodded and went outside. They were off to a bad start.

Audrey was suddenly at Libbie's elbow. She said, "Mommy doesn't let Adam use her computer either. Adam has his own for games."

"Is he okay outside?"

"That's what he wanted anyway. He's been drawing pictures of tree forts."

Audrey went to the kitchen and bounced out again. She stood, shocked, saying, "I see a dog dish. You *do* have a dog. *You do!*"

"Well, I…yes, I do, but I didn't when you were here before."

"You got one because of me!" And she was gone.

Libbie's best guess was that Audrey was looking for Max, but Max was outside somewhere. He had developed a taste for the outdoors after Alice's death. Like a working fella, he came home every night for dinner and a bed.

He had quickly trained Libbie to accept the whole indoor/outdoor dog thing. The porch was his preferred base of operations, his touch point during the day.

She paced from window to window. No sign of Adam. Apparently he was out there somewhere evaluating trees for their architectural appropriateness. The TV came on in the living room.

Audrey said, "I couldn't find him."

"He'll be back." Libbie was relatively sure he would be.

She moved through the dining room and to the screened porch, didn't see Adam, and yelled, "Adam? Adam?"

"Over here, Aunt Libbie." He was near the garage. "Look what I found."

Max was standing close to her nephew with his adoring doggy eyes fixed on the boy.

"That's Max."

"Where does he live?"

"Here."

"You have a dog? Cool." He reached over and scratched Max's head.

She was glad Adam had the dog close by. She didn't know if he would actually be safer, and she didn't expect any kind of *Lassie* action from Max, but his presence might give a stranger pause.

"Don't damage my trees unless we've talked about it first. Understood?"

Adam pouted. "Sure. Okay. I promise." He shrugged and spread his arms. "Can I climb in them?"

"I guess so. You won't break anything? I mean bones. Please be careful. Stay close, okay? I don't want to lose you. Besides, we'll need to have supper soon."

She could feel the gray hairs sprouting from her scalp. She wasn't made for this kind of sustained worry. This was definitely not healthy.

In the kitchen, she sat alone, rigid, unable to relax. She left the back door open, hoping she'd hear if anything went wrong. Her living room had been co-opted by Audrey who was spread across the floor on her belly, her eyes glued to the television. She had a book, but it was lying on the floor nearby and she showed no sign of opening it.

Adam was out in the wilds somewhere, hopefully still with Max. Libbie wasn't concerned about Adam except in terms of him falling from a tree. Or coyotes.

Getting lost was very possible. She shivered at the thought.

What would she say to Liz and Josh if she lost their son? The blood pounded in her ears.

She ran out the kitchen door shouting, "Adam! Adam!"

"I'm here." He came running from the woods. "Am I in trouble?"

Relief made her rational again. Audrey came from the living room and stared at her. She looked worried. Libbie took a deep breath.

"No, not in trouble. Come on in and let's get supper. I know a pizza place we can try."

****

"Mommy brought food." Audrey toyed with the pepperoni on her slice of pizza.

"Shut up, Aud," Adam advised. "This is better."

"But Mommy said..."

Libbie asked, "What's wrong, Audrey? Don't you like pizza?"

"Yes, but Mommy always fixes green salad and fruit with pizza."

"Audrey, if you'd like a salad, you're welcome to one. Why didn't you order a salad? They have a salad bar here."

"I don't want salad." Audrey wiped tomato sauce from her chin.

"Then what's the problem?"

"Mommy always makes us eat green salad and fruit."

This was what passed for conversation with Audrey. She kept up a steady flow of chatter and didn't require responses. Libbie kept forgetting this and kept getting dragged in. Adam had less to say and a tendency to sulk.

Audrey took a sip of her cola and smacked her lips. "And she never lets us drink soda."

"What?" Libbie looked back and forth at them in annoyance. "Why didn't either of you say something when we were ordering?"

Adam shrugged. Audrey's mouth hung open and her lower lip snapped up into a shape that suggested tears were imminent.

"Don't bother, Audrey. Tears don't impress me," She felt called upon to be disapproving since she was the closest thing here to a responsible adult.

"She can't help it. She's a girl."

Audrey sniffed loudly and threw her crumpled napkin at him.

"Dad lets us have sodas when we eat out. The milk always tastes crummy in restaurants."

"Soda is okay sometimes?" She frowned. "And other times, not okay. I have to think about this. We need to come to an understanding here or this won't work. I have to be able to trust you guys."

She saw she'd better get used to being played.

Her cell phone rang soon after they returned home.

"Liz. Hi."

"How's it going?"

Libbie leaned back against the kitchen counter. "Going fine. Audrey's watching TV. Adam is over at my desk drawing something. Would you like to speak with them?"

"Everything's good?"

"Perfect. You have lovely children."

"Josh is waiting. If you're sure everything's okay, then don't disturb them. I'll call back tomorrow."

"Go have fun. Say 'hello' to Josh for me."

"Will do."

Libbie hit 'end,' immensely pleased by how calm she'd sounded. In control, in fact. Liz had seemed to be reassured and satisfied by her easy demeanor. Encouraging signs of progress.

****

Adam was sleeping on the air mattress in one of the spare rooms. Max had joined him there. Audrey was curled up and snoring softly in the big bed.

Libbie was tired. She'd been grateful to crawl into bed, but it was emotional fatigue, not physical. The tiredness was illusory and as soon as her head hit the pillow, the drowsies evaporated. She didn't give up the idea of sleep easily. She lay there watching the moonlight streaming in over the top of the cardboard panels and listening to the yipping of distant creatures and the hum of the occasional passing car until about two a.m. That's when the regrets began to arrive.

They arrived unbidden, gate crashers. The guilt and regret party always started in the dark of night and peaked around three a.m.

Since she'd been at Cub Creek, she'd had a respite from them, almost certainly due to the difference in sensory overload compared to living in the city. One thing hadn't changed. It didn't matter if the regrets were valid. Anything was fair game for guilt.

Around two a.m. when Libbie recognized what was happening, she gave up the attempt to sleep and went downstairs.

It was dark, but strong moonlight lit the scene and her eyes were night sharpened. She pulled the cardboard from the windows in front of her desk. She sat, her head back against the chair, to watch the night and wait for the morning.

She should've been a better granddaughter to Elizabeth. If she'd been less resentful, less intractable…

Grandmother Elizabeth would never have loved her, no matter what. They were too different. Or too much alike. Either way, it came down to the same thing—Libbie wasn't her father.

How many days had she spent locked in her bedroom? Tucked away on the third floor of Grandmother's city residence, safely out of sight? Out of *her* sight. At first, because Libbie goofed. Later, because she goofed on purpose. Ugly can flow both ways.

Tonight, the night sky was lighter than the trees. A wind had sprung up, tossing the branches. She closed her eyes. The sound of the fitful breeze became the color of a sapphire night entwined with the deep emerald green of the fir trees.

Her hands pressed upon the warm wood of Grandfather's desk and the smell of the waxed, antique wood was seen by her mind's eye as ochre. It swirled and mixed with the deep green-blue and filled her head. She allowed the colors free will and they pushed Grandmother and the regrets off-stage sending them back, spinning away into the lost, dusty corners of her brain.

The colors—the perception of smells, sounds and images as colors—Dr. Raymond called it synesthesia—had probably help save her sanity after she understood she could use it to shut out what she couldn't control, what she couldn't bear.

Unfortunately, at some point, pushing unpleasantness away became unhelpful. Eventually, you had to deal with stuff.

What had Barry Raymond said? *Libbie, you have the reality, the synesthesia, so wrapped up, so interwoven with your childhood trauma and your anger and imagination that you don't know where one ends and the other begins. It's a kind of box you've built, tightly woven, and when someone gets close, or you're in an uncomfortable situation, you pull it over your head and turn off the lights.*

Trust yourself. Forgive yourself. If you don't, you'll never leave the unhappiness behind.

If he were sitting here now, she'd say, "Easier said than done."

Libbie dropped her hands into her lap, almost spent and more relaxed. She'd been in this position before and expected to be again. The wee hours of the night, those long hours before dawn when sleep would not cooperate, must simply be endured. When the sun began to break the horizon the regrets would flee. She just had to hold out for the sunrise.

Little fingers were tapping her cheek. She couldn't think where she was. Sleeping deeply, but not in her bed, and there was a tap, tap, tap on her cheek.

A whispery voice said, "Aunt Libbie?"

She drew in a ragged breath as she struggled to pull herself up from the deep pit of sleep. The sky was barely lightening. It was not yet dawn, but close enough.

"I had to go to the bathroom. I got up because I had to go and you weren't there."

"You came looking for me?" Libbie's arms were heavy. Her muscles felt drugged.

"I was afraid."

Audrey's eyes were dark pools in the dim light. Libbie felt oddly warmed.

"You were brave to come downstairs to find me."

"Can we go back to bed now?"

Hand in hand, Audrey and Libbie climbed the stairs. Libbie tucked her back in, and herself too. Instantly, they slept.

****

The bathroom window was open a few inches to vent the steam. The air was mild and the day seemed promising. Libbie stood in the hot shower until she felt her joints loosening, then took her time with the rest of her morning preparations.

Voices rose from the backyard, including happy woofs. Judging by the sounds, Adam and Audrey had finished breakfast and were out enjoying the morning with Max.

She yelled from the window, "Adam. Audrey. Don't run off, okay? I'm almost done and I want to talk to both of you."

They'd bought whistles, among other things, after their pizza last night. They were cheaply made, but she hoped they'd serve. Each was attached to a plastic string.

"Line up, kiddos." They stood in the kitchen and she hung a whistle around each neck: orange for Audrey, green for Adam, and red for her.

"What's it for?" Adam asked.

Audrey whistled, whistled and whistled. Piercing. Max jumped back and forth, barking.

"Stop it, Audrey," Libbie said. "These whistles have an important purpose. When you go into those woods keep the whistle around your neck. Don't go far. You don't know your way around here yet. If you get lost or need help, blow the whistle. If I need you, or want to check on you, I'll blow the whistle and you'll answer by blowing yours. Understand?"

Adam's dignity had been insulted. "I won't get lost."

"Wear it anyway."

"I'll wear it, but I won't get lost."

"Good. Thank you. Now, Audrey, don't blow the whistle just to make noise, okay? If you do and there's a problem, I might think you're fooling around. Understand?"

"I understand. I promise. Can I blow it one more time? For practice? We should all practice. Let's all go outside and practice."

"Chill, kid. Remember what I said."

They'd also purchased contact paper—an exotic assortment—but that project was for later.

After Audrey had honed her whistling expertise, she settled in the living room to watch television. She did that a lot. Adam was outside doing whatever ten-year-old boys did. At Libbie's request, every so often he'd stick his head in the back door and yell that he was okay and not lost or hurt.

She sat at the desk and stared out the window. The sky was a strong blue and the temperature was perfect. Her camera was on the side of the desk. She experienced a rush of annoyance, of frustration. She'd planned to photograph fences today and the weather, the lighting, was perfect. Yet, where was she? Tied here by a couple of ten-year-olds.

She pulled at the neck strap idly, wondering if she could sneak away for a while. But no, she was the adult, the responsible one.

On the computer screen the graphics program faded to the screen saver. This was the perfect opportunity to do a few more pages for the photo book she was putting together, but she wasn't in the mood.

Engrossed in thinking about herself, suddenly she felt eyes on her. Audrey took a seat in the chair next to her desk.

She pulled her skinny legs up into the chair and rested her chin and hands on her knees.

Libbie raised her eyebrows, silently questioning.

"Who is the lady? She's pretty, Aunt Libbie. Is she you?"

Audrey was staring at the far wall where the portrait of the unknown lady hung over the fireplace, the portrait that had been in her grandfather's study.

"Me?" She laughed. "No. I always thought she looked a lot like your mom. But, whoever she is, it's an old picture. It was drawn a long time ago. I believe she's our grandfather's mother. That would make her our great-grandmother."

"Mine too?"

"Sure. If she's your mom's great-grandmother, then she's your great-great-grandmother."

"I wish I knew her name. Do you know her name?"

"No. Remember I said I didn't know who she was?"

"Mommy and me, we had a picture taken and we dressed up funny for it and it was all black and white, but not black and white, but kind of brown."

"Sepia. It's called sepia-toned. This isn't a photograph. It's a portrait done in charcoal pencil, I think, but the paper has yellowed."

"Yeah. Anyway, we were real old-timey. Like that lady. I thought maybe you had one of those pictures taken too. You should. You'd look like that lady if you put your hair up on top of your head." Audrey bit her lower lip and then let it go. "Elizabeth."

"The lady in the picture? We don't know her name, remember?"

"You and Mommy are both Elizabeth."

"We are." Libbie had the name first by about a week.

"Like your grandma?"

"Yes, that's right."

They were both named after Grandmother. For love or respect? Not likely. No one wanted to risk getting cut from the will by one who fawned better than the other.

"Because your mommy and daddy died? You lived with your grandma?"

Small breath.

"Yes, with my grandmother."

"Were you sad?"

Breathe out.

"Yes, I was." The fist in her stomach slowly unclenched. "It was a long time ago."

"I wish I had a picture of my great-great-grandmother. I could take it to school."

Well, why not?

"Sit over here on the floor next to the fireplace." Libbie lifted the portrait from its hanger and set it gently on the hearth, leaning it against the fireplace bricks.

Audrey scooted up close. "Sit? Like this?"

No shyness here. She smoothed her rumpled hair, fine reddish-brown hair that cascaded with chaos from a clip she wore in the back. She moved next to the portrait, almost like a cheek-to-cheek pose with a real person.

Libbie adjusted the camera for indoor light a little worried the cast would be too cool, but rather than take the time to make more adjustments and risk losing the attention of the model, she knelt on the floor. The tiny viewfinder offered a perspective the human eye and brain alone couldn't achieve.

The light streamed in through the window, not too brightly, but it was the kind of light on which dust motes danced. It grazed Audrey's check and highlighted her hair like a feathery crown.

To avoid the reflection cast by the glass over the portrait, she changed her position slightly and with one click did something she'd never thought of doing before—she took a photo of a person, deliberately and with care, thinking about the love that might show in it.

She snapped a few more before Audrey broke the spell.

"Can I see? Can I see it now?"

Suddenly Libbie was unsure, but Audrey wasn't a critic. She was happy to squint at the small LED screen and wasn't at all concerned about artistic effect.

They reviewed the photographs. Audrey thought each was perfect.

Through her larger window on the world, the one in front of her desk, she saw Max. He was jumping and barking as Adam ran onto the scene. Adam stopped short and grabbed his chest. He fell and rolled down the grassy slope.

In horror, she stood, then realized Adam was playing. He wasn't hurt.

She switched the camera setting to be suitable for semi-shady outdoor light.

"Aud, I'll be back."

Audrey was right on her heels. As they exited the house, she ran for the hill and rolled down too. Max went crazy, delighted beyond bearing. He ran to Libbie, barking, as if informing her she was late to the party and missing the fun.

Libbie knelt, her elbow on her knee for stability, and as Adam ran up the hill Max jumped on him, knocking him down. Adam laughed as they landed and Max gave his face a bath.

The slobber was disgusting, yes, but Libbie loved what she saw through the viewfinder.

Then the background disappeared and her lens filled with gray hair and wet tongue. She snapped a photo just before the doggy and she wiped out.

She knew she'd love the last one best—the one she snapped as Max looked down at her, framed with her niece and nephew in a triangle of smiles.

As she dug out from beneath them, laughing, she wondered if the dog slobber had gotten into her lens, but didn't care, because she could always buy a new lens.

She only had to move a few yards to get back to the steps, but it felt like her personal continent had shifted. She was almost dizzy.

Audrey collapsed next to her with a loud "whoo!" and leaned against her arm. "That was fun, wasn't it, Aunt Libbie? Wasn't that fun?"

"Yes, it was." Almost too much. Could one overdose on good feelings? She needed to find a balance, but first, she needed to know how.

"Are you hurt, Aunt Libbie?"

Audrey's eyes, suddenly serious, were focused on the hand Libbie had pressed to her chest.

"No sweetheart. My heart is full from so much fun."

Audrey touched Libbie's hand. "Mine too."

Libbie cleared her throat. "Okay, kids. Ready to get to work? We have decorating to do."

Audrey blasted up from the steps. "The contact paper? I'll get it. Where do you want it? Can we sit on the rug in the living room?"

"We'll use the card table, but let's have lunch first. Adam, you hungry? We'll do the decorating after."

"Adam won't help. He'll say it's girl stuff." Her voice trailed off as she ran into the house.

Max followed her, scrambling to catch up.

Adam was grimy.

"Have you been tunneling?" She asked as they walked

into the house at a more sedate pace. "Wash up and be sure to throw some soap and water on your face too."

She cooked grilled cheese sandwiches for lunch. Audrey ate one and toyed with a second. Adam ate four at which point Libbie called it quits.

Adam joined the contact paper party. Max napped nearby while Adam covered panels for the bedrooms. His manner was serious and business-like. When he was done he got up quietly and went outside with Max close behind.

Audrey, on the other hand, made a joyful mess. Her scissors flashed with creativity. Libbie was grateful no one was stabbed. She covered the panels for the study and kitchen. Audrey decorated the panels for the dining room and living room.

Together they cut, peeled, placed and smoothed until they ran out of contact paper. It was a lot of contact paper.

Audrey volunteered to pick up the bits and pieces of paper and cardboard rolls left scattered on the table and floor. Libbie walked outside to check on Adam.

The trees were greening up. The new leaves were fresh and light. The crisp woodland carpet of dried leaves smelled fresh. No signs of passage marked the ground. Every few yards she'd stop and listen for sounds of Adam or Max nearby.

She heard the creek. The water sound was soft, almost whispery. She closed her eyes and listened to its voice and saw it as a light, shimmery, silvery blue.

"Adam? Max?" Libbie called out, but not too loudly. No response, so she moved forward.

A rough two-board bridge crossed the darkly opaque water of Cub Creek. Not shimmery or silvery at all, and far from blue. Near the banks, the water was shallow as it streamed in and around rocks and boulders, interspersed with fallen tree trunks and other debris. But mid-stream, the water seemed almost stationary. Deceptively so. It was impossible to tell how deep the still-seeming water ran.

A noise broke into her thoughts.

"Adam?" She spun around.

No one, but she felt a presence. Eyes touched her and cold prickled down her spine.

It was reasonable that people would cut through these woods, but the silence around her was profound. Even the creek's voice had faded.

And she didn't feel alone.

Chapter Eight

Libbie's grip tightened on her camera. She didn't remember picking it up from the desk and it didn't give much comfort, but it did restore a little common sense to the circumstance.

She listened. Noises were suddenly magnified. Leaves rustled on the ground. The restless feet of a pack of coyotes? A bear nearby? Leaves moved higher up. A squirrel jumping from branch to branch? A bit of breeze? A person?

Her heart raced. She tried to appear casual and unafraid, and started walking back the way she'd come. Casually.

She didn't find Adam. He and Max found her.

"Aunt Libbie."

He headed in her direction. Max ran up and licked her fingers. Adam asked, "Did you get lost? Why didn't you blow the whistle?"

She shrugged some of the tension from the knot at the back of her neck. "Thanks for finding me. I wasn't actually lost. "

"Want to see my tree? I mean your tree. The tree I picked out for my fort?"

Oh, bother. She didn't want him nailing the trees, but he'd come searching for her. How could she be harsh?

Adam was right. It was a great tree, the kind of tree you'd never notice until you truly saw it and once everything was leafed out, it would be hard to spot. Adam showed it to her like a proud first-time homeowner giving a tour. The tree had a large trunk. At about shoulder-height the trunk twisted and forked before resuming its natural shape. The result was a giant chair. The "seat" was large enough for someone Adam's size to sit in comfortably. Another oak. Libbie ran her hands over the rough gray bark.

"Watch this." Adam scrambled up the trunk and onto that "seat." He stood. "Look at me."

She did, but through the camera lens. He cooperated for about five seconds.

Libbie sighed. "You want to put nails in this tree?"

He dropped to a seated position. "Nails wouldn't hurt it, you know. But, nah, I don't have to. I'm going to build a fort on the ground over here in these bushes and use the tree as a lookout."

"Okay." What were ten-year-old boys on the lookout for?

"I need a saw and a shovel."

He said it casually as if she had the power to pull the tools out of her pocket.

"Check in the garage. It's not locked."

"I already checked. It's all there."

She appreciated initiative, but a short time ago she'd felt the menace of someone or something watching her.

"I wish this was closer to the house. I'm not happy with the seclusion."

"This is close to the house and I have the whistle. I'll be careful, I promise." He rolled onto his stomach and dropped to the ground, landing softly, with bent knees. "Max is with me." He reached over and scratched the dog's head.

"Okay. Keep the whistle handy and be careful. It's almost suppertime. You'll have to wrap it up soon. Don't stay inside the garage any longer than you have to and keep the door open, okay?"

She left him to his fun.

Later, when they were seated at the kitchen table enjoying a delicious, home-cooked meal of cheeseburgers and tater tots with salad on the side, plus milk, Adam mentioned seeing a man in the woods.

"What?" She exclaimed, startled.

"He was walking on the path. He didn't say anything or do anything. I don't think he saw me."

Libbie was disturbed, but tried not to let it show. People did walk in the woods. On the other hand, one heard of children vanishing every day.

"What did he look like?"

Adam shrugged. "Regular. Not old. He had on one of those green army jackets."

"Why didn't you tell me sooner?"

From the corner of her eye, she saw Audrey watching carefully. She put a reassuring hand on the girl's shoulder.

"It didn't seem important," Adam said. "I stayed real quiet. If he'd seen me, I would've run because I don't know him. I can run fast and besides, I have my whistle. He wasn't doing anything wrong. He was just walking."

Adam was worried she might forbid him to go into the woods. That consideration might influence his judgment; however, other than the fact that he was ten years old, she had no reason to doubt his common sense.

"You're smart, Adam, no question about it, and I think you've got good sense, but here's the important thing: your mom and dad told you not to talk to strangers?"

Audrey's mouth was hanging open.

"Right, Audrey?"

She nodded. Her eyes were big with worry. Libbie feared her poor handling of it was causing her unnecessary anxiety.

"It is very important to be careful when you're by yourself or if you're in a place where you don't know how to get help. That makes sense, doesn't it?" They all nodded at each other. "It's okay to play and have fun, but you have to be smart too, and you have to be careful. When in doubt you run or yell or blow your whistle. Don't wait to see if there's a problem. Run first and ask questions later. Will you remember that? Don't worry about hurting someone's feelings or looking silly."

Adam looked subdued and thoughtful. Audrey still seemed scared. At this rate she'd be returning Liz's children to her either physically damaged or emotionally traumatized.

"Okay," she said, "let's get this kitchen cleaned up and play some Canasta."

"Canasta?" They asked in unison.

"Canasta. With cards. Oh, good grief. You don't mean to tell me your mom never taught you how to play Canasta! You gotta be kidding me." She waved her arms with dramatic flourish. "Why, we used to have tournaments that lasted for days. Her dad, your granddad, taught us how to play."

"You knew our grandfather? Mom's dad?" Adam asked.

"You bet. He was my Uncle Phil. He was a great guy. Would you like me to tell you about him? Then let's get moving and clean this kitchen."

They stayed up too late, slept hard and woke long after dawn. She made pancakes for breakfast. By the time they were fed, washed and packed most of the morning had fled. This was like a holiday for Adam and Audrey, a vacation at Aunt Libbie's Exclusive All-Inclusive Woodland Get-Away complete with fried foods and late night Canasta. Well, one weekend of bad choices wouldn't kill them.

She spent time at the computer while Audrey watched television. Adam had washed up and gone outside to play in the dirty, leafy woods. The morning was chilly and she'd insisted he wear his jacket. Audrey had pulled the rose throw off the couch and wrapped it around the length of her body.

Libbie leaned forward. Through the open door of the study, past the foyer and into the living room, she could see most of her. She was encased like a big pink sausage. Looking at her cocooned on the floor, Libbie felt a yawn coming on. She stood up and stretched, then went out to the screened porch. She sat and swung with a lazy rhythm.

The day was warming and the sky was a deep blue. Spring was underway and a few more azaleas were about to bloom over near the wood's edge. Adam had been gone for a while, but it was such a perfect, placid day she couldn't work up any concern. She'd over-reacted the day before.

Almost noon. Nearly lunchtime.

The screen door squeaked as she pushed it open and walked onto the concrete step. A flagstone walk might be a nice addition. She should talk to Jim about it. His business was landscaping, so he'd have good suggestions and useful contacts.

Libbie tried to envision how the flagstones would run with a border of small plants, something flowery, on either side. A patio to fill in the area between the porch door and the back stoop would be nice.

"Hello."

She spun around. Jim. He stood there as if her thoughts had conjured him. This was scary. But also kind of cool. He was dressed in khakis and a cotton shirt. Nice, but casual.

"I knocked on the front door, but no one answered. The car was here, so I thought I'd look around back. If I'm interrupting, or if this is a bad time, it's okay to say."

"Why, I..., no, it's fine. I was thinking about you." That didn't sound right. "I mean I was thinking about talking to you. That is, about putting in flagstones back here."

His expression changed from concern to amusement. His eyes were a deep hazel blue today, matching the color of his shirt. The lines at the corners of his eyes deepened when he smiled. They suited him.

"I brought the estimate for the lawn care." He held out the paper. "Now, about flagstone. You should come by the nursery. Mitchell's Farm Nursery. We have displays you might find helpful. There are lots of options when it comes to stone for patios and walkways. I'd be happy to suggest a few." He held out his hand. "Here's my card. I wrote a couple of names and numbers on the back. These folks do papering and painting. Reliable and reasonably priced."

Libbie felt eyes on them. Audrey stood just inside the door of the screened porch staring with her mouth agape. Jim saw her. He stepped back abruptly.

"Audrey, say 'hello.' This is Mr. Mitchell."

"Hello," she whispered. She sounded shy. It was difficult to see her clearly through the screening.

"Jim, I appreciate you coming by with the names." Before she completed her sentence, Adam wandered in from the homestead, dirty and disheveled, dragging a shovel and a stick.

Jim backed a few more, quick steps. "No problem." He frowned.

"This is Adam and Audrey. I–"

"I'm interrupting. Sorry, I should've called first."

"No, it's okay."

"I'm on the way to meet with a new client, so I have to run. Let me know if you want to talk about flagstone or alternatives."

He waved and disappeared around the corner of the house.

Gone in a flash. They stood and listened to the sound of the truck engine gunning. Audrey was still peering through the screening of the door. Adam came to where she was standing and Max was panting behind him.

Did Jim think these kids were mine?

"Aunt Libbie, who was that man?" Adam asked.

"He's her boyfriend. She has a boyfriend. Do you have a boyfriend?" Audrey bounced in her excitement.

"Why'd he leave?" Adam asked.

She tried to clarify. "He's not my–"

Audrey interrupted, "He was nice. You can go on a date with him."

"–not my boyfriend." She finished. "It's lunchtime. Adam, you need to do some serious washing. You're covered with dirt. What will your mother say?"

"Mom won't be here 'til later. I'll get cleaned up in time."

"If he's your boyfriend, you can go on a date. You can kiss him. Did you kiss him?"

"Audrey," Adam was firm, "it's not polite to ask."

"He's not my boyfriend. Subject closed." Libbie slammed the door.

****

Over lunch, Adam invited her to come out to his homestead to view his progress.

"And please don't call it a homestead. It's a fort," he added.

"Sure, Adam. No problem."

"Homestead. Homestead. Homestead."

"Shut up, Audrey," Adam said with a groan.

"What's a homestead?" Audrey asked.

"Hush, Audrey." Libbie turned to Adam. "I'd love to see what you've done."

She followed him into the woods. He'd created a natural-looking mesh of sticks entwined with living branches such that when the small trees and brush had fully leafed out, the fort would be difficult to see. He'd dug out an entrance through which a child could move with ease and he kept it covered by sticks and leaves, like a hidden door. There was also a gate-like entrance roofed with brush. It required a certain amount of stooping and crawling, but was more suitable for grown-ups.

"Nice camouflage," she said.

Adam glowed. He explained he'd kept the area around the lookout tree undisturbed so no one would suspect it was being used.

"You haven't seen anyone out here today, have you?"

"Nope. No one. I checked out the path. I don't think too many people use it. I didn't go far enough to tell where it comes from or where it goes."

"Please don't go down the path on your own, and stay away from the creek. Next time you come to visit, we'll walk the path together. Come on back to the house now."

"Mom won't be here for a while. I'll be back in plenty of time to wash up."

"When she called this morning, she said she'd be here about three p.m. Don't lose track of time."

Adam's expression dropped from earnest to solemn.

"Are you going to tell Mom about my fort?"

"Why do you ask?"

"She worries about ticks and snakes and stuff."

Libbie stared into his dark eyes. "Adam, are you asking me to lie to your Mom?"

"No, ma'am." He scuffed at the dirt with his sneaker. "She worries. I don't want her to worry."

"Adam, I won't lie to your Mom, but I won't volunteer

the info either. I'll give you the opportunity to speak to her yourself about it."

He nodded, but didn't say anything. He might be an honest kid, but he also knew what he wanted. She respected that. She didn't look to see whether he might be crossing his fingers behind his back.

The children were well-behaved, but this nurturing, good-example stuff was a tough balancing act. Her sympathies were with Adam, not with the adults. Libbie had a low-grade headache lurking and she was ready to have her homestead back all to herself.

By three p.m. the kids were washed and packed and sitting on the steps of the front porch watching for their mom. She gave her new trick a try: think about someone and they appear. She thought about Liz very hard, but apparently the trick only worked with Mitchell's Lawn and Landscaping.

Overall, she thought the visit had gone well, but with Liz's arrival imminent someone could still be injured or get lost or worse. The possibilities were almost endless.

She went through the house checking for items the kids might've left behind. A toothbrush in the bedroom, a lone sock abandoned in the downstairs bathtub. She was amazed. They hadn't brought much with them. How had they lost track of so many things? The groceries were gathered in the fridge or the freezer waiting for Liz. Most of Liz's food was unused so she could take it back home with her in addition to the children and the dirty laundry.

Liz arrived, fresh-looking and smiling from a weekend alone with her husband, but when she saw them, a glow lit her face. She kissed them, hugged them, thanked Libbie, hugged Libbie, packed up their belongings in the car and, with a large wave, was gone.

The chemistry of the house had changed, losing the

liveliness. On the other hand, the peace was welcome and it was a relief to be responsible for no one but herself and Max, and Max had proved he could manage on his own.

After supper, Libbie took the memory card from her camera and inserted it in her laptop. As the photos downloaded, she scratched his head.

"We had some fun, huh? Just us now. I hope you're ready for some quiet."

Thumbnail images flashed by as the download progressed. She was getting excited.

Audrey's pixie chin. Adam's grin. A flash of Max.

When the download was complete, she put it on slideshow and sat back, her fingers still absentmindedly on Max's head, her brain on overdrive. She had plans for these.

Ordering enlargements online would be a breeze. She'd buy frames on her next trip out.

Beneath her fingertips, Libbie felt a tiny vibration, a faint rumble, a ghost of a growl.

"Max?"

He was staring at the front wall, so he couldn't possibly see anything. Was he reacting to a sound or a smell?

A dog's low-voiced growl was guaranteed to raise great big goose bumps all along one's arms. She rubbed her arms as she stood and stared out through the window.

Darkness was falling fast. Deliberately, and without rush or panic, she rose from her chair and retrieved the panels. She put them into place and when done, stopped holding her breath.

The new contact paper covering the panels added dash to the neutral rooms. Audrey had combined blue-flowered paper with strips of solid orange and strips of bamboo-patterned contact paper. It was unexpectedly striking in its coordination. She felt a sudden pang of loss on top of the goose bumps.

Max had moved on to the kitchen and was eating as if nothing had ever troubled him.

She picked up stray chunks of dog food.

"Sure, fella. Get me stirred up and then move on."

She meant it as a joke, but the words fell flat.

****

There's a special quality to spring that smells of earth—fresh earth, not dirt—ready to burst into life. The early bits of green that peek out in March come into their own during April. By early May the new growth would be the freshest green known to man and the pink azaleas in the front yard would be gaudy with blossoms. The profusion of buds on the white azaleas promised a magnificent display. The breeze had a hint of sun with the cool of winter still behind it. Come summer, the greenery would be lush and dark, and the air, thick and sultry. But this was spring, and the urge to stretch her muscles and joints in the warmth of the sun and to walk barefoot in the grass was almost irresistible.

But resist it, she did. She pulled on her sneakers, picked up her camera and gear bag, and climbed in the car. She was going to go check out some fences.

****

No one was in sight at the Pettus Farm. Libbie recalled seeing a truck parked by the barn before and a horse trailer or two. No vehicles today. The family might be in the house, but she hadn't knocked on the door yet. A flock of guinea hens rounded the corner of the barn, chirping and clicking, bound upon their own business. They passed her by. She watched them, not quite trusting them, but she wasn't on the menu and soon they were gone.

She wandered over to the nearest fence, eyeballing it from different vantage points. The elements and lines didn't seem to have the composition 'oomph' it had promised before. Perhaps it was as simple as the angle of view or the slant of the sun's rays. She kept trying to make the composition work through the viewfinder. The distance shot lacked punch too. It was more effective when she zoomed in on a joint in the fence or a slightly warped board with a popped nail head.

It looked like she'd be packing up and taking off pretty quickly. She was glad she hadn't disturbed Ann or Allan for such a brief, fruitless field trip.

The air shifted. She had company.

A dark brown horse nickered. He and a pale, larger horse wandered to within a few yards of where she leaned on the fence. The dark horse bobbed his head. Was it a friendly gesture? She remembered what Ann had said about biting.

Libbie pretended not to notice and instead, focused on the camera, fidgeting with it, slowly bringing it to her face.

A close up of a muzzle. A shot composed of the long, glossy plane between eye and quivering nostril. Locks of hair framed between ear and eye. Light glinted and glittered in the coal black eye of the brown horse. The tail swished up, feathering the air beyond his rump.

She kept snapping photos.

The dark horse made a snorty noise that the pale horse echoed before they both trotted off.

Had they expected a treat in payment for posing?

No one had emerged from either the house or the barn, but it didn't matter because she was finished. She turned off the camera and picked up the gear bag. She cast a last glance, almost in longing, at the run of fences, appealing in their clean lines and simplicity, but now lacking in some way.

Lacking because something had changed? Not with the fencing, but in her. A change in the brain? A difference in seeing, maybe. Perhaps a new appreciation for the animate versus the inanimate?

She suspected she couldn't go back to the old way even if she wanted to.

****

That afternoon Libbie went out again, but into her own back yard. She might pick up sticks and litter, or perhaps she'd work out how she wanted the patio, though she now thought of it as a terrace. She liked the sound of the word 'terrace.' It spoke of the Mediterranean and Sicily and vineyards. She thought Jim was probably correct—there were better, more interesting options than flagstone.

The sun was bright. The colors were fresh and everything smelled like new beginnings. From the back stoop she surveyed her little kingdom.

Between the back stoop and the screened porch there was an open area. Some hapless bushes grew next to the stoop but mostly it was dirt. Fill it in with stone for a terrace, extend it around the two sets of steps and it would make a pleasant area to grill or relax in. A nice patio set with an umbrella would complete it. A chaise lounge, for sure.

Her feet started down the path that led to Adam's fort and his lookout tree.

It was peaceful. There were no sounds except birdsong and the scramble of squirrels scooting through the brush. She stopped near Adam's tree and closed her eyes. She listened and was reassured by the silence. She climbed Adam's tree. Sitting cross-legged, resting her forearms on her knees, her palms dangling, she laid her head back against the rough, solid trunk. A breeze lightly touched her cheek. She closed her eyes and opened her mind and reached out into the woods around her.

She could hold an object and read recent influences. In

that same way, Libbie allowed herself to be enfolded by the air and environment. The woods received her gently. Impressions, smells, memories, flashed through her mind as colors. Pieces of earth and nature, all pleasant and nothing disturbing with fleeting bits of Adam intermixed as if some part of his essence was still here.

When she was in harmony with her surroundings, it was like a silent symphony. Impossible to be troubled by bad memories in this state. She relaxed and was almost asleep when an acorn hit her on the head. It bounced and landed in her lap. It looked like it was from last year's crop.

A gray squirrel chittered from a branch high above. Definitely a suspicious proximity. An intentional nut bomb. He scampered back and forth on the branch, clearly agitated. He'd dropped the nut on her head. Apparently she'd overstayed her welcome.

She was grateful for the warning. She understood he could've dropped something more disgusting than an old acorn.

Chapter Nine

Tuesday, April 30th.
Happy Birthday to Libbie.

One more thirty-something year. Thirty-three to be precise.

She usually celebrated her birthday by buying herself a nice, expensive present. For this birthday she couldn't think of anything she needed or wanted that money could obtain.

Libbie lay in bed and tried to visualize the day ahead, but the picture wouldn't form. She wasn't depressed. This was a post-move slump. She'd passed through that first hectic excitement of buying and selling homes, of packing and moving. The unpacking was done and she'd made some minor improvements in the form of painting. There was plenty more to do, but there was no rush, no urgency.

As she moved through her morning routine, she wondered about Dr. Raymond. What was he doing now? He started as her therapist, but they'd become friends. They stayed close for a while, but life was all about change and relationships were no exception. Had he found what he was seeking? Everyone needed companionship from time to time, be it a friend, psychiatrist or sweetheart.

Sometimes it was nice to have a sweetheart—someone to hang around with, to laugh with, to share special moments with. The downside of having a sweetheart is they didn't always disappear neatly when you'd rather be without them.

Through the window she saw a brown station wagon

pulling up the drive. She went to the door.

An old man was holding flowers. Fresh-cut flowers in a vase. Some sort of spring bouquet in purple, pink and white. The daisies added a touch of yellow. She felt like crying when she saw the yellow. No reason. Just felt like it. This was the sort of gift that would dry up and drop pollen on every surface, yet it was beautiful.

"Ma'am? Are you all right?" He looked rickety. He passed the vase to her. "There's a card in there, ma'am."

"One minute, please." She set the vase on the coffee table while she dug her wallet out of her purse. Lovely flowers. Big tip.

"Thank you, ma'am. Have a nice day."

Libbie pulled the card from between a pink carnation and a tall purple flower.

"Happy Birthday to our favorite Aunt. Love, Audrey and Adam." There was more to the note. "Please come to supper. Love, Liz and Josh."

She thought she could fit it into her schedule.

Plus, she had a special gift for Liz. A set of framed enlarged photographs of Audrey and Adam. Liz would get her birthday present a few days early. She'd love it and Libbie was glad to have finally found the perfect gift for her—one of which Liz would absolutely approve.

****

A van brought her new front porch furniture on Saturday morning. The set included a bench, two rockers with curved backs, a couple of chairs and two end tables, all in white wicker—Libbie's birthday presents to herself. The day before, on her way to Liz's house, she'd stopped at a home improvement store where, on impulse, she bought the furniture and paid a bundle for quick delivery. A pickup, driven by the installer, brought a storm door.

The porch was now furnished, and the hardware store called to say her "Cub Creek" sign was in. She decided to drive into Louisa and maybe stop in Mineral on the way back for groceries and barbecue. It was a sunny day outside, and she felt sunny inside too. The fun of the cake and ice cream the evening before had carried over.

When she returned home a visitor was sitting on her porch on her new furniture, rocking and looking smug.

"Ms. Inman. Joyce. How are you?"

"Nice furniture. A little hard. You can get cushions for the seat and backs, you know."

"Indeed. I'll give it some thought." Libbie shifted her purchases to sort out the door key. "Would you like to come in?"

"That'd be nice. Door's already unlocked. I had to use the facilities. Hope you don't mind." The rocker squeaked as she rose. "Nice storm door, too. Worried when I saw it. No key for that one."

"Don't mind at all." Why should she mind since, obviously, she had no choice? "Did you put the key back into its hiding spot?"

"Oh, yes. Alice was always particular about where she hid her keys."

Keys? Did she say keys?

They went to the kitchen. Joyce hung her cane over the back of her seat. Libbie got out the plates and utensils.

"You got rolls this time and extra hush puppies, too," Joyce said. "Good thinking."

"Yes, ma'am. I was expecting you." She was joking, of course.

Joyce chuckled in appreciation. "Alice used to do that."

"Do you prefer water or iced tea? And what did you mean? What did Alice used to do?"

"Expect me. Always said she knew I was coming. Water, please, with two cubes of ice and a wedge of lemon." She smoothed the tablecloth.

"Sorry, no lemon."

Joyce sighed. "Well, then."

She lived to disappoint.

They enjoyed their food in relaxed silence until Libbie judged her guard was down.

"You mentioned 'keys.' There are several keys hidden outside?"

"Oh my, yes." Joyce took a sip of water.

"Why?"

"Alice got locked out once. Many years ago. Back when she used to drive. She had to break a window to get inside." Joyce took another bite of roll.

"Wasn't one spare key enough?"

"She had a key hidden, but when she went to fetch it, it was gone. Or maybe she forgot where she hid it. She hid a bunch more keys so she'd be likelier to find one the next time she needed it.

"She didn't do it all at once, but over the years. Every so often she'd get to worrying about locking herself out again. Next thing you knew, she'd get another key made and hide it somewhere outside."

"Do you know where they're all hidden?"

"Oh, no. Only the one."

"Well, then, we'll leave it there in case you need it." Even if she got her hands on that key, there were unknown quantities still available in the yard. She'd have to figure out what to do about that and the solution would likely involve a locksmith and new locks.

"I should've asked sooner. Should I call the Home? Are they out searching for you?"

"Dear me, no. I got a ride over here today." She chuckled, but with a mischievous edge. "I got a ride with one of the nurse's aides. I told her I was going to visit my niece."

"You lied."

"That may be. I had to get away from all those old women for a while. Old people can be so annoying. Don't get me started on the aides. They mean well, but they're bossy. Or they talk to you like you're a two-year-old. Sometimes you have to do what you have to do."

Libbie understood that fine.

"You got people of your own?"

People. "Yes, my cousin Liz and her husband and kids."

"No mom and dad?"

She shook her head. "They died."

"Long ago, I guess, judging by the way you say it."

"I was young. Five."

"You grow up with that cousin of yours?"

"No. Well, sort of. My grandmother took me in."

"Took you in? Like you had nowhere else to go?"

"Not exactly." Libbie shrugged. "Sort of."

"Not looking to raise more kids, I reckon? Wouldn't be the first grandma that had to."

"Maybe so. She adored my father and uncle. I was a poor substitute."

"That so?"

Enough. "Did you have children?"

"No. Never did. Didn't work out."

Maybe they had something in common, after all. She gathered up the dishes and changed the subject.

"Would you like to hang around here for a while? Watch TV or something? I have things to do, but you're welcome to stay and amuse yourself."

She shook her head. "I might like to sit out on the porch

for a while. Maybe nap on that fancy new furniture."

Joyce folded the cotton throw into a cushion for the rocker. She settled into her seat and went gently to sleep. The air was fresh and wonderful, but Joyce liked it warm so Libbie found a lightweight shawl in her closet and brought it out to drape over Joyce's legs. The birds chirped. The road was distant enough that the occasional car didn't disturb her. After a while, Libbie chose a book from the armoire and joined her, sitting in the other rocker. When Joyce woke, she'd drive her back to the Home.

She dozed off. The crunch of tires in the driveway woke her. She was disoriented, but Joyce was already awake and waving at the new arrival. Dan. The deputy.

She stared at Joyce. "You didn't lie to me, did you?"

Joyce got a "who me?" expression on her face and shrugged.

The deputy came straight up the steps and he didn't look pleased. "Ms. Inman, you took a walk this afternoon. They're worried back at the Home." His voice was soft when speaking to Joyce. His frown was directed at Libbie.

What had she done wrong? Her temper rose.

He continued, "Ms. Havens, here, was going to call and let the Home know if you took off again. I guess she forgot."

So they were back to surnames? Libbie turned to Joyce, her eyebrows raised in question fully expecting Joyce to inform the deputy that she'd left with permission, but she didn't. Instead, Joyce appeared puzzled and sweetly elderly.

"Dan Wheeler, it's nice to see you. Been so long. How's your mama and daddy doing?"

"They're fine, Ms. Inman."

"Well, you tell them I asked after them."

"I will, ma'am." He'd taken off his hat and was rubbing the back of his neck. "Are you ready to go back?"

"Why sure. Elizabeth will take me."

"Libbie," she said. "Call me 'Libbie.'"

"Well, of course, dear. Libbie. My friend Libbie will take me back. No need to worry, Dan. You were always such a cute little boy. You're all grown up now."

Rather syrupy, she thought, but Joyce pulled it off nicely considering he was long past adolescence. Joyce was overdoing the folksy thing, treading a fine line of manipulation. Dan looked like he thought the same, but wouldn't challenge her and risk being proved wrong and rude. Only a brute would insult an elderly family friend. Joyce was pretty wily, so Libbie figured that was a good decision on his part.

"Ms. Inman, you can't keep going off like this. It's not safe and it's not fair to the folks at the Home."

Joyce said, "I'll visit the facilities before we leave, if you'll excuse me."

Libbie tried to catch her eye and failed. Why didn't Joyce speak up and get her out of trouble? On the other hand, she enjoyed a perverse satisfaction seeing Deputy Dan flushed and irritable. A smile tugged at the corners of her mouth. She reminded herself that this man had toted rugs for her and had introduced her to her neighbors. A little extra consideration was called for.

Joyce made a big deal of getting out of the chair and managing her cane. Dan held the door for her. As soon as Joyce had gone inside, he turned to Libbie.

"You said you'd call the Home if she showed up again."

"Yes, I did say that." She stood and hooked her thumbs in her pockets. "Rather, I was going to call if she left without permission. That wasn't the case this time."

"No one at the Home knows where she is." He left the sentence hanging there as if expecting her to finish it.

She shrugged.

His eyes narrowed. He looked like he was contemplating her fate and his thoughts weren't pretty. Perhaps he deserved more cooperation, but she didn't like his attitude. Also, there must be a reason why Joyce didn't speak up about getting the ride over here with an aide.

She didn't mind playing the bad guy, at least until she understood why Joyce didn't want to come clean with the deputy.

In the silence, as they waited for Joyce, Dan seemed to examine the distant trees, the porch, his eyes travelling wherever.

She asked, "Is there a problem? Aside from Joyce, I mean?"

"No. I heard your children were out here with you. Just noticed how quiet it was. No problems I hope."

Her children? What did Dan know about her children? He and Jim had been talking about her, about her personal business. Gossiping. It annoyed her, on top of already being aggravated.

She crossed her arms. "I don't have custody."

He nodded. "I see." After a short pause, he asked, "How's it working out with Max?"

"Okay. He comes and goes as he chooses."

Dan frowned, but before he could express his thoughts on her pet management skills, the storm door hinges squeaked.

"Here she is." He offered his arm to assist Joyce down the steps.

"I'll get my keys." She wanted to speak with Joyce alone. Joyce had put her into an uncomfortable position. Libbie wanted to know why?

"No need. She's ready to go. I'll drop her off."

"Oh." Joyce hooked her cane over one arm and used her free hand to fumble in her tote bag. She pulled out an envelope. "I almost forgot what I brung you. Brought it for you." She handed Libbie the envelope. "A clipping. You can read it later. Thought you'd be interested, considering."

Considering? Libbie felt like she'd been out-stepped.

Dan helped Joyce into the cruiser and Libbie waved as they drove off. The next time she saw Joyce, if she saw her again, she could ask her why she'd lied, either to her or to Dan, or both, but would Joyce remember the conversation? Her memory seemed hit or miss.

Libbie sat on the wicker settee and opened the envelope. As Joyce had said, a newspaper clipping was inside. It was an obituary for Alice Carson.

ALICE L. CARSON - Alice Lambert Carson, 92, of Cub Creek, died Sat., Jan. 1, 2014 following a fall at her residence. A private graveside service was held Wed., Jan. 5, at Apple Grove Baptist Church by the Rev. Albert Simms who officiated at the interment in the church cemetery. Mrs. Carson was born June 27, 1922, daughter of the late John M. and Agnes Peyton Lambert of Cub Creek. She was preceded in death by her husband, Roy W. Carson, Sr. in 1999 and is survived by a son, Roy W. Carson, Jr. of Montana. Excepting four years when Roy Carson, Sr. served in the US Navy during WWII, Mr. and Mrs. Carson were lifelong residents of Louisa.

She was touched Joyce brought this to her. Alice had been Joyce's friend. This clipping was almost a personal introduction to someone she'd cared about. In some weird way, Libbie felt included.

Keys. She should get the locks rekeyed. They were so

old, she'd probably do better to get them replaced. That would be the smart thing to do.

But then, Joyce might walk all the way here and not be able to get in. She was accustomed to finding the keys in the bushes or rabbit holes or wherever.

It had been an interesting day: furniture delivered in the morning, unexpected company for lunch, and a spitting contest with Deputy Dan in the afternoon. What more could a woman ask for? Especially a woman who didn't have custody of children who weren't hers, who encouraged wayward behavior in little old ladies and, for whom, the truth of her life was even stranger than what she allowed others to see.

Restless, she paced the porch. Dan Wheeler was irritating. She thought about Jim too. Very different men.

Jim. While she was having so much fun, maybe she'd burn a little gas and cap off the afternoon with a visit to Mitchell's Farm Nursery. There was some stone she wanted to see.

Maybe Jim would be there.

****

A gravel road led from the main route and curved around to the nursery entrance. It had been a farm. The Mitchell farm, no doubt. No crops were grown and harvested here now except as rows of potential Christmas trees and deciduous trees. There was a large beige steel building containing indoor plants, pots and such. Two long greenhouses stretched back behind the main building. To the left of the main building were most of the outdoor plants, artfully arranged with artificial pond displays and other outdoor decorative features like trellises and arches.

There were a number of customers. Some were looking. Others were focused on selecting their purchases and loading them into the backs of their pickups or SUVs.

She strolled between the rows of plants keeping an eye out for the patio blocks and flagstone. A petite girl with a blonde ponytail tipped in purple was carrying a large potted plant. She paused to ask if Libbie needed assistance.

"I'm looking for stone for my terrace."

"Around the end of that H-frame. I'll be back in a few minutes if you need help."

Jim was right. Flagstone was one of many choices. She knew what she wanted the instant she saw it. They were beautifully textured blocks in mellow hues that looked soft and warm. They weren't, of course. She ran her fingers over them. They'd feel wonderfully smooth under bare feet and the aged appearance would blend well with her old house.

She took a brochure and flipped through it. The pictures were colorful and glossy and there was no pricing information so the blocks were probably expensive. Also, she'd have to pay someone to do the work.

There was nothing like a new project, a quest, to get the heart pumping.

The girl was back. "Did you find what you wanted?"

"Yes. How do I arrange for an estimate?"

"They're out today. If you'll write your name and number down, one of them will call you on Monday."

The ride home was pleasant. Libbie liked to drive and had the speeding tickets to prove it. All paid, of course. She tried to keep an eye on the speedometer and enjoy herself too. She wasn't expecting to see a white van and Liz's Benz parked in her driveway.

She pulled off to the side and into the grass to ensure Liz and the strangers would have an easy exit. The van had a sign on the side for a decorating company.

Liz rushed over. "At last, here you are." She took

Libbie's arm, urging her forward. "It's my fault. I should've called first, but I wanted to surprise you."

"What's up?"

"My present to you. I wracked my brain trying to think of the perfect gift. Impossible to thank you for those wonderful photos of Adam and Audrey. Please, don't say no. I want to do this for you."

Two men exited the van.

Liz followed Libbie's gaze.

"They're here to do the measurements."

"Measurements?"

She practically jumped in her excitement. "Draperies. I know exactly what you need. Please say yes."

Libbie unlocked the door and allowed them inside. There were so many thoughts and words juggling for attention in her brain that she couldn't pick out what to say.

"You don't like 'fussy' so we'll keep them simple and classic." Liz hugged her. "I need to repay you for those wonderful photos. So amazing. I never saw you do anything like those photos before. And my children... I don't know how to say it, but they looked, gosh this is going to sound odd and it was probably a trick of the light, but they looked bathed in love."

She hugged Libbie again, almost squeezing the breath from her. "It can't be as wonderful as those pictures, but I want to do something for you. You'll love it. Trust me."

Libbie sat in the rocker with her feet propped up on the rocker opposite. Kind of numb. Not sure how she felt about curtains. Drapes, was it? Whatever.

In the end, they were nothing more than window coverings and if, ultimately, she didn't like them, she could take them down.

The men left and Liz was gone right behind them,

beaming in her shiny Benz and waving like a beauty queen on a float.

Libbie shifted in the hard seat. The back slats were unyielding against her spine.

Actually, cushions weren't a bad idea at all. Joyce had a point. Maybe Liz did too.

Chapter Ten

On Monday morning, after breakfast, Libbie walked into the dining room and gave it a critical look. This room hadn't made her renovation list yet. She spent no time in this room other than to walk through it to reach the screened porch or the kitchen. There was remarkably little wall space in this room. It was all windows and doorways.

What was she going to do with a dining room anyway? Still, the more painting she did in the rest of the house, the uglier these walls looked.

There was a lot of glass in the windows and doors and it might be interesting to incorporate the reflective quality into the decorating. The wall at her back, between the kitchen and dining room, was the only place a china cabinet would fit. A low buffet would fit beneath the windows. She ran her hands through her hair and shook her head. A terrace and a dining room. This was shaping up to be an expensive few months, but it sure was a lot of fun.

When considered rationally, why not paint the dining room? She'd do it sooner or later.

And the terrace? Well, that was an investment in the property. A good business decision.

What about other good decisions? What about seeing that figure in the shadows and feeling watched down by the creek? Yet rarely did she set the house alarm when she was away during the day. Because she had someone else to consider? Someone prone to unannounced visits and who knew where the keys were hidden?

Heaven forbid she should return home one day and find Joyce on the threshold having had a heart attack because the alarm was blaring. She'd rather risk burglars.

She didn't need a jacket today. She picked up her purse and headed to the car. She hoped to reach the Home shortly after their lunch.

Libbie rang the doorbell. The woman who answered wore pink scrubs patterned with little kites. When she told her she was there to see Joyce Inman, the aide stepped aside to let her enter. She was a short, scrawny woman, but she looked wiry and tough.

"What's your name?"

"Libbie Havens."

They entered the living room which functioned as a common area. Through a wide doorway she saw an expanded dining and kitchen area.

"Ma'am, come this way."

She had muscular calves and walked like a sprinter. They turned left and followed the long hallway, bypassing rooms on each side. Tiny rooms opened off each side of the hall. Most were decorated with personal items, but the occupants weren't in sight.

At the far end of the hallway there was a long room perpendicular to the main house. The curtains were drawn and the walls were lined with recliners. Most were occupied by elderly residents of all shapes and sizes, almost exclusively female, deep into their post-lunch nap.

The aide opened the door at the end of the recliner room and they entered a sunroom. It was filled with light that spilled over everything including the padded, white wicker furniture. Joyce sat in the corner with her eyes closed, her head slightly tilted forward.

"Ms. Inman, your niece is here. Come to visit you. You wanna wake up and visit?"

Her niece?

Joyce opened her eyes, but without recognition. She'd been sleeping soundly.

She raised her voice, "You wanna wake up, Ms. Inman? Ya' got a visitor!"

Annoying.

"Thank you," Libbie said to the aide. "Joyce, I'm sorry we disturbed your nap." She turned back to the aide. "I'll sit here while she wakes."

Apparently satisfied, the aide sprinted off to other duties.

Libbie pulled a chair nearer to Joyce.

"In the mood for a visit? Or would you rather nap?"

"I can nap anytime." Joyce rubbed an eye and stretched her fingers. "What brings you here? You ain't here with some no-good do-good group are you?"

"Joyce. Do you remember me? Do you know who I am?"

"'Course I do. I got my wits." She scratched her arm and then reached up and scratched her cheek. "We always nap after lunch."

"It's very warm in this room."

"When you're old, warm feels good. Good to the bones. You didn't bring barbecue, did you? 'Cause I already ate."

"No, no barbecue. What did you eat?"

She shrugged and threw up her bony hands. "It doesn't matter. No matter what it is, it all tastes the same. No salt and too soft. Old people food. Ugh." She made a face.

"They think I'm your niece, don't they? You left me looking stupid yesterday. Why didn't you tell the deputy you had permission to visit me?"

Joyce didn't answer, but held up her hand as if commanding silence. She stared at the window. The bright sunlight washed the color from her already faded eyes. The brown spots on her cheeks and hands were prominent. Her fingers plucked at a food stain on her slacks.

"Close that door," she whispered.

After Libbie closed the door, Joyce said, "Cause I didn't. I never said I had permission."

"But you told me you had permission."

"No, I did not. And keep your voice down. They're bad as jailors here and snitches are everywhere. Those old women might seem like they're sleeping, but oh my, no." Joyce wagged a bony finger at the closed door. Her voice was sharp. Ornery.

"Listening for all they're worth is what they're doing. I told you I asked the nurse's aide to drive me over to visit my niece. She was on her way home and it weren't no problem for her at all. I never said I asked permission."

"That's what I figured," she said with a trace of self-satisfaction.

"Oh, that's what you figured?" she mimicked.

"Why didn't you tell that to Deputy Dan?"

Joyce tilted her head and gave Libbie a crooked look.

"I don't guess you called him that to his face? Humph. If I told him and he told the matron, that girl could lose her job."

She leaned toward Libbie and stared, eyeball to eyeball. "You don't want that to happen, do you?"

Libbie stared back. "Well, maybe she shouldn't have done what she did without checking first. Maybe she should lose her job. And maybe you shouldn't have put her in a position where she could lose her job for doing you a favor."

"You won't tell."

"No, I won't, but don't do it again. There's something else I need to tell you. I have an alarm in my house."

"An alarm? A clock?"

"No, Joyce. The house is alarmed for security. I don't always set it during the day, but I might and if you show up unexpectedly and open the door, even with a key, you could trigger it. It's very loud and the alarm people will call the police."

She deflated.

Libbie relented. "I'll show you how to work it the next time you come over."

"They won't let me leave if I'm walking."

"Fine. Call me. I'll come and get you." How had that happened?

"Write your number down and we'll give it to the matron." Joyce smiled, satisfied, and changed the topic. "You don't call him that, do you?"

"Who?"

"Dan Wheeler," she said.

"Deputy Dan?"

"It ain't respectful."

It was Libbie's turn to "humph."

"You have to know someone better, be their friend, before you take liberties with their name." She gazed straight ahead and added, "Ain't that right, Elizabeth?"

"Libbie."

"That's what I mean." She smiled with satisfaction and reached for her cane. "Now let's go visit Mrs. Hughes, shall we?" She stood and said in a scratchy whisper, "And remember you're my niece."

When Libbie opened the door to leave the sunroom, she noticed several old women had migrated nearer the door. They appeared to be napping, except one who made no pretense of sleeping. She grinned and waved as they went past.

Apparently, there were spies and perhaps there were snitches too. She wondered, with some amusement, if she could get into trouble with the law by posing as Joyce's niece? No, just another courtesy title. Legal trouble or not, there was likely be a decided degree of inconvenience as she'd suspected at their first meeting.

When she returned home there was a pickup parked in her driveway blocking her way. At first, she thought it was Jim Mitchell's truck, but the man standing beside the vehicle wasn't Jim. He introduced himself as Victor Smalls and apologized for blocking the drive.

"I called first, but no one answered. I was out this way, so I took a chance on stopping by. I hope it's not inconvenient? I'm here to do measurements for a patio."

"Terrace. What I have in mind is a terrace." She walked him around back, explaining how she envisioned the layout. She left him with his tape measure and went inside to grab the glossy brochure to show him what she wanted. He promised to have an estimate to her within a few days.

****

Liz called the next morning and invited Libbie to meet her for lunch in Charlottesville. Josh was traveling overseas again and the kids were in school. She had an appointment to get her highlights touched up and expected to be done by noon.

"Sure you don't want to join me, Libbie?"

"I don't have an appointment."

"I'm sure they'll fit you in if I ask them."

"Nope. Thanks for checking, but I'm good."

Libbie arrived first and secured a table in the corner near the window. She saw Liz crossing the parking lot. She walked into the restaurant as perfectly put together as ever.

The only highlights Libbie had ever had were bleached by Mother Nature. The simpler approach suited her. She might not be gorgeous in the same way as Liz, but she knew was attractive even if her hair was out of control.

Liz said, "Are you doing something different? You have a certain glow about you. You always had the most amazing complexion. I've always been jealous."

"No need to lie, Liz. You, however, just walked off the page of a fashion magazine." She nodded toward Liz's three-inch heels. "How can you walk in those?"

"I walk just fine, thank you. And thanks for the flattery. Excessive or not, it's appreciated." She reached up to smooth her hair. "I mean it, you know. You look like you've got a secret."

Over lunch, Liz talked about Josh, the kids, her friends. Libbie listened and part of her was curious, almost envious, but part of her was relieved that when she returned home she would be alone with no demands on her time, no confusing social signals, no added emotional drain.

"Audrey and Adam had a great time at your house."

"I'm glad. It's kind of boring for a couple of kids. I don't lead an exciting life."

"You taught them how to play Canasta. They're bugging me to death over it." Liz frowned, but it was a pretend frown that didn't dim the sparkle in her eyes.

"Have you lost your touch? You used to win all the time."

"I told them to save it for their next visit to you, *dear Aunt Libbie*." She leaned forward. "Speaking of visitors, have you met anyone interesting?"

"What do you mean? Like the mailman? Cashier at the grocery store?" It sounded like the kids, probably Audrey, had been talking about their visitor.

"Don't be dense. You know what I'm talking about."

"Well, I do have a friend of sorts. Visits from time to time. Of course, she's ancient and tends to wander in a number of ways." Libbie smiled, delighted to frustrate her.

"Fine. Be like that. I'll just say it. Audrey says you have a boyfriend."

"Now I understand. Audrey has jumped to unwarranted conclusions. He's the lawn and landscape guy."

"Oh." Liz sighed. "She'll be disappointed. She said he was handsome. I'm disappointed too. I thought maybe it was our deputy friend. You have a look about you. I thought maybe you were in love again. I don't like you being so alone."

"I'm fine. I'm busy. Let me tell you about my plans for a terrace..." The last thing she needed was her cousin's help with romance.

Libbie was on her way home when Jim called her cell phone. He had the estimate for the patio and was hoping it was convenient to drop by.

"Terrace," she corrected him. "I'll be home in about thirty minutes. Any time after that is fine."

Max was on the porch. She opened the door to let him in, but instead he dropped down on the floor next to a rocker, so she sat outside with him and waited for Jim. Within a few minutes, he drove up.

"You two look cozy," he said.

"We are. Do you mind talking out here? Can I get you something to drink?"

"Nothing to drink, thank you."

Jim chose the bench. His cotton shirt was a blue and black plaid that worked well with his blue-hazel eyes and dark, almost black hair.

"I never asked you, but I want to know so I'm going to ask. Did you want to buy this property? That's what Dan said."

He answered slowly, "I was thinking I might."

"I saw your nursery. It's a big operation. Did you have plans like that for this property?"

He laughed and put his clipboard on the seat next to him. "I'm glad you feel comfortable enough to ask, but it seems more like an interview. Are you curious? Or actually concerned?"

He had an interesting way of speaking, of phrasing with short pauses, as if always ready to stop and listen. Like an invitation to conversation.

"Curious. Maybe concerned that I caused a problem for you without realizing it. If so, I might want to apologize, but that depends upon what you'd planned for the property."

"I see. No particular plans. Thought I might use it to store some equipment to have it on this side of the county, but nothing more than that."

"That was a big price for a few parking spaces."

Jim tapped his fingers on the arm rest. "Maybe a drink would be good."

This time, she smiled. "Water or iced tea?"

"Tea."

Max watched as she stood and went inside, but stayed where he was. When she came back, Jim had laid a diagram on the end table between their seats.

Plans for her terrace. But she wasn't ready to be distracted yet.

"So...for parking, you said? You can say so if it's none of my business."

Jim stared off across the distance, as if at the horse farm. Finally, he said, "I didn't want Alice's property denuded of timber. Figured I'd buy it, hold onto it, maybe make a profit on the resale when a good prospect came along. I know the developers in the area. They'd have beaten us both to it if Sam hadn't gotten the property on the market a few days earlier than expected."

"That's almost funny."

He frowned and picked the clipboard up. "Not intended as funny."

Libbie leaned forward. "Not what I meant. I meant that my impulse to buy this property was prompted by the idea of the woods being leveled. Something that Sam Graham said to me. It was by chance, you know, that I happened along that day."

"That's what he told me. By pure chance, he said."

She shrugged. "Well, it was, and when he said that about selling it for timber, well, something happened in me. So, that's what's funny. We were both motivated to buy Alice Carson's property to keep it safe."

Jim nodded. "Can't say I'm surprised."

That seemed a mysterious remark, or a supercilious one. "How's that?"

He groaned. "Don't make me sorry I said this. I know it sounds foolish. There's something about this property that's different."

Was he testing her? Had he learned about her special gifts? No, of course not. Not possible. She relaxed her neck and shoulders.

She asked, "Different? What does that mean?"

"You haven't noticed? I was sure you had since you felt the need to protect it too."

"Maybe I have. Maybe."

"It's more...just more. I don't know how to explain it better. There's something about the property here. I remember my grandparents saying the same, but they called it the old Lambert Place back then. It's just a little more 'there' than most places. That's the best I can explain it." He grimaced. "And if you tell anyone I said that, I'll deny it."

His grin told her he was kidding. Sort of.

"Hold on." Libbie got up and went inside. She returned with her sign. She held it up.

"Not the Lambert Place and no longer the Carson Place."

"Cub Creek?" Jim was silent for a few seconds, then added, "Sounds right."

"Right enough for you to help me hang it? I tried hammering the pole into the ground, but messed it up."

He took the sign from her hands and brushed his fingers over the deeply carved letters.

"I can do that." He handed the sign back with a smirk. "But if you don't mind, and if you don't have any more questions, maybe we could discuss the estimate for your...terrace?"

They reviewed the layout and the numbers while Max lounged nearby, head resting on the cool, smooth boards of the porch floor. Every so often his haunches would shiver as if running in his dreams.

Victor had drawn the terrace layout on graphing paper. Jim explained the costs. The terrace would be expensive, but it was decided. There was no point in acting coy.

"I have one concern. Here where the screened porch meets the terrace." I touched the drawing. "And here where the back steps come down. How will that work level-wise? I can't tell from this."

"Why don't I show you?"

"Sure. Let's go out back." She went through the front storm door and held it open for him, in invitation, rather than walk around the exterior of the house.

He paused in the foyer. "Wow. Bears no resemblance to when Alice and Roy lived here. I like the paint job." He saw the antique desk in the study and gave a low whistle. "Nice."

As they moved into the living room, he paused to stare at the photo collections.

He stood in front of the road group. He turned to survey the train rails. He moved closer to a select few, especially those of the kids that she'd interspersed.

"You did the photography?"

"Yes."

"They are…beautiful…well, maybe not beautiful, except for the kids. But compelling."

Compelling. She liked that.

"They're a hobby."

He looked around. "Are they here?"

"The kids? No." She added, "Not now." She couldn't resist. "Too bad I had to run off so quickly last time."

"Yep. Had that appointment." He paused in front of the country roads photos.

"People usually ask what the pictures mean," she said.

"I suspect they mean different things to different people."

"I like that and I think you're correct."

"Maybe one day you'll tell me what they mean to you."

She paused, mentally processing his words and tone. He was being friendly, no more. He was a pleasant person as well as a good businessman, so of course he'd say nice things.

"This way." She led him out the back door.

He explained how the terrace would accommodate both exits.

"When could we start and how long will it take?"

"I checked this morning. The block can be delivered here in two days. Usually takes several weeks. We got lucky." Jim paused, smiling. "Also, I have a crew available. They finished the Baxter job early. They have a week before the next job is scheduled and can take on yours if you're willing to move ahead immediately. I have to tell you I've never had a job fall into place so smoothly, so quickly."

Libbie wasn't surprised. Her property on Cub Creek seemed inclined toward happy coincidence. Plus, Jim already understood about this place. Remembering what he'd said amused her and made her smile.

Jim smiled back. "The terrace is a relatively simple job. With good weather and continued good fortune, they'll wrap it up in a few days. Maybe Monday. Maybe Tuesday. Now, what about plants for foundation beds around the terrace?"

Jim suggested some plants. She didn't recognize many of the names.

"I want plants that stay green year-round and don't require upkeep." She smiled again, sweetly and sincerely.

He raised an eyebrow. "There are plants, evergreens, some azaleas and rhododendrons, that stay green year-round, but all plants require some basic care."

"I can sprinkle them with water from time to time, but I don't want to be digging things up and replanting. Or having to prune them all the time. Azaleas are good, I think. They don't seem to be much trouble." Libbie started it as a joke, then realized she also meant it, at least in terms of not wanting to have to replant and such.

"I think I understand. You'd like plants that stay green and attractive, don't require pruning or other care." He said it slowly as if trying to decipher her words.

"I've considered plastic. Some of it looks very realistic."

Jim's face went blank, then without change of

expression except a tiny quirk at one corner of his mouth, he responded. "Yes, we have a lovely line of plastic plants. Resistant to disease and pests and they never require pruning. Perhaps a bit of watering occasionally to dust them."

"With plastic mulch, I hope. I don't want to have to redo the mulch every season."

"We can also supply plastic mannequins to enjoy your patio—excuse me—terrace."

"Sold." She laughed and Jim laughed with her.

"Should I sign something?" she asked.

They walked back to the front porch. Max was still there, but had moved to a sunny spot.

"He's looking good. Kind of you to take him in."

Kind? "I think he's doing me a favor."

Jim slid the paper with the numbers from among the others and turned it to face her, handing it to her.

"Sign here to show we reviewed the estimate. I'll put together a separate contract for the plants. We usually require half up front and the remainder on completion. Please read the print about possible additional expenses. That's always a possibility, but unlikely in this case. I'm familiar with the ground around here and we aren't likely to run into anything unexpected. Well, nothing that would affect this project."

He folded the contract and placed it in his portfolio case.

"I'll get my checkbook."

"No hurry. Wait until the block's delivered. I can't believe the good luck will hold." Jim didn't stand up to leave. He leaned forward with his elbows on his thighs, his hands clasped in front of him. "I'll be here when the block arrives."

A sense of expectancy filled the air. She waited, wondering what it meant.

Jim spoke. "Hope you don't mind if I ask, but how do you like living here? You've been here about two months?"

"About two months, yes." Small talk. She could handle that. "You already told me you grew up around here. I guess you liked it, or you wouldn't have stayed."

"I had my son to take care of and it helped being around family."

"A son? How old?"

"Seventeen. He'll graduate from high school next year and then off to college. I hope."

"I suppose it's not easy to raise a son."

"Your son is much younger. Wait until he's a teenager."

"Oh." It was time to tell him the truth. She was formulating the right words, when he changed the subject.

"Any regrets about moving here?

"No, I like the peace." She leaned forward. "You know, about the kids–"

"Sorry. Didn't mean to worry you. Teenagers are teenagers. Just keep a good relationship with him and he'll be fine." Jim stood. "Let's get that sign hung."

She'd almost forgotten about it.

"Thank you. That's kind of you. I appreciate the help."

A smile and a nod that said 'friendly,' but also something more, passed across his face.

Something more. *Just more*, hadn't he said? Like the property. Like her.

****

Jim's contractor, George Roza, knocked on Libbie's front door about ten a.m. and asked if he could see the site for the patio. He was broad-shouldered, built like a weight lifter on the downhill side of fifty.

She showed him where she wanted the terrace. He seemed happy with the accessibility and with the level, hard-as-a-rock surface. He moved his arms around with lots of pointing to show how they would excavate the dirt to ensure a proper base. He was an artisan who understood his medium, block and stone, and the requirements of the construction, as well as good drama. Libbie felt confidence in Mr. Roza despite his annoying insistence on calling the project a "patio."

After Mr. Roza left, she prepped the dining room by wiping down surfaces, spackling small holes, and taping the trim. The walls had aged to a muddy gray. She planned to paint the entire room with the flat champagne beige. It would serve as a good base coat regardless of what she chose to do next. She felt like an artist preparing her canvas. Artisan. Artist. Creativity and energy seemed to infuse this place, inside and out.

She'd barely dipped her brush when the doorbell rang. She answered the door with paintbrush held aloft. A guy from Mitchell's Lawn and Landscaping informed her they were here to spread various magical potions in her yard to encourage the lawn to green and thicken and discourage the weeds—or words to that effect. Another man was backing a riding mower down the ramp of a trailer. She gave them her blessing to proceed and returned to painting.

The phone rang at three p.m.

"Aunt Libbie?"

The "Aunt Libbie Club" had a limited membership. "Adam? Is everything okay?"

"Oh, sure." He paused. "I told Mom."

"What? Told your mom what?" She held the phone in one hand and the paint brush in the other.

"About the fort. Remember?"

"Oh! Of course, I remember. What did she say?"

"She's okay with it. Kind of okay. She said she'll let me show her what I built. Can we come over on Saturday?"

She shrugged and nodded as if he could see. "Sure.

Come on Saturday for lunch."

"Aunt Libbie?"

"Yes, Adam?" She spread the paint.

He paused significantly. "It's still there, isn't it? I mean, no one's knocked it down or anything?"

"So far as I know, it's fine. I haven't gone out to check it in a couple of weeks, but it was fine the last time I saw it."

"Cool. Thanks. Uh, bye."

"Bye." She clicked off the phone and dipped the brush, but couldn't deny she felt touched. Adam trusted her.

****

Jim called the next morning to say the blocks were en route to the house. He was coming to meet the driver and take delivery. She was impressed by the personal attention he was giving to her project.

George Roza and his crew were already behind the house performing some minor excavation, staking corners, and running string.

The flatbed hauling the pallets of block was equipped with its own forklift. Jim was on site before the delivery was complete. They stood together and watched the man maneuver the forklift. After the truck left, Jim spoke with Mr. Roza. Jim seemed satisfied with their discussion and rejoined her.

"Any problems, Libbie, any problems or concerns at all, please call me immediately." Jim reassured her. "George and his guys are professionals. You can count on them to deliver great results, but, I repeat, any concerns, call me."

"I will."

Jim's eyes met hers. "Are you worried about this? A change of heart?"

She shook her head. "No, not at all. A little disconcerted by all the activity, that's all."

"These guys are pros, Libbie. Ignore them, unless you *want* to speak to George, in which case, feel free."

She walked with Jim around to the front of the house. He paused beside his pickup truck.

"Libbie. Is that short for Elizabeth?"

"It is."

"Elizabeth." He said it as if trying it on for size.

She met his eyes and spoke softly, but clearly, "No one calls me Elizabeth. Libbie is my name."

He looked embarrassed. She decided to lighten the moment.

"Is Jim a nickname for John? Or short for James?"

"No, not James. Jameson. No one calls me Jameson."

"Deal."

He laughed. "Deal."

Jim left and instead of jumping back into painting, she sat at her desk and watched for the horses to appear on the hillside across the way. From time to time, with more curiosity than anxiety, she peeked through the kitchen window to check on the progress of the terrace builders. After lunch she settled into the rhythm of painting.

At some point vehicle doors slammed. Her terrace builders were departing. She waited for them to drive away and then stepped out the back door and onto the stoop.

The dirt had been carved out shallowly into a neat depression. Mr. Roza was taking advantage of the rock-hard ground. The fill sand had been tamped down into the excavation and some of the edging blocks and interior blocks were in place. He walked back around the corner.

"I rang the doorbell, but you didna' answer. What you think? It's good?" His light accent was clipped and lyrical.

"Yes, I think so. I like how it's coming along."

"Yes, very good. Very nice patio."

"I'm sure it will be a lovely terrace."

"Don't walk on, okay? Not 'til we are done tomorrow. Okay?"

"Oh, no. I promise. I won't walk on it."

"Very good. Thank you. See you tomorrow."

He left. She walked down the steps to the terrace. The blocks were laid above ground level at the base of the bottom step. They curved in a semi-circle to meet the main area of the terrace which was raised and whose outer edge also curved. This same method was repeated at the screened porch steps such that the main raised arc was intersected on each side by the smaller, almost ground level arcs. It was pleasing in balance and appearance.

Libbie went to the woods to check on Adam's fort. It was possible, though unlikely, that it could've fallen. They'd had a little rain here and there, but no storms or strong winds.

There was the lookout tree. She ran her hand over the rough bark of the trunk and stepped around it to the fort. The fort seemed undisturbed. The smell of earth and green was strong. The leaves had grown apace and the camouflage was complete. It was good she knew where to look for it. She stooped and pushed aside the covering over the people entrance. Her heart took a leap. A dead squirrel lay on the floor of Adam's fort. She dropped the covering branches back into place and jumped up quickly.

Well, what to do? Her stomach was queasy. She didn't want to handle the little corpse, but she couldn't leave it for Adam and Liz to find. Crap.

The shovel was in the garage.

Libbie paused with her hand on the garage door. No, she didn't want the shovel, not if she had to go into the garage to get it. There must be something else she could use.

Trash can lid.

She unhooked the bungee cord, removed the plastic lid and looked for a stick. A wooden stake left behind by the terrace builders would serve the purpose.

Steeling herself to keep her imagination damped, she pushed aside the foliage covering the door and stooped into the fort. As she averted her eyes from the squirrel, she noticed the pine tags and dirt across the floor area had been disturbed. She held her breath, almost closed her eyes trying to see just enough to perform the task. She pushed and pulled the little body over the lip of the lid.

She pretended it didn't bother her as she carried it all the way back to the trash can. Safely inside. Safely stowed. Lid replaced. She tossed the stake back over to where she'd found it. Now that it was dealt with and she didn't have to look at the poor little guy, she could consider what might've actually happened.

There'd been no visible marks. Presumably, squirrels could drop dead of bad hearts or sudden illness like people. Funny how when you thought about it, you only saw them dead when they were road kill. She suspected this particular squirrel had died of a broken neck. It was something about how his head hung. Hard to imagine how that could've happened accidentally. A cat or dog, maybe, but wouldn't an animal have left marks? A cat or dog surely would've taken home its prize.

Libbie had no answer and there would be no autopsy for the squirrel. It left her unsettled and sad.

It was simply an unfortunate event. It made sense that things like that—like finding dead squirrels in the woods— happened in the country where there were so many creatures of all sizes running around. It was just bad luck that it happened to be in Adam's fort.

That's what she wanted to believe.

Chapter Eleven

George and his crew were back at work early in the morning. Judging by their quick, quiet efficiency they were planning to start their weekend early and her terrace stood in their way.

Libbie stood at the kitchen window and watched the terrace come to completion block by block. Some of the final blocks required chipping to fit the angles, then a special filler was spread across the surface of the block and swept into the crevices.

Jim arrived and spoke with George briefly, then came back around to the front of the house and Libbie met him on the porch.

"What do you think?" he asked.

"It's going to be beautiful."

Jim grinned. "I'm glad you're pleased."

"Should I write the check for the remainder now?"

"No. Let George finish up. He'll want to drop back by, probably on Monday, for a final look. That will give you a chance to use it, to consider if there is any problem, anything you are unhappy with. After that, we'll work on those foundation plantings. How does that sound?"

"Perfect. Thank you, Jim."

"My pleasure." He paused. "I have another project to check on, but I'll drop by later to see how the terrace comes out."

This time when George and his crew left, she went

outside and walked all over her new terrace. She stepped down from the raised part and then up to the screened porch step. She stepped down to the ground and up again onto the terrace. Up and down and all around the curved perimeter of the terrace, almost like a dance. The stones were mellowed tones of gray-blue and reddish tan. She couldn't have been more pleased.

She visualized how the terrace might be furnished. A table here. The chaise lounge in this spot. She could hardly wait to show Liz and the kids tomorrow.

The kids. Funny. Libbie realized she'd never set Jim straight about Audrey and Adam.

****

About three o'clock in the afternoon she heard tires crunching up the driveway and assumed Jim had returned to view the finished terrace. She had some ideas about the foundation plants and was eager to talk to him.

She pushed the lid down on the paint can. The doorbell rang and she went quickly to answer it. She'd left the front door open with the storm door latched and saw immediately it wasn't Jim. Dan stood at the door and he wasn't in uniform.

Libbie unlocked the storm door and stepped out to the porch.

"Yes?"

"Hope I didn't interrupt?" He looked down at her painted jeans.

"No. What's up? Did Joyce escape again?"

"Joyce? As far as I know she's where she belongs. I'm here for another reason. Would you like to go to dinner?"

"Dinner?" She stalled trying to figure out his angle.

"Food. A meal."

He was smiling but in an embarrassed kind of way. She hadn't thought of Dan as shy.

"It's early, I know, but I want to eat before going on duty tonight. Nothing fancy. Interested?"

Libbie started to ask if he'd heard of telephones, but bit the inside of her cheek instead. His style was lacking, but he'd gone out of his way.

No was a one-syllable word. Two simple letters. A word with which she'd had a lot of practice. But she didn't say it because he was flattered.

"I'll have to change."

"No problem. I'll wait."

How could she resist?

****

Dan drove to an Italian restaurant in Louisa. It was early and they were ahead of the supper crowd. The hostess greeted them and obviously knew Dan well. She led them to a table in the corner. It was set apart somewhat from the other tables and booths and felt almost private.

The waitress brought the menus. She knew Dan too, and greeted him by name. A man walked past on his way to the door, nodded at Dan and at Libbie.

"Dan. I get the feeling you're well-known around here."

He shrugged. "In my capacity..."

Certainly that made sense. "I hope you don't mind me asking, but is there anyone special who may not like us dining together?"

His eyes met hers squarely and he shook his head. "No, no one." He leaned forward. "I should ask you the same question."

Libbie folded the menu and set it aside. "Same answer."

The waitress came to the table and took their orders. They handed her the menus and Dan said, "Thanks, Sue."

After she'd walked away from the table, he said, "I think she wants me to introduce you. If you don't mind, I'll let her wait awhile."

She liked the twinkle in his eye. Let Sue wait and wonder.

"Have you lived here all your life, Dan?"

"No. I went away for a few years. Jim and I both did. He didn't go as far. I went to college and then joined the service."

"Military service?"

He nodded. "Yes, and it was good in a lot of ways, but I came to the conclusion I had more interest in local events than international."

"You came back home?"

"About eight years ago. That's when I joined the sheriff's department."

Dan had his hands on the table, fingers clasped, like he wanted to rap his knuckles on the wood. He'd become increasingly fidgety. He cleared his throat and said, "You probably wondered why I asked you to join me for dinner."

She'd assumed it was because he was interested in her company, but his remark poked a hole in that assumption. I shrugged. What could I say? "Why?"

Dan stretched his fingers, straightened his hands out on the tabletop and sat back in his seat. He rubbed the back of his neck. "I don't know how to say this. It's embarrassing and I'm not sure it's fair to you."

"What's this about?"

"Alice Carson was a real lady. I'm sorry you never knew her. She'd like that you have her house." He paused. "She was born in that house. Alice Lambert. It's called the Carson Place now, but for many years before, it was the Lambert Place.

"This is where it gets strange." Dan paused, before resuming. "I don't like to say this because you live there and you live alone, but the Lambert Place was believed by many to be haunted." He sighed loudly. "You can see why I didn't want to say this."

"Haunted?" She was incredulous. This was a fully mature county deputy sitting across the table from her telling her that her house was haunted and, somehow, this was a deeply difficult thing for him to say. Of course, he didn't know about the more exotic aspects of her reality. She must've looked dubious and unimpressed because he leaned forward and spoke intently.

"I'm not saying it is haunted, but that it has the reputation."

"The house isn't haunted. I would've noticed."

"Understood. I'm glad to hear it. I'm–" Dan stopped. Sue had arrived with the food.

"Sorry to interrupt the conversation." Sue smiled and asked if they needed anything else? "No? Fine. Well, just yell." She lingered for an extra moment before moving off.

Dan's steak smelled wonderful. She'd ordered a large salad.

"Well?" Libbie prompted him to continue. "I don't believe you went through all this just to tell me my house is haunted."

"I'm relieved you aren't upset. I had to tell you that part, to tell the rest." He took a sip of iced tea. "From time to time, kids or others, have shown up there. Sometimes a dare to touch the house, or some misguided trespassers. I confess Jim and I did some of that when we were kids. But, back to the present. It hasn't happened recently that I know of, but I overheard a kid the other day saying something about it and knowing you're out here alone…well, I wanted you to be aware."

She opened her mouth to speak, then closed it again. She shook her head and found the words she wanted.

"This was so difficult to tell me? I mean, I don't like the idea of trespassers, but for the rest? The house isn't haunted. Take my word for it."

He answered between bites, "Of course not."

"But you said..."

"Many have spoken of it, some believed it. Pays to be prepared, and to be prepared you have to have the information." He paused. "All of these reality ghost shows don't help. Puts ideas in people's heads and they lose good sense.

"If you see anything or anyone that doesn't seem right, feel free to call me." He reached into his pocket and retrieved a card. "My number. You don't have to worry that I won't take it seriously."

"Well, thank you."

The last bite of steak was gone. Dan sat back.

"You know that Jim and I are related?"

"Yes, I know." Now what? This was the strangest date she'd ever been on, but then it wasn't a date, was it? It was some kind of weird information session.

"Understand that Jim and I talk. We're family, plus we've been friends all our lives.

Sue materialized beside our table. "Would you care for dessert?"

Dan looked at Libbie and she shook her head. He asked for the check. Sue's expression was sour. She pulled the order pad from her pocket, tore off their tab and slapped it on the table, just missing Dan's hand.

Dan kept his face carefully bland and asked, seemingly unaware of Sue's annoyance, "Sue, have you met Libbie Havens?"

Sue's face lit up. "Why, no, I haven't."

"Well, then, please allow me. Sue Kersey. Libbie

Havens. Sue has served me lunch and supper more often than I can count. Libbie, here, is new to the area."

"Well, honey, I am pleased to meet you. Welcome to our little town. I hope you'll come back by here real soon."

All the while Sue was speaking Libbie was aware she'd already assessed her single state—no ring on the finger—and she wondered what Sue had made of the intense conversation she and Dan had shared. Nothing casual in the picture they'd made. Sue had summed her up, but Libbie wondered how well she could add. Libbie didn't care about local gossip. She noticed Dan tipped well.

They walked out to his SUV and were quiet for most of the ride home. Libbie was annoyed with the whole haunted house thing, but touched that he'd given her his number.

Finally, as they turned into the driveway, she said, "Okay, fine. Have it your way. If I need help with ghosts or ghost-seekers, I'll call on you to chase them away." She couldn't resist chuckling at the mental picture. "It's a deal, then. I'll call you as long as you let me watch. I'd love to observe your technique."

To her ears, that sounded provocative. Flirting, maybe. Dan might have thought she intended exactly that because he stared, and then she saw something else in his face and in the tension of his body. She was certain he was going to reach out, to touch her arm or her face. For the briefest second, she wondered what she'd do if he did.

It passed quickly. Dan laughed, cut the engine, and opened his door. She didn't wait for him to come around the vehicle, but opened the door herself and slipped out on her own.

It was still light outside, but the day was fading. The sunset showed promise of developing nicely beyond the ridge. Dan walked her to the porch. Should she invite him in?

He'd made no pretense of this being a romantic date. As they walked up the steps, she saw a piece of paper stuck in the storm door.

Libbie pulled the paper from between the doors and unfolded it. It was a note from Jim. A short, simple note saying he was sorry he'd missed her.

Jim had said he'd drop by to check the finished terrace. She'd lost track of time. Without design, she said, "It's from Jim. I forgot he was coming by."

Dan's expression change as she finished the sentence. She stopped short.

"Is there a problem?"

"No. No problem. I'll be on my way."

No problem? Obviously, he'd made an assumption. She wouldn't explain. Libbie extended her hand to him. She thanked him for supper, and bid him 'good evening.' He and Jim could have one of their conversations and sort it out themselves.

He stopped halfway down the steps, turned and looked back. He started to speak, then appeared to change his mind. He shook his head and resumed his walk to the car. She watched him back his vehicle down the driveway, but the daylight was fading and she couldn't tell whether he waved or not.

What might Dan have said if she'd given him encouragement? She felt adrift, suspended, waiting for a moment that had passed unfinished and wouldn't return.

Unfinished conversations.

Like the last time she'd seen Dr. Raymond, about five years ago over lunch.

He'd sat across from her at the bistro where they'd met for lunch. She was still his patient officially, but hadn't felt like one for a long time. They treated each other as friends, but with respect, careful not to cross intimate or sensitive lines. Their discussions were comfortable and companionable.

Barry Raymond wore a small, close-cropped beard that didn't fail to remind Libbie of those in his profession before him. He was balding, but it gave him dignity and emphasized his sparkling blue eyes. He was twenty years older than her and his soft assurance evoked confidence. Libbie always enjoyed their conversations.

They'd nearly finished the meal before she noticed there was something different about Dr. Raymond's manner. They'd been discussing her lack of employment—she'd walked away from another job—when Dr. Raymond said, 'I've decided to take leave.'

Libbie was surprised and concerned.

"Why?" she asked. "I had no idea you were unhappy in your work."

"I've lost my objectivity."

"What does that mean? You care about what you do. You care about your clients. Maybe it's reasonable that you can't always be totally objective."

"I do care about my work and my clients. Sometimes I care too much." He paused. "Mine is a position of trust and in losing objectivity, I betrayed that trust. Perhaps I've been focused on helping my patients for too long and lost sight of my own needs. I spoke about a patient to that patient's family, without permission."

"Has the patient complained? Will it cause trouble for you?"

"The patient doesn't know. I haven't told her yet. I've kept it from her. She's special to me." He stared down at the table.

"Maybe she won't find out."

"But, I know. I betrayed her trust, and I don't have the courage to be honest."

She felt sad for her friend. "I think, Barry, you've lost your objectivity about more than your client. I think you've lost it about yourself and the job you do. In fact, it might be kinder altogether if you don't tell her. Easing your conscience might damage her."

Her friend sat quietly, listening. She continued, "Do something different. Maybe for a while, maybe forever. What might you do instead?"

"Travel. I'll call it early retirement." He looked up from his hands. "Have you considered traveling, Libbie?"

She frowned. There were meanings within this conversation she couldn't catch hold of. It made her edgy.

"Travel where?"

"Just travel. Get away."

"Thanks, but no. I prefer to stay closer to home. Maybe someday I'll travel, but not now." Anxiety nibbled at me. What was wrong? Was I afraid of traveling?

"Libbie, I'd like you to consider stepping outside of your small, controlled space. Trust a bit. Take a small leap of faith. A hop of faith." He smiled at his little joke, but his eyes spoke of sadness.

She shook her head. "You've said that before, but I'm content in my space."

"Take a risk. You're a strong person. Trust yourself so you can trust others. Learn to forgive yourself and you'll be able to forgive the weaknesses and failures of others."

"I'm okay alone. I don't need anyone else." Her voice was almost belligerent. Sharper than she'd intended.

"Libbie." He touched her hand. "It's okay. Do something for me, for yourself? Remember I asked you to reach out to other people?"

"Of course."

He shook his head. "Step away from your family for a while."

She frowned. "What?"

"I'm not saying forever. Find other congenial people. Make friends. New relationships will give you a better perspective on your relationship with your aunt and cousin."

"We've discussed all this before. I meet new people all the time. Liz and I are fine, or will be. I thought we were talking about you now."

Dr. Raymond stood. His shoulders slumped. He reached out and took her hands in his.

"As you wish." He released her hands. "I don't know how long I'll be gone." He placed a business card on the table and slid it across. "John Franklin is a fine therapist. Call him. I recommend it."

"I don't think I will. I've been fine for a long time now. You're a dear friend. You, our friendship, can't be replaced."

He nodded, but didn't speak.

"Send me a postcard when you think of me," she said. It seemed an inadequate farewell, but at the time, she didn't understand it was a forever goodbye.

Dr. Raymond walked away. He didn't look back. She sat alone, troubled by a vague sense of dissatisfaction, of unknown things left undone. Loss.

Communication works well only if both parties are willing to listen. She wondered from time to time whose trust he'd betrayed, but she didn't want to think about it too much. It wasn't her business.

She received a couple of postcards from Dr. Raymond, but that was all. The last postcard was from Rome and now two years old. It was a picture of a fountain.

Libbie hoped he was happy in his travels.

Chapter Twelve

Saturday morning she drove to the hardware store to buy champagne flat paint for the dining room ceiling. Returning by way of Mineral, she stopped by the barbecue place to get their lunch. She bought plenty of everything.

Someday she'd find an alternative takeout place, but not yet. Why change what was working?

Liz and the kids arrived shortly after noon. They admired her new front porch furniture, the painting efforts in the dining room and her new terrace. Adam escorted his mom into the woods to view his fort. Audrey started to follow them, but Libbie grabbed her hand and asked her to help rustle up lunch.

Audrey pushed a chair over to the kitchen counter and climbed up to reach the cabinets. She got the plates down and set the table. The kitchen window was open and Libbie listened for Liz and Adam's return. Without question, Liz was a good mom, but you could never tell for sure what people would do or how they'd react. People were usually unreliable.

Audrey was fidgeting at her elbow with her hands full of silverware.

Libbie looked down at her. "What?"

"Can we eat on the terrace? On your card table? I think we should eat on the terrace. Please can we?"

"An excellent idea, Audrey. Fetch the card table. I'll help you carry it outside and down the steps."

Liz and Adam emerged from the woods while they were setting up the table. Adam walked behind his mom and gave a thumbs-up. Together, they all carried the chairs, food, and drinks out to the terrace.

"It's beautiful out here," Liz said.

Libbie was pleased to hear her say it.

She continued, "I hope it's not too quiet, too lonely for you."

Adam and Audrey were gobbling up the hush puppies. Libbie grabbed a few more for herself.

"I enjoy the solitude," she said. "I've kept busy working on the house and the yard."

"Who did the patio? It's very nice."

"Terrace. I call it a 'terrace.' Mitchell's Lawn and Landscaping. They'll do the foundation plantings too." Libbie told her about how it had all come together so smoothly, so quickly.

Liz said, "Terrace. Nice word. I like the sound of it. Makes me think of sweet Mediterranean breezes."

The kids ran off, whistles around their necks, into the woods.

Liz stacked the lunch plates. "Have you considered going back to work?"

"Not yet. I have things going on around here." She sipped the iced tea. "On the other hand, if I keep on with these home improvements, I'll need to go back to work."

Liz arched an eyebrow. "You can afford it."

She shrugged. "I can, but there's no telling what the future will bring. You have Josh. A partnership, if you will. I have only myself to depend on."

"That's not precisely true." Liz shook her head in disagreement. "You have family. Libbie, do you ever think about the items we set aside?"

"Think about them in what way?"

Their grandmother, Elizabeth, left a number of benevolent bequests, but willed the bulk of her estate to her granddaughters. Money buys ease, but not happiness. There was so much of the former that Liz and Libbie felt unworthy, especially considering their negative feelings about the woman who died and dropped it in their laps. Also, there were lots of items they simply weren't ready to dispose of. They put a portion of the estate aside—monetary, furniture and keepsakes—and agreed they'd dispose of the property as they jointly saw fit when the time seemed right. In her own mind, being childless, Libbie had assumed it would go to Liz's children when they grew up, unless something pretty drastic changed in her own life.

"Libbie, I've been thinking about all the work you're doing here. You should take the dining room furniture. Neither of us wanted it when we were dividing the estate, but we kept it because it was from Grandfather's family. We're paying a lot of money to store it properly. I think you should take it and use it."

Libbie couldn't recall a single happy meal at that table.

Her mood had soured. She turned her face away. A silence fell uneasily between them.

Liz said softly, "Think about it. It's your choice. Whatever you decide is fine."

Libbie stood. "I need more tea. Shall I freshen yours?" She picked up the leftover barbecue and took it inside the house. She pressed her forehead against the fridge. The cool, smooth metal against her skin was calming.

Voices engaged in conversation filtered in from outside. She told herself to shake off the gloom. She poured the tea and picked up the chocolate pie. Dessert time.

Catching the storm door latch with her elbow, Libbie

backed the door open because her hands were full. She recognized his voice before she saw him.

Jim was standing by the table in a relaxed mode, a study in casual charm. Jim and Dan were about the same size, but Jim's build was slightly trimmer. Liz and Jim were talking. Liz stepped away and walked over to take the pie. She used the opportunity to give Libbie a pointed, speculative look.

"Jim, hello! Sorry I missed you yesterday." Libbie sat the glasses on the table. "Would you care for some iced tea?"

"I don't want to interrupt," he said.

"No interruption at all. Has my cousin, Liz, introduced herself?"

"I'm pleased to meet you," he said, and extended his hand to her.

Liz shook his hand, grinning.

Libbie said, "Jim, have a seat and join us for dessert. Liz, Jim's the person responsible for this beautiful terrace."

Adam and Audrey came walking out of the woods.

"Pie. Adam. Chocolate pie. Mommy, can we have pie? I want pie."

"Audrey," Libbie held up her hands to stop the flow. "Go inside and get more plates and forks, please? But, first, you and Adam wash your hands. With soap." She said it no-nonsense, so they would know she was serious about the hand-washing. "Stop. Halt. Say 'hello' to Mr. Mitchell first."

"Yes, Aunt Libbie." They turned to Jim, "Hello."

Jim gave her such a look. She pretended not to notice,. She'd never said they were hers. She'd told Dan she didn't have custody which, of course, was the absolute truth. Truth could be surprisingly flexible. And gossips got what they deserved.

She went back inside to pour a glass of iced tea for Jim. She heard Liz asking him about the terrace.

They chatted over chocolate pie. Jim asked Liz where she lived.

"Charlottesville." Liz pushed a napkin toward Adam who had chocolate on his face. Apologetically, she smiled at Jim. "Do you have children?"

"A son. A teenager."

"Children are great, aren't they? Rewarding, but challenging. I don't know how I'd manage without my husband. Especially with a boy. I'm sure your wife feels the same."

"We're divorced. Matthew and I have been on our own for many years."

"Well. I'm sorry. Maybe. Sometimes it's for the best." Liz was sweetly sensitive and sympathetic—and shamelessly fishing.

Jim replied, "Yes. Our divorce was friendly. She left long ago. She lives on the West Coast. We don't hear much from her." He took a sip of iced tea and turned to Libbie. "It's nice you have family nearby. Family you're close to." He turned back to Liz. "That's one reason I stayed here to raise Matthew. My family's in the area and there's no substitute for grandparents, aunts, uncles, etc."

Score one for Jim. Liz was thoroughly impressed by that last statement, especially since he was single and appeared to be available. She'd have to have a serious chat with Liz to reset expectations or she'd drive her crazy with matchmaking.

Audrey had been staring at Jim for several minutes. Her mouth was ringed with chocolate and her eyes were fixed. Suddenly, everyone became aware of her stare and an awkward silence fell.

Audrey spoke, "I have a boyfriend too."

Okay. Enough. Who knew where she was going with

that? Libbie stood, grabbed her hand and said, "Let's go wash your face."

She dragged Audrey past the surprised faces at the table and into the house. Let them think what they would.

When they returned, Liz said it was time to go. She gathered the napkins and pie box and walked over to the trash can. As Liz unhooked the bungee and lifted the lid, Libbie remembered the squirrel corpse lying on top of the garbage.

"Liz." She moved to intercept her, but Liz lifted the lid and dropped the items into the can without incident. Liz showed no sign of seeing anything unusual or distressing.

"What?" Liz asked as she replaced the lid.

Libbie was puzzled, but let it go rather than try to explain.

Jim walked over to Liz. He looked at her and said, "I hope I haven't caused your visit to end early."

Liz assured him, "Not at all. We came for lunch and have errands to run." As soon as her back was turned to Jim, she winked at Libbie.

Liz winked? What next?

The kids carried the chairs inside before going around to the front of the house.

Jim said, "I'm blocking the driveway, but I have to leave anyway." He turned to Libbie, "We still have to talk about those plants."

She was relieved Jim was leaving now. Things seemed to be getting complicated too quickly, growing beyond her control. They walked around to the cars together.

Jim opened the car door for Liz and told her how much he'd enjoyed meeting her and the children. Libbie walked with him to his pickup.

"I'll trust you to choose the plants, Jim. Whatever you think will work best is fine with me."

"If you're happy with the terrace, we'll move forward with the plants on Monday."

"Yes, the terrace is beautiful. Better than I could've hoped."

"I'm glad. I'm sorry I have to leave now. I made a commitment to Matthew." He spoke softly.

"I understand. I have obligations myself. Monday, then."

"If it works out, I'll bring the crew and plants with me on Monday morning. The landscaping will take a couple of hours."

Jim shut his door and started the engine. Libbie walked back to Liz's car.

"I'll call you later," Libbie said, frowning.

Liz laughed. "I can hardly wait. Seriously, I'm glad there are signs of life out here on your acreage. I promise I won't meddle."

Her mouth gaped. "What do you call the grilling in my back yard?"

"Fact-gathering my dear. Just getting the facts, ma'am, and letting him know you have family. People who care about you. And, by the way, that lucky coincidence you told me about? About how the brick and crew became available unexpectedly?"

"You mean, for the terrace?"

"Looks to me like you might've gotten a little extra-special customer service." Liz waved, put the car into gear, and started down the driveway without waiting for Libbie's response.

Libbie waved at her family as they drove away. Liz's innuendo was silly. They were definitely going to need a firm talk to reassert reality.

It was still early afternoon, but she felt drained. Frankly, it didn't pay to establish relationships. They might be briefly satisfying, but they only complicated your life.

Suddenly, standing there in her front yard alone, she felt like the little boy in *Peanuts* who walked through life with the dirt cloud swirling around his head, except her little cloud was one of sad, gray confusion.

Quiet was restored, yet she felt emptiness. She went back to finish the cleanup. She folded the legs of the card table, then saw a stray napkin in the dirt and remembered the trash can.

How had she forgotten?

She steeled herself to lift the lid, as if something might jump out at her, snapping. Nothing but jumbled garbage was visible inside. Beneath the items Liz had deposited, she saw the newspaper on which she'd placed the small, furry body, but the body wasn't there.

In the edge of the woods, she found a likely stick. Gently, she pushed the stick around in the can. Papery trash, but no squirrel.

This made no sense. Only another animal would want the squirrel's remains. Even if a cat or dog had been able to get into the can, they wouldn't have replaced the lid. The answer seemed obvious, but that answer posed other questions.

Either she had totally dreamed up finding that dead squirrel and putting it into the can, or a live person had removed the squirrel. She didn't dream it, therefore...but why would anyone want a dead squirrel?

She replaced the lid. How did someone, anyone, find the squirrel in her trash can?

Unless they watched her put it there.

She felt a prickling on the back of her neck. Impossible to tell whether it was genuine, or a response to the thought of being surreptitiously watched. Due to the timing, she presumed the latter.

Enough. There was a simple explanation she was missing. She carried the card table up the steps and into the kitchen.

****

Grandmother Elizabeth sent Libbie to her room. Often. Maybe for something she'd done, but she was pretty sure Grandmother mostly just wanted to forget she was there in the house. The cook sent up meals so there was no danger she'd starve. At some point, she pulled out her markers. She had lots of paints and markers. She was ten and it was the one activity that kept her quiet, so Grandmother supplied them generously, but Libbie was out of sketch paper.

The perfect white walls offered themselves. For five years, she'd watched the shadows play on the walls as they shifted with the changing lights coming from both inside and out. To her, the shadows had color and form. The colors were before her eyes and in her head and she imagined capturing them by outlining them and filling them with color, maybe even tracing them in their shifting shapes as they progressed across the walls.

She knew she'd never actually do it, of course—until she did. Even then, with each stroke of the marker, she knew it was wrong. She didn't care.

First, she traced the outer edges. She looked at her plastic container of markers and knew there wasn't enough ink to fill in the shapes properly so she drew landscapes inside them instead. Tall, fluffy trees. Paths. Flowers with faces.

She worked for hours, lost in the work, but then elation gave way to chagrin, then to fear. There was no way to hide this.

Even the maid, usually filled with sympathy for Libbie's lonely state, couldn't ignore what she'd done.

Grandmother was quietly, eloquently livid.

You can't be trusted. You've spoiled your room. You spoil everything. If they hadn't gone to pick you up that evening..."

As Grandmother escorted her through the kitchen, her fingers firmly gripping Libbie's upper arm, her manicure pinching the flesh, Libbie looked around frantically for the cook, for the maid, for help. There was no one.

Instead of being sent to her room, she was shut in the basement.

And you'll stay here until you appreciate what you have.

Grandmother closed the door and Libbie heard the slide bolt hit home.

It was only a small piece of time. A fragment. These moments would pass and someone would retrieve her. She sat on the stairs with the light filtering in through the small, barred windows high up on the walls. Her anger and resentment had drained away, leaving her empty and wondering why she'd marked up the walls. Soon even that ceased to matter. Waiting. It was chilly. She was wearing a light cotton shirt and slacks. She stayed on the steps. They were like a little island surrounded by dim light and the smell of dirt. Libbie remembered what Uncle Phil had said and tried to imagine him and her dad playing make-believe down here. She could almost do it, but it wasn't long before the light changed.

Someone would be here soon because the shadows were creeping out and deepening. Darkening. Dark. It almost made her hopeful. And terrified.

What would they think when they carried the meal up to her room and she wasn't there? When Grandmother dressed for dinner out, and left, would they think to look for Libbie? Would they think she wasn't in the house at all?

She could've yelled. Maybe she would have if she'd known for sure that someone would hear her.

The air turned cold and damp. The smell changed, intensifying with the night. She huddled with her arms around her legs, resting her head on her knees, going to sleep without actually sleeping. Drifting. When the door opened light spilled down the stairs. She didn't move. The light above seemed less real than her current state.

Uncle Phil walked down the steps cautiously. He lifted her to her feet and picked her up. She was too big to be carried, but he did anyway.

She found out later that the maid had called him. When she didn't find Libbie in her room, she thought she might be spending the night with Liz. Bless her—she made it her business to find out.

He helped her pack an overnight bag. He smiled with his lips, but his eyes were bright with anger. He said she was coming to visit Liz for a few days.

Libbie was delighted.

Liz and she had a great weekend. She tried so hard to be nice to Aunt Margaret. Uncle Phil was funny and sweet. Regardless, on Sunday afternoon, they returned to Grandmother's house. He sent her to take her bag upstairs while he spoke with his mother.

Before he left, Uncle Phil came upstairs and hugged her. He gave her a card with his name and phone number on it. "Call me," he said, "if you need me." He ruffled her hair, and left. She watched from her bedroom window as he stepped out onto the sidewalk. The sunlight made his hair golden. He walked to his car to return to his home and to his wife and daughter.

Libbie's heart broke.

Grandmother and she shared Sunday dinner. Her feet dangled from the chair. She swung them more and more vigorously beneath the table, until the chair rocked and even the water in the glass near her plate, rippled. Grandmother pretended not to notice. No words were spoken. Not one.

Elizabeth's dining room table was a dark, glossy walnut, hand-rubbed to a mirror-finish. Grandfather's desk, at which Libbie was seated in the present day, was a warmer wood that invited the human touch. But then, she'd never known her grandfather. He died before she was born. Maybe he and Libbie wouldn't have liked each other either.

She never had the chance to thank the maid. Grandmother dismissed her that weekend while Libbie was at Uncle Phil's house.

She pushed away from the desk and walked out to the front porch. It was a while yet before sunset, but clouds were rolling in. Rain was forecast for tomorrow.

Every time Uncle Phil took her to his home, she cherished a secret hope that he would announce to one and all that she, Libbie, now lived at his house, never to leave again. It didn't happen, of course.

When she was fifteen, Grandmother suggested she go away to school. Libbie was angry. Why did she care? Because sometimes the home you know, however unsatisfying, is better than the unknown? She called Uncle Phil's special number, the one he'd given her that day when she was ten. She expected his support. He'd promised. She told him, her champion, that Grandmother was trying to send her away.

Uncle Phil was silent at first, and then agreed that it might be a good idea.

He died of heart failure while she was off at school, so

she never officially forgave him.

Libbie made her grandmother pay by behaving badly. It cost Grandmother a lot of money to persuade those schools to keep her. That's where Libbie learned the 'slather the bucks' technique. Anything inconvenient, unpleasant or embarrassing could be remedied by a generous application of greenbacks. Money couldn't buy happiness, but it could get you pretty close to satisfaction.

Libbie went back inside her house, her home on Cub Creek, and shook off the memories. It was time to paint the ceiling.

****

She was losing her mind. When she closed her eyes the strips of blue tape remained, the negative afterimage burned into her retinas in bloody hues, and the strips were crooked!

No matter what she did, no matter how many times she peeled the tape from the wall and started over, it wouldn't square because clearly the room wasn't square. After several hours of taping and re-taping, she threw the tape roll aside in disgust. It was an old house. Expecting trim, ninety-degree angles was unrealistic.

A light, misty rain had fallen for most of the day, but had let up, so she slipped on her shoes to take out the garbage. Pickup was in the morning. She lifted the lid of the first can. A dead squirrel lay on top of yesterday's picnic trash.

Libbie lowered the lid, counted to ten.

When she lifted it again, it was still there. Yes, indeed, one very dead squirrel. It had to be the same one as before.

In the woods, the leaves were heavy and the shadows were especially dark due to the overcast. Anyone or anything could be watching her.

She lifted the lid of the other trash can and deposited her two bags of garbage into the empty can. There were no

165

footprints in the wet dirt, except hers. There hadn't been enough rain to create mud, especially beneath the spreading branches of the oak.

This was a sick joke. What sane person would play such games with a dead squirrel? What would be the point? There were more effective ways to frighten someone. If it was a message, why deliver it this way? The trash guy picked up every Monday morning. If she hadn't come out here this afternoon, she would've missed seeing it altogether.

She felt alone. She sensed nothing negative or threatening in the air around her.

That squirrel hadn't jumped back in there by itself, and thus, while she didn't know much, she knew for sure that someone was roaming her property, regardless of intention.

****

For the second time since moving in, Libbie had trouble settling down for the night. An unknown person or persons was moving around her property and she didn't like it. Not one little bit.

Chapter Thirteen

Everything looked better in the light of day and that was true this morning. The sun was shining, the sky was an amazing, forever shade of blue, and the trees were well on their way to being fully dressed for spring. She'd figure out what was going on around her property sooner or later.

Libbie tidied up around the house, except in the dining room. For now, those blue strips could consider themselves abandoned. She was on hiatus from house painting.

Around noon she drove to Mineral. Some of the old houses had caught her eye, in particular an old, dark colored house that sat a ways back from the road, almost hiding in the wild overgrowth. She wanted to photograph something different from roads and rails. Given her experience with the fences, she thought that maybe she had narrowed her world too much. Maybe it wasn't about living subjects. This was an experiment and she was going to try a little architecture.

She sat in the parking lot at Miller's and chose her lens. Carrying the gear bag usually attracted attention and she wanted to walk around unnoticed.

The area around the house was too dark. There was a restored train station and she tried different angles before moving on to a nearby church. Whether it was the buildings or her, she didn't feel the connection and didn't stay long.

When she returned home, there was no Joyce waiting, no deputy and no Max. She boiled an egg and buttered some toast for a light lunch.

The day called to her. The sun was singing her song.

She sat on the screened porch, but wasn't content. Could it be she was missing Max?

He hadn't been home two nights in a row.

She walked out into the yard and called his name. She went down the path to the lookout tree and called again. She paused there, realizing she was reluctant to go farther on her own.

Chicken?

No, I'm not. Here I come.

The rough bark brushed beneath her fingers as she passed the tree, following the path she'd taken the weekend the kids had visited, when she'd gone looking for Adam and been afraid. Today she would face that fear.

With luck, she might even find her dog, or he might find her.

The back property line followed Cub Creek. Most of what she'd seen of the creek, especially on the Loop at the two concrete bridges, was of water, opaque and silently swift, running between high banks. Near the small, improvised bridge on her back boundary, the water was shallower where it flowed around water-worn rocks alongside the banks. The water between the rocky banks was deeper, surely, but she didn't plan to go swimming.

As she stood on the little bridge the air held the scent of innocence. The creek music, as it washed around the rocks, was soothing and inviting. There'd been no sign of Max or any other creature. He hadn't come home last night. Was he out here somewhere reverting back to that wild time in his life after Alice was gone? Should she report him missing? Did one do that with dogs?

"Max?" She called out his name. "Max, are you out here?"

The bushes and low growth were thicker now that spring was well along. She watched closely for signs or sounds of Max pushing through. No Max, but a distance beyond the bridge, on the far side where the undergrowth was sparse and the skinny pines reigned, a flash of pink caught her eye. It drew her forward over the bridge and beyond her boundary. It was low, near the ground. Likely it was litter marring the otherwise clean woodland.

As she walked up the gentle slope and drew level with it, she saw it wasn't trash, but a flower.

She'd never seen one of these before in person, but she knew instantly it was a Lady's Slipper.

Traces of black marred the trunks of some of the trees. It was obvious there'd been a fire at some point in the past year or two. Pine needles carpeted the ground. Lady's Slippers spread across the area growing near the base of the trees. Trite phrases like 'pink profusion' registered in her brain. It was the closest her mind could come to embracing this awesome, idyllic spot. Libbie half-expected pixies and fairies to dance out of the shadows.

Kneeling for a closer look at the slipper, she held her breath, afraid she'd damage it. It was a wild orchid—she knew that much. Out of habit, she reached for her camera. Nothing. She hadn't brought it.

Libbie wanted to capture this, desperately, all the more urgently because despite common sense, she felt like tomorrow would be too late. She stared up at the sunlight sparkling through the leaves overhead. How much time did she have? Could she run back to the house, snag the camera, and get back out here with enough sunlight left to take the photos?

The flowers wouldn't disappear overnight. They looked fresh and no storms were forecast. She could return tomorrow, prepared. Except, that she couldn't wait because, when urgency hit, patience simply wasn't in her nature.

She double-checked her laces to ensure they were securely tied. She left her sweater lying on the leaves like a promise. Nothing would change as long as part of her was still there.

Down the slope she ran, wary of leaves and twigs. When her foot hit the bridge, one of the boards snapped.

She stumbled to the side. Her shoe hit one of those rocks peeking above the water. It was wet enough to be slick. As she launched into the creek, her ankle bent and her knee twisted. The cold water drenched her to the waist.

Frantic, she grabbed and hugged one of the rocks with everything she had while Sam Graham's voice echoed in her head, warning her about underestimating Cub Creek.

Luckily—if there was any luck involved in this—her impetus had carried her to the far side. She didn't try to stand, but settled for crawling across the rocks to what was left of the bridge and the muddy bank.

Her ankle hurt. So did her knee. Thanks to her heavy wet jeans and socks she'd suffered no scrapes or broken skin.

She shivered.

No problem, she told herself. It would be fine. She'd hobble back to the house, clean up a bit and then head back here if it wasn't too late. If it was, then she'd do the sensible thing—what she should've done in the first place—come back in the morning.

On her feet, she tested her weight on the injured ankle. She could walk. Slowly. Gingerly. In squishy shoes. It was a ways back to the house, but she could make it, especially with the help of a convenient stick.

Rustling. Libbie heard it somewhere behind her, then off to the side. She couldn't pin the direction down.

She looked this way and that, unnerved. The noises stopped. She re-gripped the stick and tried to focus on getting back to the house. She got a pretty good rhythm going and then the rustles resumed. They seemed to come from around her, but were no closer.

Maybe those coyotes she kept hearing about? If so, they were probably just curious. As long as she was upright and clutching a big stick, they weren't likely to bother her. But she was ready to swing the stick if need be. That was the thought that kept total panic at bay.

By the time she reached the lookout tree, her confidence was pushing out the fear. Considering she was wet, cold, muddy and injured that was saying something. She refused to let down her guard until she was in the house with the doors locked.

Just getting home was enough for today.

The high point was that no one had witnessed her pitiful retreat home.

****

Libbie woke in the early morning while the mists were still lifting from the pastures.

She would do it better today and she wouldn't be intimidated.

Her ankle was bruised, but not swollen. Her knee was sore, too, but nothing serious. Crossing the creek might be tricky considering she'd broken one of the boards.

Max wasn't on the front porch. His water bowl was still full. She called his name but received no response. She was worried, but he'd proved himself to be a survivor. Like her.

She waited until mid-morning for the lighting to be close to optimal for the photos. She tied her laces firmly for good support and screwed the 50mm lens on her camera. She didn't want to carry much. She wanted her hands free for other things, like the stick that was still leaning against the back steps.

There was a board in the garage. She'd haul it out and take it with her to drop across the creek. She might be able to manage the crossing on the one board, but she could see it now—Joyce creeping up the path with her cane. She'd find the single plank. What if she tried to cross anyway?

She dragged the board out, brushed some of the dirt off and balanced it under her arm. She tried to walk but the board swayed. It was long and she didn't have the strength to keep it balanced. She stopped, readjusted her camera strap on one side and the board on the other, and then moved forward again.

Barely into the woods, she had to pause again to adjust her grip.

"Libbie?"

She turned halfway around. The board swung wildly and the momentum nearly pulled her over. Between the camera, the stick and the board, she knew she made a pretty ridiculous picture.

"Jim?"

"Good morning." He was holding his clipboard. "Going for a walk?" He came toward her.

"To take some photos."

"Of a board? With a board?"

"No. Longish story, but the board's for crossing the creek."

"I see." He grinned. She thought he probably wanted to laugh, but kept it in.

"Hang on a minute." He went to the back steps and left his clipboard there. When he returned, he extended his hands.

"Hand it over."

"Oh, no. I wouldn't dream of inconveniencing you. I can

manage."

"Happy to help."

He wasn't moving. This wasn't some personal or secret journey. She wouldn't mind not having to fight the board all the way to the creek. Besides, there'd been the rustling. If there'd actually been anything following her, other than her imagination, it wouldn't dare to bother two adults with a big board.

"If you're sure."

He handled the board easily. They moved forward and had barely reached the lookout tree when he asked, "Is that a limp?"

Had she limped? She looked down. Her sneakers were stained with mud. She'd tried to clean them, but they needed a real wash, or replacement.

"I had a misstep yesterday." She changed the subject. "Are you curious about where I'm going?"

"Aren't you curious about why I showed up at your house?"

Libbie stopped. "Yes, now that you mention it."

"I did a rough layout of the plantings I have in mind. I'd like to go over it with you."

"Oh. Thanks. I trust you though. Didn't I make that clear? You're the expert."

"I'm expert enough to understand you're the customer and the customer should give the go-ahead."

"We're going to see some flowers."

"Flowers?"

She didn't have to see his face to know he was looking around at the forest with not a flower in sight.

"Just wait. You'll see." She plunged ahead. "We'll check that layout when we get back."

With Jim along, the trip was a breeze.

They situated the board across the creek, then walked up the slope.

"Fire got this a couple of years ago. I remember it was a bad fire season."

"Lady's Slippers. Look."

He stood, observing before stepping into the growing area. "Very nice. I haven't seen any in a while. They're tricky to grow if the conditions aren't right. Rather, there's not much you can do to make them grow or not grow. They're picky."

"I'd like to take some back with me. I should've brought a spade and a box."

"Nope. You can't dig them up and transplant them. Doesn't work with Lady's Slippers. They'll die."

"So, when these are gone, I'll have to wait until next year to see them again?"

"They may be here, may not. Probably not."

"But..."

"Just how they are."

She snapped photos. Jim never complained. She took a bunch of pictures all the while knowing there was no way she could capture their otherworldliness with her camera lens.

Finally, feeling a bit silly at the quantity of photos she'd snapped, she stopped and sat on the forest floor with Jim.

"That it?" he asked.

She laughed. "Enough, don't you think? Thank goodness for digital."

Her sweater. She'd almost forgotten it. She'd expected to find it damp from being out overnight, but she did expect to find it.

"What's wrong?"

"I left my sweater out here yesterday. Where did it go? How... I left it by this tree. I remember."

What were the odds someone had come along and picked up the sweater late yesterday or first thing this morning—just happened along during the time her sweater was here unattended?

Her mood down-shifted, but only slightly. Jim was here. She wasn't alone, not this time. Yet someone must have been out here yesterday while she was. She spoke aloud without intending to.

"I don't buy it for a minute."

"Buy what?"

She shrugged. "I don't believe a coyote ran off with my sweater."

Jim shifted position and scanned the area. "We can look around. It might not have traveled far."

"It doesn't matter. I hope the sweater is making some creature's nest nice and cozy."

Jim stood and helped her to her feet.

"You sure?"

"Not important." She situated the camera strap around her neck. "Maybe it'll turn up." She added with a sigh, "And Max too."

"I wondered where he was. Out roaming?"

"Maybe, but I'm worried."

"Check with the animal shelter. If he got picked up, he'll be there. Alice may have had him implanted with one of those chips. He's a valuable dog, has papers. You know, like registered. Speaking of registrations, if you didn't update the county registration, the animal shelter probably wouldn't know to contact you."

"I did. The vet explained it to me."

When they reached the bridge he took her arm to assist her over the creek. She shot him a look.

"Hey, not taking any chances here. We already have a

history with ditches. Don't want to add creeks to it."

Libbie groaned. "Funny."

He delivered her to the far side with a flourish.

They chatted as they walked. After a while, Jim said, "I hope you don't mind me asking. What do you do for a living? The photography, maybe? You seem to be home most of the time."

"I'm between jobs. Taking a little time off." She made a sweeping motion encompassing all her projects in a virtual sort of way. "Between painting and the terrace and landscaping, it's been busy and expensive. Maybe I'll go back to work soon."

"Not too soon, I hope."

The lookout tree was just ahead.

"We're back already? A quicker trip with company. Thanks for the help with fixing the bridge. Shall we sit on the screen porch and review that layout?"

On the swing, each of them holding a corner of the paper, Jim shared the plans.

"Looks great to me. Hope I don't kill it all. You thought I was kidding about those plastic plants, but seriously, I would've dug up those Lady's Slippers if you hadn't stopped me."

"You wouldn't be the first, which makes them all the harder to find. They don't propagate and they fertilize differently than other flowers. Seeing a patch of Lady's Slippers is rare. I've never seen so many in one place."

"It's something one never forgets."

"Which is true of most things that are special or rare."

He smiled at her and they both went silent, rocking gently in unison in a comfortable silence. He was steady and calm. Libbie enjoyed his company. She was very comfortable with him. He was becoming a good friend.

Too bad love couldn't be that way. A relationship this easy and pleasant could never be love—at least not in her experience. Love was more likely to hurt.

A whine, then a bark. Max scratched at the door, his eyes fixed on her.

"He's back!" She rushed to let him in.

He jumped up, dirty paws on her arms, then barked and went to greet Jim. Jim scratched his head, but even then Max didn't relax until she was seated back on the swing. He arranged his long body incongruously around their feet and legs.

"Where've you been, Max? I missed you."

Jim said, "Wherever…he's happy to see you."

She let the question go because wherever he'd been, he was back now. He was dirty, but safe and sound and home. It was as simple as that.

Chapter Fourteen

Jim arrived at noon on Monday with a truck full of plants and gardening supplies, and accompanied by helpers in a second vehicle. He wore tan slacks and a white cotton shirt—definitely not dressed for digging in the dirt.

"Take anymore walks?" he asked.

"Not me. Enough adventure in my own backyard."

"I doubt that. How'd the photos come out?"

"Gorgeous, but they still fell short of capturing the beauty of the real thing."

"Why don't we tackle more mundane matters?"

He gave her a brief rundown of the plants he'd chosen and introduced the workers. She handed him the check for the remaining balance on the terrace.

"You can leave the invoice for today's work or bill me. Whatever works best."

"Yes, ma'am." He put the check into his portfolio case.

Jim cleared his throat. "Would you join me for lunch? By the time we get back, the landscaping will be almost done."

"Lunch?" Good grief.

"Lunch. You haven't eaten yet, have you?"

"No. I'm not dressed for a restaurant."

"You look great."

It was lunch, that's all. "Okay, then. If you're sure. I'll be right back."

"Certainly."

Same routine as before: change the blouse, don the earrings and fluff the hair. Not primping.

The workers had unloaded the goods from Jim's pickup. Jim held the door for her and she climbed in. Should she mention the meal she'd shared with Dan?

The question was decided for her when Jim drove to the same restaurant.

Didn't these two talk to each other? Well, she could just about guarantee everyone else would be talking about them.

The waitress, Sue, did a double-take when she saw Libbie at the table with Jim. She wasn't their waitress. Their waitress was a small, quiet woman named Margie. After Margie took the order, Sue cornered her near the door to the kitchen and appeared to be conveying some sort of whispered information. Libbie shook her head in wonder.

"Is something wrong?" Jim asked.

"No." She spoke a little tenuously. "I've eaten here before. I think the waitress over there recognized me."

He cast a glance back over his shoulder. "That's Sue. We were in high school together. Long time ago." He narrowed his eyes in studied concentration. "She married Dave Kersey. Again, long time ago."

"Jim, when I was here the other day, I was with Dan."

"Oh." He looked back at Sue again and she waved.

Libbie said, "I'm guessing there might be some gossip."

"Why did you and Dan come here?" He shrugged, then nodded. "For a meal, of course."

"Yes, and it's very nice of you to take me to lunch today."

"My pleasure." He paused briefly, fingering the silverware. "One of the hazards of living in the same town, in a relatively small community all your life, is that everyone knows you and your family. Everyone knows, to some degree, everyone else's history and current events. It's a hazard of small town life and of having roots. On the other hand, it's also a blessing. For all those years I worked in the city, sometimes the relative anonymity was a relief, but there's also comfort and security in recognizing the faces and sharing the lives of other people over a lifetime."

Jim paused again while Margie brought their drinks. The sound of the work day lunch crowd was all around in the low hum of voices and the rattle of dishes.

"You, however, are an unknown quantity." He sat back in his chair and tapped his fingers on the table. "You will inspire curiosity in a number of folks. Imaginations will be working overtime. Should I warn Dan?"

"You're asking me? I thought you two talked."

"We talk a lot." Jim shrugged. "We're related. Family. We've been friends all our lives. Best friends. What about you? I enjoyed meeting your cousin and her children."

She couldn't resist laughing. "They're delightful, aren't they?"

Margie brought their lunch orders. Jim ate fish and a vegetable medley. Libbie stuck with the same kind of salad she'd eaten on the last visit.

They shared general conversation until near the end of the meal when Jim returned to the subject of family—her family.

"So, Libbie."

"Yes?"

"Libbie. Liz. You're both the same age and you share the same name, Elizabeth. You look a lot alike. I'd have to be dead not to notice, not to be curious. Is there a story you're willing to share?"

"Jim, I'm sorry to disappoint you, but there's no story. Or, at least, not an interesting one. Our fathers were identical twins. They named us after their mother, Elizabeth. I'm a week older, so I guess my uncle just liked the name."

She shrugged and shook her head. "That's not true. Everyone wanted to be on her good side. You know, for the inheritance and all." She fidgeted. "Too much info, probably. Our family was pretty messed up."

"Most families have problems. What about your parents? You lived with your grandmother?"

She never liked to talk about this. It wasn't her shame, but she felt it anyway. Ashamed for her grandmother. Ashamed that she, Libbie, could be tagged with the blame and have it stick in anyone's mind as having any validity. Shame that she wasn't loved.

"They died in a car accident when I was five." Libbie looked at Jim and decided to tell more. "I was at a birthday party for some child I've long since forgotten and they were coming to pick me up. If not for that…but that's how it was."

"Wow. That was terrible for you. I guess it was good you had your grandmother." He observed her face. "Or not."

"We didn't get along." Again, she felt the words pushing past her lips. "She adored her sons and that was about it. She blamed me for my father's death."

"In her grief, you mean. People can be irrational when they're grieving."

Libbie had stepped much farther past her comfort zone than she ever had. She couldn't do more. She tried to smile and failed. She settled for a nod.

Jim said, "No one is perfect. Worth saying twice. No one. We can only try." He checked the time on his watch. "Let's go see what the landscapers have done. I think you'll be pleased. I hope so, anyway. If you aren't happy with the results, you have to be blunt. Promise?"

As they left the restaurant, she was almost surprised by

the sunlight and to see that the day was still progressing at its normal pace. She turned back to look at the restaurant wondering if her gloom, those bad memories, might've left something in their wake, maybe like a tainted shadow? "Do we leave pieces of ourselves behind?"

"Pardon?"

You said that aloud.

Her face heated up. "I just meant that…well, you know how one person's mood can affect others?"

He nodded. He looked interested, not judgmental.

She said, "Sometimes I think we leave pieces of our happiness or sadness behind us. In the air, you know? Like some kind of pollution?"

Jim opened the car door, but didn't move back to let her in. He watched her face, as if reading it, then said, "Maybe we have to, at least with unhappiness. Otherwise the burden might grow too heavy. Maybe we have to shed it like we shed…well, that's not a good analogy. How about like a tree sheds dead leaves?"

She nodded and rested her hand on the top of the car door between them. He opened the door wider and she took her seat inside.

Is that what her grandmother had done? Did she shed her grief and spoil the air? Whatever she was shedding, or sharing, the by-product was poison.

Jim climbed in and shut his door. "You're thinking about your grandmother, aren't you?"

Libbie half-nodded, but stared straight ahead. A slip of a thought, a realization, shimmered beyond her, just out of reach, then it was gone.

She sighed and relaxed her hands. Somehow they'd become fists. Closed fists. Fists were for fighting, not for grabbing elusive thoughts.

"Libbie."

His voice brought her back.

"I'm sorry," she said, rubbing her temples.

"Don't be. You've given me a lot to think about."

Sure. Like you're nuts, Libbie, and he's going to drop you off at your house and run like the wind.

"Seriously," he added. "We can't control what people dish out, but we can control what we pass on to others. Easy to forget. Sometimes hard to do."

She looked over at Jim, smiling. Speaking of easy, he was almost too easy to be with. And nice. She almost found that difficult to trust.

By the time they arrived back at the house, the workers were sweeping dirt from the terrace and packing their tools into the trucks.

Jim stood quietly while Libbie took in the scene.

The foundation plants set the terrace off beautifully. The planting bed ran along the side of the screened porch, the wall of the house and the back stoop. It was filled with azaleas, hollies and nandina. Rhododendron anchored the ends.

"It's perfect, Jim. Now I need furniture for the terrace."

"If you find what you want and need some help getting it home, give me a call. I'll bring the truck and some helpers."

"Thanks for lunch."

"I'm heading to Richmond now. For business, and nowhere near as much fun. Won't be back until late, but don't hesitate to call if you have any questions."

The vehicles pulled out and everyone was gone.

It was a sunny, warm afternoon and she wanted to enjoy her terrace, to sit out here and visualize it with furnishings. On impulse, she brought the card table and two chairs outside. It wasn't stylish, but the best she could do for today.

She brought her book outside too. She'd sit out here and

read, but she needed something to sip on so she brought out a bottle of water.

Comfortably situated at the card table with her feet on the chair opposite, she lost herself in her book.

Crack.

She looked up without raising her head. A dim, shadowy figure moved through the trees. She saw him briefly and then he was gone. She held her breath. Head still down, but eyes fixed on the area before her, she watched for movement. There was none. She fought the urge to look around more obviously. She resisted the instinct to run inside the house and lock her doors.

The cracking noise had probably been a stick broken when stepped upon, sounding loud in the comparative silence.

Libbie didn't like being spied on any more than she liked being the object of gossip.

What to do? She wouldn't be driven into the house. She refused to be intimidated. Several minutes passed with no further sign of a trespasser. Her heart was racing and the blood was pounding in her ears. It was all she could do to stay seated.

She took slow, calming breaths. Her feet were still propped in the chair opposite. She forced her eyes away from the woods and pretended to return her attention to the book. She wanted to present a picture of having been disturbed, but being satisfied nothing was amiss, had returned to reading.

The air began to change. It shifted as if the molecules parted and re-formed to accommodate another, more alien, mass. There was a smell—a whiff on the breeze. She stared forward and her heart stopped.

A young man stood about thirty feet away, near the garage, under the oak. His hair was dark and straight, about chin length. He wore a baseball cap and an old fatigue jacket in olive drab.

He didn't move. His arms hung at his sides and his hands appeared empty of weapons except for the broken sticks dangling from each hand.

Libbie slipped her feet off the chair. She moved and the spell broke. The man hastily backed a few steps, then turned and loped off into the woods in the direction of Adam's fort. A limping run.

She checked her forward motion and didn't chase him into the woods.

Who was the intruder? What did this mean?

Should those broken sticks trouble her? They suggested a deliberate act, not an accidental step.

Maybe he'd just wanted to get her attention?

She was missing information. She lacked expertise.

Libbie thought of Jim. He was on the road to Richmond.

She went inside and grabbed Dan's card from under the magnet on the fridge, plus her cell phone, and returned to the terrace. He'd offered, hadn't he? In case anything odd happened?

As she dialed the number Dan had given her, she walked back and forth with quick steps.

"Dan. There's someone in my yard. I don't think he's what you were talking about at dinner, but he's a stranger. And very strange." She hung up.

She paced the perimeter of the terrace. As handy as an adrenaline rush can be, it's terrible when it stops pumping and you deflate.

Exhaustion edged in, but she wouldn't go into the house and hide. There was something wrong with the man, wrong beyond trespassing. What did he want? What was his purpose? The fact of his presence on her property, lurking around her house, coupled with the disappearing dead squirrel mystery, couldn't be a coincidence.

The thought of a good fight revived her and suddenly, she was hungry. She went inside to grab chips. She brought the bag out to the terrace, then went back inside for a fresh bottle of water and grabbed the bag of oatmeal raisin cookies too. She settled back down at the table, but leaned forward in her chair, staring at the woods.

"You're in another world. Are you okay? I got your message," Dan said. "I knocked on the front door, but no answer."

"You were fast."

"I was in the area. What's up?"

She looked at this uniform and asked, "Who are you today? Deputy Wheeler? Or Dan?"

"Who'd you call, Libbie? Who do you need me to be?"

The words were said so sincerely, with such directness in his brown eyes, her sharp wit dried up and blew away with the breeze.

"I need a friend, Dan. Especially one who has experience in solving mysteries."

Dan placed his hat on the table and took a seat. "Well, you seem fine and look wonderful, so, if you don't mind waiting a bit before jumping into mysteries, what's all this?" He waved his arms at the new terrace and plantings. "I know Jim's nursery was doing work for you, but this...this is amazing. Almost overnight."

"Yes, it's terrific, isn't it? They did great work. Mr. Roza is an artist. The terrace was finished Friday and the bushes were planted earlier today."

"Wow." Dan shook his head. "So, you called?"

"Are you thirsty? Would you like some water or a soda?"

"No, I'm fine."

"It isn't an emergency. I hope I didn't give that impression."

"Okay."

"So, I hope nothing important was interrupted...that, you weren't in the middle of something big." Now he was here, she didn't know where to start.

"I think you're stalling."

"Yes. I think I am."

"You can talk to me."

"Can I?"

Dan shrugged. "I've seen a lot of things in my time. Remember our conversation at dinner?" He paused before continuing. "So, regarding your mystery, start at the beginning."

"Well, a couple of things have happened." She tapped her fingers on the table. "I can't be sure they're connected."

"Start chronologically. I think I'll want water, after all. That's if you're planning to share those cookies."

She laughed and went inside to grab the water. She used those few minutes to frame her opening statements. Back outside, Libbie handed him the bottle of water.

"Okay," she said. "Here goes. A few days ago I found a dead squirrel in the woods. I disposed of him in the trash can. On Saturday, he wasn't in there. I checked thoroughly. On Sunday afternoon, he was back in the can again, on top of the most recent trash and with the lid on tight." She sat back and waited for Dan's reaction.

"Where's the squirrel? Still in the trash can?"

"No. Pickup was this morning." She shrugged. "He was very dead. It seemed wrong to keep him around. I think his neck was broken. Maybe he fell out of a tree?"

"Maybe. Go on."

"Okay. It made no sense that he would disappear and then reappear. Then, today, a man walked into my back yard from the woods. I think he's been around here before, but stayed in the shadows, in the trees. This time he walked out into the open, but when I moved he ran away."

Dan's face stayed neutral. He didn't seem surprised or concerned, but he wasn't dismissive either. "You saw him? Describe him, please?"

"He had dark hair, straight, about chin-length. He was wearing a baseball cap so most of his face was shadowed. Hard to tell his age. Not old, but not a kid either. When he ran, he kind of limped. Loped. Very odd."

"Was he wearing an old Army jacket?"

"Yes. How do you know?"

"Tommy Lloyd. I should've warned you about him, but I didn't think he'd come around here anymore. He's harmless. I'll talk to him and make sure he understands." Dan rubbed the back of his neck. "I don't think he'll come back. He's probably pretty scared."

"Wait a minute. What do you mean 'not come around here anymore'?" He knew about this odd character and didn't warn me?

"Tommy visited Alice Carson regularly. After she died, I went by his house and explained Mrs. Carson was gone, but he may not have understood, or maybe he forgot. Maybe he was hoping she'd come back. I'll explain it to him again."

"What's wrong with him?"

"A combination of things. He was disabled from birth and his home environment wasn't helpful. But he's harmless. I wouldn't mislead you about that." Dan looked down and then back up at her, considering.

"He wanders a lot. Mostly around the woods. I don't know of a single incident where he's ever done any harm to person or property. Not beyond startling folks, anyway. He doesn't speak much and he's timid. If he's been loitering around your property, then I think he's hoping to see Alice. Alice was kind to him."

"What about the squirrel?"

Dan shrugged slowly and shook his head. "Can I have a cookie?"

"Brain food?" Libbie pushed the package toward him.

He chewed on the cookie, appearing to give great consideration to the mystery presented by the squirrel. He seemed in no hurry. She began to be amused. Perhaps he intended to be amusing. Or he may simply have been enjoying the cookie.

"Well?" she asked, finally.

"I don't think we have enough facts. I need to investigate." He finished the cookie and brushed invisible crumbs from his fingers. He stood up, took a drink of water.

"The trash can?"

Libbie pointed to the garage.

"I see two cans. Any chance you could've confused them?"

She gave him a look with attitude and didn't bother to verbalize.

"Understood. So, please show me where you found the body."

"Yes, sir. This way, Officer."

Libbie led Dan into the woods and along the path to the lookout tree. They ducked around the tree and she showed him Adam's fort.

"See the door he made?" She brushed the branches aside carefully.

Dan was suddenly close. Legitimately so, looking past her into Adam's hideaway.

She stepped away quickly, practically elbowing him in the face. She spoke quickly to hide her discomfort.

"I found him in there." She turned to point at the can. "And put him in there."

He scanned the trees above their heads. The branches were high. "I've known squirrels to fall from trees. I saw it happen once. From way up, he fell. Hit like a rock. Actually sounded like a boom. But he got up and shook it off. I've never heard of one breaking its neck in a fall. That's what you said, right?" Dan's voice was low and calm.

Dan had no more idea of what had happened with the squirrel than she did. They didn't have enough information. Still, she found it unexpectedly comforting that someone else shared the knowledge of it and wasn't laughing at her.

"Tommy must have moved the squirrel. But why would he?" she asked.

"Anything is possible, but Tommy? I don't see it."

Dan walked away, following the path for several yards. She'd never cared much for uniforms—probably that authority figure problem—but Dan wore his khakis well. He stopped before he reached the ridge and looked up and down and around. He turned and asked, "Have you followed the path?"

She pointed northeast. "To just beyond the creek."

"Joyce's path. I haven't been out that way in years."

He stood still, deep in thought. As he turned, she moved toward him. There was a current of energy in the air between them. He reached out and lightly touched her cheek with the tips of his fingers.

"Dan, someone's watching us. I can feel them." She spoke in a quiet, even voice.

It took him a second to process her words. He dropped his hand to her arm.

"I don't want him spying on me, but I don't want to frighten him either."

Dan nodded. "You don't feel threatened."

Libbie closed her eyes and waited before answering. "Not threatened," she said. Her heart was beating faster than normal, but it wasn't due to a stranger in the woods.

They stood in the backyard. Dan faced the woods and called out loudly, but gently, "Tommy? This is Deputy Wheeler. I'm here as your friend. You aren't in trouble. Come out and let's talk. Come on out, Tommy." Dan turned to her.

"Why don't you go into the house? Maybe he'll show himself if I'm alone."

She went inside and stood at the kitchen sink watching through the window. She was already feeling odd about that moment in the woods with Dan when they shared a brief, but undeniable connection. She was thankful Tommy had been nearby. It saved embarrassment and complications.

After a few minutes, it became apparent the young man wouldn't respond. She went back outside to Dan. This time she was better armored against inconvenient feelings.

Dan said, "He's probably run off."

"Are you sure he's not dangerous?"

"He's not violent. That said, if anything odd happens, no matter how silly it seems, call me."

She struggled to re-establish distance between them.

"I'm accustomed to taking care of myself. I don't scare easily."

"I'll speak with him."

He met her eyes directly. She read warmth in them.

"Thank you, Dan. Thank you for responding so quickly. I appreciate your expertise." Libbie clasped her hands together to prevent them from reaching out.

Dan looked puzzled. "Yes, ma'am." He put on his hat and walked away.

She felt downcast.

Taking her book inside with her, she left the card table and chairs outside. She sat in the living room, on the sofa, feeling quiet and subdued.

She'd never been casual and never convenient. The closer she got to something real, the more erratic she became.

Her truth was her history. Other truths? Not even her grandmother had loved her. Aunt Margaret couldn't have been all wrong. And pity parties were repulsive. But here she was yet again.

Dan didn't realize what a lucky escape he'd had. He should be thanking her.

Libbie lay on her side and put her head on the sofa pillow. A dark mood was descending and she was helpless against it.

Snippets of their conversation kept surfacing. Could she have said anything differently? Not said anything at all? And what about Jim? She'd said way too much at lunch and afterward. His kindness had been a cover for his disgust.

She reached up and grabbed the throw blanket from the back of the sofa and pulled it down. She covered her face against the darkness. If only it was as easy to shut out the negative voices.

Every time something looked like it might be good, she folded. She lost her guts. She was more comfortable *not* being comfortable with people. Giving up rather than risking certain failure? She was a coward.

Dan should count his blessings.

Chapter Fifteen

Morning wasn't good. Libbie had fallen asleep on the sofa. She awoke during the night and moved upstairs to her bed, but sleep didn't return easily. Guilt and regret tried to start a party, but she was emotionally exhausted. They gave up and went home early. Finally, Libbie slept, but sleep didn't resolve her problems or the heavy gloom.

In the kitchen, making her morning coffee, she looked out the window and realized she'd left the card table, chairs, chips and cookies outside overnight. The food would be stale and probably full of bugs.

Libbie went out to the terrace. The table and chairs were wet with dew. She touched the bag of cookies and it was empty. She snatched her hand back.

Empty. Empty. Her gloom-shrouded brain didn't think nimbly. She picked up the bag and peered inside. Barely a crumb remained.

The chair caught her as she sat. With her elbows on the table and her face in her hands, it overwhelmed her—the image of Tommy creeping through the woods in the dim twilight to sit at her table and eat the cookies. So lonely and pathetic, a person carelessly cast aside. She cried into her hands, then dropped her head to her arms and sobbed.

Great, gulping sobs couldn't be sustained and eventually the storm eased. Libbie wasn't crying for Tommy only, but also for herself, or rather, the person she might've been if her family had been different.

Was that true for Tommy, as well? Was Alice Carson the only person who'd been kind to him?

The chips bag was empty too.

She carried the empty wrappers over to the garage to toss in the trash cans. The cans were empty. Thank goodness for that, at least. She was still wrapped in despair, but the deepest, darkest shadows were lifting. Light was beginning to peek in around the corners.

If she didn't like the current state, then it was up to her to change it.

Libbie left the table and chairs outside to allow the sun to dry up the dew.

As so often happened when she was especially down, the phone rang and it was Liz. She said Libbie had been on her mind this morning.

"Believe it or not, I was thinking about you when the decorator called and said the draperies were ready. Said time had opened up on their schedule. I told them today would be fine. If not, say so and I'll call them."

Drapes? Libbie had almost forgotten about them.

"Is today okay?"

"I guess so. As good as any other day."

Or no day.

"Seriously. You're going to love these. Trust me."

She shook herself. "Sure. You're right. Let's go for it."

Liz arrived immediately after the decorator van. She kept Libbie occupied.

"Stop pacing. I repeat, you're going to love these." She pulled Libbie out onto the porch and they sat in the rockers.

"They'll yell if they need us."

They used the end table for their coffee, and for the lunch Liz had brought with her. Liz seemed to go out of her way to be witty and charming. They spent a lovely two hours chatting. Libbie enjoyed herself so much that draperies seemed a small price to pay for the time spent with her cousin, and closest childhood friend.

When they called us in to inspect the work, Libbie was amazed. The drapes delivered on Liz's promise.

Liz touched her arm. "What's wrong? They look wonderful."

"They do."

The workers stared at Libbie. "Problem?"

The cream-colored fabric was light and lustrous. Semi-sheer. The drapes dressed up the rooms, but they didn't look like the rooms in Libbie's house. More like Liz's house. Maybe even Grandmother's house.

She didn't know how to say that to Liz. She re-shaped her cheeks by force, pulling her expression into a smile.

"Lovely. Thanks so much, Liz."

"Belated happy birthday, Libbie!" She hugged me. "You don't need that cardboard now. You can throw all that out."

Liz hooked her arm through Libbie's and they walked out to the porch.

"I have to run. But first, I have another brilliant idea. We need to christen your new patio."

"My terrace? Christen? We already used it."

"A real party. Don't panic, silly. Just family."

She was still trying to come up with reasons why it wouldn't work when Liz added, "Don't delay. You'll fret yourself to death. How about Saturday afternoon? Josh will be back in town by then." She finished, "He's been wanting to see your house."

"I don't own a grill," Libbie reminded her.

"We can fit ours into the SUV. No problem." Liz dismissed her concern.

"I don't have furniture for the terrace yet." Her excuses sounded feeble.

"Give me a break. You'll own a full set of outdoor furniture before the end of the week."

Libbie considered. The thought of shopping lifted her spirits. She did need the furniture since she now owned a terrace and it would be nice to host a cookout. The idea of re-paying some of Liz's hospitality was appealing. Plus, she had a mission.

"Okay. Sounds good. That is, if I can find the terrace furniture I want."

Liz made a rude noise. "Nonsense. If you don't get the furniture by Saturday, we'll bring lawn chairs and use your card table."

****

A mission. A goal. A purpose. Libbie's kind of motivation.

She checked the home improvement stores in Charlottesville, but couldn't find what she was looking for. Nothing came close to her mental image of the terrace furniture. Finally, she gave up, but for the day. She'd try again tomorrow. She stopped by the Home on the way back.

Joyce was sitting in the living room waiting to be called for supper. Libbie invited her to the cookout on Saturday afternoon. She spoke loudly so the other residents, including spies and snitches, could overhear easily. Joyce beamed and was pleased to accept. Libbie told her she'd pick her up at noon, then she spoke to the matron and told her she'd be picking Aunt Joyce up at noon on Saturday.

Mrs. Hughes said, "I'm actually the administrator. Some call me the supervisor and that's fine too."

"Oh, sorry. Not matron?"

She grimaced. "No. This isn't a prison."

"Of course not." Did she hear Joyce chuckling in the background? Libbie almost laughed herself.

No confusion. No worries.

"Thank you, Mrs. Hughes. I'll pick Joyce up on Saturday."

As always, Libbie felt welcomed as she drove up the gravel drive. It was an intangible, but unmistakable '"welcome home" extended to her by the property.

The view was especially pleasant now. The lawn was responding to the attention of the lawn service and the wicker furniture on the porch looked as though it belonged there, as though it had always been there.

Home.

She carried her groceries into the house. Her brain was full of all the tasks she needed to accomplish during the week to prepare for the cookout.

Before dark, she went out to the terrace and left four oatmeal raisin cookies wrapped in foil on the card table.

****

The day dawned bright and her plans were set. Showered and dressed, she went downstairs for her coffee. Today, she planned to check around Fredericksburg for table and chair sets. First, she peeked out back to see if her gift had been appreciated by the intended recipient, or whether a squirrel or mouse had enjoyed a midnight feast.

The foil was on the table. Someone had tried to wrap it back up, presumably after the cookies were taken, because it was smaller. Too small for the four large cookies. Curious, Libbie stepped outside and stood by the table. She sensed he'd been here. The air was now settled, but a trace of energy remained. She picked up on a trace of color. Dark, but dispersing. Libbie picked up the hunk of foil, intending to throw it away, but it was heavier than empty foil would've been. Something was wrapped inside.

The crumpled foil package sat in her palm.

She cupped both hands around the foil package. Tommy was in her mind.

Carefully, she peeled the foil back. A small figurine was inside. Carved ivory. A small, eastern-looking guy with a pudgy tummy. He was dirty with smears of dark earth and red clay, but interesting.

Was it a thank you gift, or perhaps a trade for the cookies? Libbie dropped the foil into the trash can, but kept the carving. When she reached the back steps, it occurred to her Tommy had probably been carrying this little guy around, possibly for a significant period of time if the grime was any indication.

Fresh from Tommy. He was unknown, an enigma. Libbie cupped her hands around the figurine.

She closed her eyes and saw the absence of color. Black. She put her cupped hands to her cheek and slowed her breathing.

Fear. Surprise, then fear again, swirled down through her, black and oily. Not her fear. Other fear.

Her stomach twisted and her knees buckled. Her shin struck the edge of the cement step and she caught a glimpse of a flowered housecoat on the steps below her. Blue flowers.

She fell

Libbie hit the steps hard. The abrupt fall shook her cupped hands away from her face, but she didn't drop the figurine.

She'd never experienced anything like this. Her face was wet and she was perched on the edge of the second step, clutching the figurine. She reached up to wipe her cheek. There was a thin smear of blood on her hand and her cheek was stinging. Enough.

There's more

Yes. There was more to know. The compulsion almost overwhelmed her.

Self-preservation rushed forward pushing back the compulsion to read further. She wouldn't place the figurine near her face again and yet, she continued to sit, caught in a moment. It was a past moment that had a flavor, almost had form. She pushed herself to her feet and went carefully up the steps to the house.

She didn't wash the gift. She left it as given and set it on her desk. She sensed no malice specifically from Tommy, but the deep and penetrating fear that he, or someone, had experienced in the past while carrying the figurine on their person.

Her cheek was mildly abraded. She soaked it for a minute with a warm cloth and let it go at that. It would be barely noticeable in a day or so. A bruised knot had raised on her shin and ached when she walked. All in all, it was a reminder that nothing good came from being nosey.

It was a lovely day for a drive. Libbie had a pleasant trip to Fredericksburg, but no luck with finding a table set.

On her way home, she stopped by Miller's Grocery to purchase some sandwich makings and to pick up items for the cookout. Her focus was everywhere except on what she was doing. Thoughts about the cookout, about the furniture, about Tommy and Dan and Jim were all mixed up, but kept returning to Dan. On the upside of a dark mood, she was always more clear-headed. Venting strong emotion seemed to distill the worst of the poison she'd accumulated throughout her life, at least temporarily.

Dan had offered kindness and concern and she'd responded to her own fears. She'd brushed him off so abruptly she might as well have turned a fire hose on him.

If she'd been prepared, she could've handled it better. She could've said something like, 'Dan, I enjoy your company, but I have to tell you–' No, no, something more like, 'Dan, I'd like to thank you for all of your help and I want you to know I enjoy your company, but I don't have a good history with relationships–' No, again. It sounded self-serving and whining.

Maybe there was no good way to prepare for such a conversation and perhaps there was no need. Maybe Dan had decided to wash his hands of her and that might be for the best.

While Libbie was doing all this thinking, she was also shopping, paying the cashier, and walking across the parking lot to her car. Her brain was so full of her own conversation there was no attention to spare for anything occurring around her. She didn't notice the man walking toward her until they collided. The groceries were caught between them. She dropped one grocery bag and another bag split, sending cans of baked beans and assorted veggies rolling across the asphalt.

"Are you hurt, ma'am?"

The young man was tall and thin, gawky despite his uniform, a tan one like Dan's.

"I'm fine. Thank you. It was my fault. I wasn't paying attention to where I was walking."

"I noticed you were limping. Are you hurt?" He was speaking about her limp, but his eyes were fixed on the abrasion on her cheek.

"No, truly, I'm fine." Libbie reached up and touched her cheek. "I fell this morning and scraped myself up a little. I appreciate your concern."

He was very polite. His drawl added extra syllables to every word. "Not at all, ma'am. My pleasure. Name's Deputy

Hoskins. I believe this is yours?" He held out a can of chocolate syrup.

"Thank you, again."

Kneeling and stooping to grab the spilled groceries aggravated the bruise on her shin and reminded her that her ankle wasn't fully healed yet either. When she stood she was limping again. Ridiculous. She was limping from one injury to the next. It was time for her to pay attention to business and let the rest go for a while. Liz was right. If she didn't find a table set, they'd use the card table.

Realistically, she was already out of time. There was a slim chance that if she found a set by tomorrow she could have it delivered the next day, Friday, but it was unlikely. Jim had offered to transport any furniture she wanted, but it would be awkward to ask his assistance when it was Dan she pictured at the cookout.

Complications? Entanglements?

Maybe it was a fresh start for relationships, too.

She opened the car door and dropped the groceries, both the bagged and bagless, onto the seat.

"Thank you, again."

He walked away. A nice young man. Hard to imagine him intimidating any criminal types.

Libbie turned the evening news on in the living room to listen to through the open windows and went out to the porch to watch the sunset. The horses were in for the night across the way and there was almost no traffic on our Loop.

Had she really lived in the city? In the metro area of the nation's capital? The city noise and chaos seemed so unreal here. She was chillin' in a major way. She wasn't sure why or how, but she seemed to have reached equilibrium again. Even the nagging, chase-your-tail thoughts running through her brain earlier in the day seemed inconsequential. She was at peace.

Roses bloomed in the sky, tipped with gold, and faded to lavender in the distance. She'd left a snack for Tommy on the terrace. Did he come late, or did he come early, or both?

****

The next morning, she sat on the front steps clutching her cell phone in one hand and Dan's card in the other. She'd been sitting out here for more than thirty minutes. Silly. Foolish. Such a simple conversation, yet, she couldn't bring herself to punch the numbers.

She'd awakened with the certainty that she should contact Dan. She owed him some sort of explanation, self-serving or otherwise.

She shifted her position to lean against the upright post and stretched her bruised leg out straight on the floor of the porch. She was wearing shorts because the weight of the jeans fabric was uncomfortable against the bruise. Plus, it was a fine day, a preview of summer. Her bare feet and shorts were a welcome change.

The morning was fine. A squirrel was running along the branches of the oak in the front yard. Birds flew from the woods alongside, saw Libbie, and flew back into the trees. They were accustomed to having the front yard to themselves. She was an interloper.

Too bad, birdies. This was her yard. In fact, she might get a feeder and put it out on the lawn where she could watch them from her desk. She could try capturing them with her zoom lens.

Libbie pressed several numbers on her cell phone, then hit "end." Maybe she wouldn't call, after all. Maybe she wouldn't need to. Maybe the little trick of thinking about Mitchell's Landscaping could be applied to deputy sheriffs.

She sat and waited.

Maybe not. She couldn't help a little laugh and a sigh. If she wasn't going to dial the phone, then it was time for her to move along. The dining room awaited with blue tape streaming down the walls.

She shifted her leg, putting her foot back onto the step to stand. Before she'd made it all the way to her feet, she saw his cruiser.

Dan drove up the driveway as smoothly as if they'd had an appointment.

He stepped from the car and walked over to the porch.

"Good morning," he said.

She noticed he'd left his hat in the cruiser.

"I'm glad you came by." She stood on the steps and greeted him.

"I–" Dan started.

"If you don't mind, I'd like to speak first."

Dan frowned, then shrugged. "Go ahead."

"I owe you an apology." She stared at him straight-on.

"How's that?"

"I was rude before. You were kind and helpful and I was rude. I'm sorry."

"No problem." He nodded again.

"What I mean to say is I was rude and–" She broke off. He was looking at her bruised shin and the scrape on her cheek. "I don't think you're listening."

"I listened. You apologized. I don't know why you feel the need to apologize, but it's done. What happened to your leg and face?" Dan put his hands on his hips.

"Nothing happened. I fell. No big deal."

"You're angry again. Why? Because I didn't show sufficient appreciation of your apology? Or because you don't want to talk about how you got hurt? It wasn't Tommy, was it? Did something else happen?"

"It's unimportant. I tripped going up the steps."

"You're sure?"

"What? What do you mean, 'am I sure'? Of course, I'm sure. I was there. I tripped going up the back steps." Her voice rose on those last words. What an irritating man.

"Mind if I sit?" He walked up the steps and sat on the porch.

Libbie felt silly standing while he was seated, so she sat. She was confused. She'd lost control of the conversation. She didn't know where this was going, so she said nothing.

Dan's elbows rested on his thighs and his hands were loosely clasped in front. With one hand, he reached up and rubbed the back of his neck.

She spoke abruptly, "Please say what's on your mind."

"Deputy Hoskins told me he'd seen you. He mentioned the injuries. I was concerned."

"But surely not about Tommy causing them?"

Dan shrugged. "No, not about Tommy." He scanned the yard and surveyed the trees as if seeking an answer. "It's this place. The Lambert Place. The Carson Place. Whatever you call it. It's different from other places." He looked down at his interlocked fingers, then back up. "It's a beautiful place, no argument, but it's different somehow. Unsettled."

Libbie tried to focus on his words, but he wasn't telling her anything about this place, the Havens place now, Cub Creek, that she didn't already know. Instead, her attention was tempted away by his smile. There was something special about Dan's smile.

There was a pause and then the words popped out, "I'm having a cookout on Saturday afternoon. Not a big deal or anything. My cousin and her family. Joyce Inman too. Would you like to join us?"

An incredulous expression passed across Dan's face

with bemusement in its wake. "A cookout?" Dan looked disoriented, like a man who'd passed too quickly from one state of being into another.

"Sure. Why not?" Libbie laughed. "It's not much notice. It was kind of a last minute decision. My cousin, Liz, is bringing lawn chairs and a grill. We'll have to use a card table since I couldn't find a table set I liked. I don't guarantee 'fun' as such, but we should be mildly amusing. That is, if you don't have plans for Saturday."

"I'd like that."

"I'm glad. You'll like my family."

She couldn't read his face without staring and she didn't want to do that, so she fidgeted.

"I have to run," he said.

"Oh?"

"On duty. Just stopped by to see about your injuries."

She shrugged it off. "As you can see, they aren't much."

He looked at her legs. Suddenly, her shorts felt too short. She resisted the impulse to tug at the hems.

He grinned and stood. "Better be on my way."

Libbie stood too, and touched his arm to steady herself. "Noon on Saturday?"

"Yes, ma'am. I'll be there."

Dan's brown eyes were on her face while she talked. Her hand still rested on his arm. With his free hand, he traced her cheek with his fingers, then lightly followed the line of her jaw and neck.

She held her breath. Moving might break the spell.

He pulled her close and brushed her lips with his. A brief hesitation—and then he kissed her slowly, deliberately. When they parted, she stood silently, afraid she was about to add more regrets to her portfolio of failures.

"Libbie." Dan's voice was low. "Please look at me."

She did. She looked up and met his warm eyes.

"Am I still invited to your cookout?"

He seemed so sincere, so sweetly troubled.

"Yes, Dan. You are most definitely invited." She ran her hand across his cheek and around to the back of his neck where she paused. "But, for now, I think you should go."

He didn't speak. He reached up, took her hand and kissed her palm. After he left, she held that fist close to her heart.

This time, she thought. This time it will be different.

Chapter Sixteen

One day to go. Libbie threw herself into preparations for the cookout.

If she could've whistled, she would've. Instead, she sang, not well, but with gusto. She couldn't remember when she'd felt this elated.

She'd never had a gourmet bent, but she could handle deviled eggs and hamburger patties. The potato salad and slaw were store bought, made by professionals and much tastier than she could have managed. Libbie stayed busy, too busy to allow extraneous, unnecessary thoughts to derail her. She pushed all unhappy thoughts away and slid the cake pans into the oven. Her reality had always been different from most people, and these days her life was getting stranger and stranger—in a good way.

It was a new day and felt like a new beginning. A happy beginning.

Mid-afternoon, Dan telephoned. He sounded rushed.

"Libbie, I heard the Bennetts are moving. I understand they're having a yard sale tomorrow morning."

She was assembling deviled eggs. "What?"

"Here are the directions–"

"Dan, I don't understand. Why do I care about the Bennetts?" Ouch, that sounded harsh. "I'm sure they're lovely people, but…"

"No, listen. I called because Henry Bennett has a patio set. He'll let you take a look at it this afternoon, ahead of the sale. It's old. It might not be much, but it'd probably get you through until you find what you want. If you like it, he'll help you get it home."

"But..."

"It's up to you. If you'd rather not, or if you go, but don't like the set, no one will be offended. I'm sorry I can't go with you or help you with it, but I'm caught up here at work."

She wrote down the directions and let Dan off the phone. The Bennett's didn't live far from her. She bit her lip and considered whether she should go. It was possible the table set might meet her needs until she found what she wanted. Almost certainly it would serve better than her card table.

She'd go. What could it hurt?

They were strangers. She was uncomfortable around strangers. Still, would a look hurt?

Libbie went and liked what she saw. She paid Mr. Bennett more than his asking price to help cover the delivery and their inconvenience. The Bennetts had known the Carson family and respected Alice and Roy. Mrs. Bennett had gone to school with Roy, Jr. With a little prodding, Gladys said Roy, Jr. was a nice boy who never fit in. All he ever talked about was leaving which he did as soon as he graduated from high school.

Gladys Bennett said she was looking forward to her move with mixed feelings. "It's hard to pick up and move at this age. We're all creatures of habit. But it's so much harder at Mrs. Carson's age and her not having a husband to help. I think it was seeing what she went through trying to decide that convinced me to go ahead and move now. Nothing gets easier with age."

Mrs. Bennett had piqued my curiosity. "Mrs. Carson planned to move?"

"Yes. She told me all about it and that's how we chose

the place we're moving to. She was struggling with the decision. She spoke about it in Sunday school and seemed so burdened with it that I went by to visit her." She picked up a brochure from her kitchen counter. "Here it is. It's one of those fifty-plus communities. Club house. Pool. Golf course. I think when she saw how impressed Henry and I were with the place it helped her make up her mind."

She added, "We played it up a bit to make her feel better about it, and ended up convincing ourselves."

Libbie glanced at the photos. "It must have been difficult for her to make that decision. She'd lived there for so long."

"Especially hard for her. Once she understood and accepted that Roy, Jr. would never live there…well, what can I say? She was real attached to that place of hers. She thought she'd live there until they carried her out to bury her. Said it more than once." Gladys shook her head. "And I guess, in the end that's what happened. It was Sam Graham who found her out in the backyard. He had an appointment with her. So she must've made up her mind but never got the chance to go through with it."

"In the backyard?"

"Yes, poor dear. She must've gone out early. She was still in her housecoat. Fell on the steps and… Well, never you mind. I should be ashamed telling you all that."

She shook her head. "We all miss her light."

"Light?"

"She was a light in the darkness. It's what we should all strive to be."

As they walked back outside, Gladys added, "If you don't have a church already picked out, consider visiting ours."

"I don't usually attend church."

She patted Libbie's arm. "Give it some thought. And remember, churches are made up of people and have different...well, personalities. If you don't feel like you fit in at one, try another. If your heart is open, you'll find your church home."

Libbie pushed away the usual objections and instead said, "Thanks. I'll consider it."

Gladys smiled like she'd read Libbie's mind and intent. "I hope you will. No one can do everything on their own."

While his wife and Libbie spoke, Mr. Bennett, a lovely white-haired man, and his stocky grandson, enlisted the help of a burly neighbor boy and the three of them loaded the table, chairs, a settee, a planter and the Bennett's gas grill, into Mr. Bennett's box truck. The truck had a ramp. Very handy. They delivered the contents to Libbie's terrace. Everyone was happy with the deal.

After the Bennett's left, Libbie called Liz. No one answered, so she left a message.

"Never mind about the lawn chairs and grill. I've got it covered."

Liz would smirk when she heard that, but Libbie could handle a little smug good will.

The black wrought iron table and chairs were old and showed wear. There were a few spots of rust. She'd have it refinished. This furniture belonged on her terrace as if it were made for it.

Libbie placed her hands flat upon the table top and closed her eyes. She'd done this at the Bennett's house too, before making the deal. Laughter, gentle, family—all in sunlit shades of peach and spring-green. Bringing this table here, was like adding the goodwill of a happy family to her own little piece of planet Earth.

Happy and solid.

The table was delicately wrought, but immensely heavy. If tornadoes barreled out of the clouds and blew away the house, even if it carried off the terrace block by block, yet this table would remain, possibly into eternity. That's how permanent it felt.

The grill was clean from last season. Mr. Bennett had fired it up to show it was functioning properly. It wasn't a high-end grill, but it wasn't the cheapest either. Libbie had no use for any features beyond the most basic in a gas grill.

The afternoon was sunny with an unending blue sky and the weather promised to hold fine all weekend. With the wrought iron table and chairs on the terrace, the mental image felt complete. She was ready for the cookout and to play hostess.

She thought about what Gladys had said. A light in the darkness. People might say things about her, Libbie, but it wouldn't be that. She would like it to be. Maybe one day.

Before she went inside for the evening, she left cookies wrapped in foil on the new wrought iron table. Next to the foil-wrapped cookies, she placed a small snack bag of chips.

****

She slept solidly and woke refreshed. She spent extra time on her appearance, curling her long hair before clipping it up loosely. Instead of jeans, she chose a red crinkle skirt with a white cotton lace-trimmed top. Casual, yet feminine, a style very different from her usual jeans. She had low-heeled red sandals to slip on before going outside. The house was clean and looked reasonable, except for the dining room with its crazy blue tape stripes still dangling from the walls.

She had a song in her heart and a spirit so light it felt like she could dance on the treetops.

Liz and her family were due shortly after noon. Libbie planned to pick up Joyce at noon. It was possible Liz et al would arrive while she was gone, so she left the doors unlocked and posted a note on the front door saying she'd be back soon. Keys in hand and shoes on feet, she walked out the front door and was almost to the car when she remembered Tommy's snack. She'd forgotten about him this morning. She half-ran around back.

The table was empty. Not even the foil was left. There was the possibility a giant rodent had run off with the cookies and chips, but her guess was he'd been to visit. She stared at the woods. Should she check Adam's fort for any unwelcome leavings? Adam was sure to go there. She'd hate for something unpleasant to ruin it for him if a quick look could prevent it.

The lookout tree was her marker. The undergrowth was lush now. Without the tree, she might've had difficulty locating the fort. Libbie stood by the tree, her hand resting on the bark. She gathered her skirt closely around her to keep it from dragging in the dirt. She stooped, pushed aside the branches, and peered into Adam's fort. All was well.

She needed to tell Adam about Tommy. She didn't want to frighten Adam, but he needed to be prepared for unexpected events or visitors. Libbie wished no harm to Tommy, but she would do anything necessary to protect Adam or Audrey.

Joyce was ready and waiting for her in the living room of the Home. A number of ladies were there, along with one gentleman. Every seat was full, in addition to the fleet of walkers that came with their own seats attached. Joyce made a show of greeting Libbie and remarking loudly about the cookout before she was willing to leave. She wore navy slacks and a flowered shirt, and carried a sweater in a small tote bag. Leaning on her cane, she moved stiffly. She was so thin it almost hurt to watch.

It was a long, tedious walk down the wooden ramp from the front door to the parking area. She felt as fidgety as Audrey, her feet shuffling along to the slow tip-tap rhythm of Joyce's cane. By the time they drove back to the house, there were two SUV's in the driveway. Libbie hadn't mentioned Dan to Liz and the family. She smiled. This should be interesting.

"You're grinning like you're up to mischief, girl," Joyce said.

She walked around to help her out of the car. Audrey came running, "Aunt Libbie! Aunt Libbie!" She skidded to a halt when she saw Joyce.

"Hello, Audrey. Mrs. Inman, this is my niece, Audrey. Audrey, this is my friend, Mrs. Inman."

Audrey stood there with round, staring eyes. Her red-brown hair was flyaway and her pink barrette was slipping down.

"Audrey?" Libbie prompted.

Her mouth firmed up. She spoke in a loud whisper. "There's a man in your back yard."

Libbie kept a straight face. "Of course, dear. Your daddy, right?" She ushered Joyce up the drive and Audrey walked at her side.

"No, Aunt Libbie. A real man. I mean a strange man." Her voice, still soft, sounded urgent.

"A stranger? Is he handsome?"

"I don't know. I think so. He spoke nice."

"Well, then." Libbie pretended to consider. "Perhaps we should offer him a hamburger?"

"Are you teasing me, Aunt Libbie?" Audrey asked, with that worried note in her voice.

Libbie smiled and pressed her shoulder. "A little, Audrey. He's my friend. I invited him."

Adam, Josh and Dan were setting up wickets around the backyard. The two men, Dan with his dark hair, and Josh with sandy-colored hair, were engaged in serious consultation with Adam. It was a hushed scene. Libbie stood, almost in awe of the picture they made, kneeling together and looking like inspiration for a new Norman Rockwell painting. Her breath stopped and her heart flipped. She felt perilously close to something like membership in a normal family grouping.

The guys looked up and she waved. Liz wasn't in sight so Libbie knew she must be in the kitchen. The kitchen window was open, but the view was limited from below. She settled Joyce in a chair at the wrought iron table.

"Would you prefer to sit in the shade?"

"No. No, I'm fine. Stiff today. The sun'll ease my bones." She glanced at her surroundings and rubbed the rough, worn finish on the wrought iron table with her fingers.

"Where did this patio come from? Alice never had nothin' but dirt back here. This furniture, don't I know it?"

"Terrace. Nice, isn't it?"

"Nice. Very nice. Ter-race." She strung the last word out with emphasis. "Plants too. Alice would like it." Joyce nodded. She turned to Audrey and said, "Alice could grow anything."

"Who's Alice?" Audrey asked.

Joyce was pleased to explain, so Libbie left them to their conversation and went over to her other special guest.

Dan was helping Adam set a pole at the head of two wickets. He wore a faded blue shirt and jeans. She walked toward them and he raised his head. The soft color made his eyes both darker and warmer at the same time.

Adam said, "Croquet, Aunt Libbie. Do you know how to play? Mom says you do. She says you'll be rusty and easy to beat."

"She's probably right. Did you meet my friend?"

Josh walked over to join them.

"Libbie." He hugged her. "Terrace, furniture and grill. All within one week. Good work." A sparkle danced in his bluer than blue eyes. The sun picked up the golden lights in his hair.

"Josh, I hope you don't mind doing the cooking. Just burgers and hot dogs."

"No, ma'am. At your service." Josh tipped an imaginary hat. "By the way, those photos—portraits, I should say—that you gave Liz for her birthday? Amazing."

"She liked them, didn't she?"

"She's hardly talked about anything else. You have a gift, Libbie."

She was pretty sure she blushed. She pretended it was all cool.

She liked Josh. He was reliable and brilliant, and he never imposed. If anything less than pleasant lurked beneath his handsome exterior, he hid it well. Once, she'd almost kidded Liz that daughters married their fathers, but decided not to. It was too close to the truth.

"Did you and Dan manage an introduction?"

"We managed." Josh nodded toward the terrace. "You have another guest?"

Libbie introduced Josh and Joyce. Josh held Joyce's frail, thin hand and spoke attentively. She was charmed. Audrey still sat by her side and appeared content.

"I'd better go see what Liz is up to." She left them all chatting on the terrace, except for Adam who was practicing croquet technique. She needed to speak with him about Tommy and other strangers, but no need to worry about it today, not with the others around.

Liz had put the macaroni and cheese in the oven and was

chopping celery sticks and carrots at the counter. As Libbie entered the kitchen Liz glared at her.

Libbie stopped short. "What's up? You seem out of sorts."

"Nothing. I'm fine. You look nice. I like that skirt." Liz said it grudgingly, as if it were some sort of concession. "What happened to Jim? The guy I met before?"

"This is the deputy who helped with the rugs. I thought you liked him. What's the problem?" She was annoyed. "Dan's a very nice man. I'm sorry you don't approve."

"It's not that. I'm sure he's nice." Liz stared down at the pile of green and orange veggies. "I guess I'm in a mood."

"Liz, what's wrong?"

She slid the veggies from the cutting board onto a plate and shook her head, "Nothing. I'm fine. Hey, you know what this party needs? Music." She dried her hands, placed the radio on the sill of the open window and tapped the tuner.

"There we go. Oldies. Perfect." Liz picked the knife back up. "Someday I'm going to bring you into the modern age."

"I have a CD player."

"Exactly." Liz smiled.

She sounded okay now, but a cloud lingered at the back of her eyes. It made Libbie uneasy.

Whack. Whack. Loud noises outside distracted them and drew them from the kitchen. They stood on the back porch and watched Adam and Dan hitting the croquet balls. Audrey had left Joyce and was watching the guys hone their technique. Dan motioned to her to give it a try.

She bit her lip and concentrated mightily, but when she whacked the ball with her mallet, she hit it off-kilter. The ball barely rolled.

Dan saw Libbie watching. He spoke to the kids and

handed Adam his mallet and headed her way. She walked down the steps to meet him, stopping only to introduce Liz to Joyce.

He was there before she was done.

"You ladies mind if I borrow Libbie?"

Joyce asked, "What for?" She watched their faces, and then laughed. "Always wanted to say that." She pointed at Dan. "You behave yourself, young man."

Liz looked back and forth between them and seemed bemused.

Joyce turned to her and patted her hand. "Always wanted to say that, too. It's one of the perks of getting old. It's allowed."

The voices faded as they walked toward the woods edge. Libbie stopped and focused on Dan.

"You okay?" she asked him.

"I'm fine. You look wonderful." His eyes were warm and inviting.

"You too." She smoothed his shirt.

He caught her hand. "You don't have any children, do you?" His voice sounded grave, but he was grinning.

"No. If you think back you'll recall I never said I did."

"It was implied. It's called quibbling."

She shrugged. "I didn't think it was anyone else's business. Not at the time. Besides, you and Jim talk, don't you? That's how you knew about them in the first place. When women do that, men call it gossiping." She gave him a fake frown. "In point of fact, you may have dozens of offspring. If I'm quibbling, then I think you may be omitting."

"Omitting." He put his hands on her arms. "I'll tell you anything. I have no secrets."

She linked her arm through his and drew them back

toward the terrace. "For now I'd like to know if you need to be rescued from the kids."

"No, they're good kids. Josh is okay too."

"What about Liz?" She was puzzled. Everyone always noticed Liz first and foremost.

"Sure. I remember her from the day you moved in. Today I was already back here when they arrived. She went inside right away. We didn't have a chance to speak."

"Probably had food she wanted to put in the kitchen. Liz is great. You'll see."

Josh was putting the hamburger patties and hot dogs on the grill. Liz had fixed iced tea for herself and Joyce. They were chatting and sipping. Music streamed softly through the kitchen window. When Dan and Libbie reached the table, Liz was her usual charming self. Libbie saw the curious gleam in her eyes and knew it was only the presence of Josh and Joyce that prevented Liz from launching directly into a full scale inquisition. She was warming up, already asking about his family, when Libbie interrupted.

"Excuse me, everyone. I'm going to start putting the food out in the screened porch. No, Liz. Stay here. Visit with Joyce. Dan will help me." She tugged him along behind her into the house.

As they reached the kitchen, she asked him, "Can you set up the card table in the screened porch?"

But he'd stopped in the dining room and moved to stand in the open area between it and the study. He looked around, obviously checking out the house.

"You've been in here before." She was puzzled by his curiosity.

"Not since you moved in. It's different now." Dan stood, hands on hips, and considered. "Seems bigger. Emptier. Alice lived in this house all of her life. Her parents lived here before her. They accumulated a lot of stuff over the years. I've never seen it this empty." He turned back to the dining room with its dangling, crooked blue strips of tape. "What happened in here?"

Libbie shrugged. "It's out of square, I guess."

Dan stared up at the motion detector in the corner near the ceiling. The red light lit up as he moved within range.

"The Carson's didn't have a security system."

"No, I added that. Mostly, I use it at night."

He took a detour on the way to the kitchen.

"What's all this?" He moved farther into the living room and turned slowly taking in the collection.

She stammered. "Just some photos."

He ignored her and walked closer to the road group, but his eyes didn't rest there. He focused on the pictures of the kids. "I like these." He looked around again. "I don't see any fences."

"No, that got temporarily derailed."

He mock-frowned. "As in fence rails derailed?"

"Nonsense." She cleared her throat. "Come give me a hand. We can talk about the pictures anytime."

He nodded and joined her in the kitchen.

She kept Dan busy toting condiments and utensils to the porch. The smell of food grilling came through the open windows and music filled the air. She heard Liz laughing with Joyce and Josh. The kids shouted as they ran through the edge of the woods. Happy shouting. Brother and sister picking-on-each-other kind of shouting, with Max in the middle of it.

They all crowded around the wrought iron table to eat. It was chaotic and fun. Even so, something was amiss in the chemistry of their little group. She couldn't pin it down. Liz would seem fine and then suddenly become still as if she'd gone far away.

Libbie tried to flatter her back into her normal state.

"Liz, this macaroni and cheese is the best." She turned to Dan. "Liz is the best cook."

No response from Liz. She tried again, this time talking up Liz's decorating skills, then her charity work. No good. Finally, Libbie gave up. Everyone was entitled to quiet moments. Certainly, she knew that as well as, or better than, anyone.

As the meal wound down, Max settled in for a nap at Joyce's feet and everyone leaned back in their chairs. Conversation had gotten soft and infrequent.

Adam brought up the question of team or cutthroat play. He proposed teams. Guys versus gals. Audrey said she wanted to be on her daddy's team. Joyce was silent. Her eyelids kept trying to close and her jaw had relaxed, her lips parting. Her next breath sounded much like a light snore.

Josh suggested team selection based on skill levels.

"Who are the best players?"

They looked at each other.

Josh said, "If I may?"

As hostess, Libbie said, "Please go ahead." She bent to secure Joyce's cane lest Joyce knock it over while she napped.

"Adam's pretty good. I'm guessing Dan is too." He waited for dissent and received none. "I propose the following teams: Liz, Adam, and Dan versus Libbie, Audrey and me. Feel free to suggest alternatives."

"Josh," she said, "You're getting the short straw. Audrey and I are both weak players. Neither of us can hit those balls like the rest of you." She was competitive by nature. With these teams, they'd lose before the first ball was struck.

Everyone had fallen silent. Audrey looked downcast. Libbie was sorry she'd spoken out. Being right doesn't always make you right.

"But Aunt Libbie," Adam said, "I can teach you how to hit the ball. You don't have to be strong or anything like that. It's knowing where to hit it. It's like what Dad told me about baseball."

Libbie shook her head. "You've lost me, Adam. I don't understand. I'm not good at croquet, but I'm worse at baseball."

"That's not what I meant." He groaned. "Dad, remember what you said at baseball practice?" He turned to his father, but Josh shrugged. Adam's forehead furrowed in concentration. "It's how, when you hit the ball right—in the right place on the bat and in just the right way—it goes farther than if you hammer it. More about 'how' than 'how hard'."

"The sweet spot, Adam." Josh spoke up. "It's called the sweet spot."

"I have no idea what either of you are talking about." Libbie was totally confused.

Audrey was confused too. She had that big-eyed, worried look again. Libbie put her finger beneath Audrey's chin and pushed it up gently to close her mouth. She seemed not to notice.

Liz spoke. "It's mostly a sport's term, I think. It's used in tennis too. It means there's always a prime spot, whether you are using a racket, a bat or a mallet, such that, when you hit that spot, you get the best and fullest effect with the least effort every time. So, when you find the perfect spot, the sweet spot, you've got it made."

Liz's words spun in Libbie's brain, sorting, re-sorting. Sweet spot. When you find the sweet spot you get the best and fullest effect with the least effort, you've got it made.

When you're in the groove, you're in the groove—permanently, if you've found your sweet spot. She was sleeping better than in years, the voices in her head were relatively quiet, and her personal relationships were more enjoyable and had more potential than ever in her entire life. She'd found her sweet spot. The property was her sweet spot.

Joyce woke up and spoke up, "This was always the sweetest spot. Alice had the sweetest water in the county. Maybe two counties. I never tasted sweeter."

Libbie reached out and took Audrey's hand.

"Come on, kid. Let's go show these clowns a thing or two about enjoying croquet."

"After we do a quick pick up," Liz added.

They all pitched in, except Joyce. She said she'd gone stiff from sitting too long. She pushed up from the chair and limped inside to use the facilities and find a better spot to nap.

Liz and Libbie put the food away while the guys bagged the trash. Discreetly, Libbie made up a cheeseburger with lettuce and tomato and wrapped it in foil. She wrapped up some leftover veggies too. When Liz went to the bathroom, Libbie walked quietly outside.

The guys had gone around to the front of the house. No one was in sight. Libbie walked into the woods and placed the foil packages in the seat of the oak tree near Adam's fort. The packages wouldn't be here long if Tommy was still around. If he wasn't, then they still wouldn't be here long because some lucky creature would have a fine feast.

Poor Josh. If he'd cherished any hope of his team winning, he was doomed to disappointment. Audrey and Libbie played horribly, but had fun anyway. The nice thing about two lousy players is that you have company at the wickets as the rest of the players leave you in their dust.

Liz, Josh and Dan talked a lot while hanging around the

wickets well ahead of Audrey and Libbie. Later, when they could speak privately, she'd find out what Liz had learned about Dan. Hopefully, Josh was softening Liz's inquisition.

Libbie offered apple cake and ice cream for dessert. She sliced the cake and Adam scooped the ice cream.

Everyone relaxed around the table. Joyce had rejoined them and she was livelier now.

"I saw that little fat man sittin' on your desk." Joyce shook her head. "I thought Roy, Jr. cleared out every last stick and crumb from the house. How'd he leave the little man behind?"

Libbie was confused. "Roy, Jr.?"

Joyce continued, "Alice was always tickled with that little man. Roy brought him back from one of his Navy trips when he was young. From the Orient, she said. It didn't look like much to me, but Alice treasured it. After Roy, Sr. died, she used to carry it around in her pocket all the time. Said it made her think of him."

The carved ivory figure? Libbie's gift from Tommy?

This required thinking about, but later. Everyone was joking, chatting and having a good time. Liz appeared relaxed until Joyce asked about the wrought iron table set.

Joyce ran her bony fingers along the patterned iron, over the chipped and rusty spots, and said, "This sure does look familiar. Haven't I seen it before?"

Liz was suddenly so quiet, so absolutely silent Libbie wasn't sure she was breathing despite the waves of strong emotion emanating from her. She was white pale and her posture was rigid.

Dan answered Joyce. "This belonged to the Bennett's. Gladys and Henry. Just up the road from here."

"Of course," Joyce said. "Why'd they give it up? Gladys favored this set."

"They're moving to Charlottesville," Dan told her.

"Like Alice wanted to do." Joyce shook her head. "Well, I always liked this set, but it's so heavy. Needs cleaning up too."

She looked at Libbie. "So, I guess you got yourself another project, don't you, gal?" She laughed.

Something in the quiet conversation between Joyce and Dan seemed to vent some of the strong emotion with which Liz was struggling. The planes of her face softened. A second later, she looked like she might cry. She reached up with one hand to run her fingers through her perfect hair. It was a measure of her distress.

"Liz, will you give me a hand with this mess?" It seemed a good idea to get her moving and busy.

She stood and stacked the plates. Audrey gathered the utensils. Libbie tossed the trash into the garbage can, then went into the house. Adam had already put the ice cream back in the freezer. Audrey dropped the utensils in the sink and hurried back outside.

"Liz." She reached across and turned off the sink faucet. The music was playing so they had privacy despite the open window. "I don't like to intrude, but something is obviously wrong. I wish you'd tell me what it is."

"There's no point it talking about it. It's stupid and silly, but it upset me. We've had a nice afternoon. Let's leave it that way."

Libbie knew what that meant. Liz was about to criticize her. It never failed to sting and she didn't want to hear it. Still, she was an adult and Liz was someone she cared a lot about.

She touched Liz's arm. "So? What? I'm listening."

Liz shook her head roughly. Her words sounded like an accusation. "Remember, you told me to speak. It's your wrought iron. You like it, don't you?"

"Of course. It's perfect for the terrace. It needs refinishing, but otherwise it's great."

"When I saw it, I recognized it immediately. Or, rather, I remembered one exactly like it." Liz paused significantly, her silence heavy with meaning.

The picture bloomed in Libbie's head: the brick patio in the rose garden from Grandmother's house, and from the vantage point of Grandfather's study.

The fourth-floor study overlooked the backyard patio and the wrought iron table and chairs. Maybe the pattern was similar. She didn't recall. It was just a wrought iron table and chairs. Pretty generic in appearance.

Liz watched Libbie's face closely as she remembered the scene. She continued, "I thought…don't get upset, but I thought you'd somehow gotten hold of that same table set. I thought you might be re-creating…you know, like you did with Grandfather's furniture here in your study." She shuddered. "How can you do this? How can you stand it?"

"For the life of me, Liz, I don't understand. I'm not angry, but I am confused. This is furniture for my terrace. I got a great price on it." Her voice sounded rigid, almost fierce, and she forced herself to take a deep breath.

Liz seemed to have run out of words, yet unsaid words dangled in the air between them. Liz turned away and shook her head. "Call me later if you feel like talking, okay?"

She walked past and Libbie let her go, bewildered. She didn't understand why this bothered Liz.

You know.

No, I don't know.

Libbie waited a few minutes, then followed Liz outside. Liz was speaking with Dan and Josh and she seemed better already. The kids had gathered up the croquet set. Josh walked away and picked up a load to carry to their vehicle.

Libbie was almost out of time. She held up her camera.

"Hey, everybody. Can we get a group shot?"

Libbie pulled the camera in close and held it against her.

Josh said, "That's a great idea."

Liz added, "It sure is. Audrey. Adam. Straighten your clothes."

She combed their hair with her fingers and blotted a spot of food on Audrey's face.

The kids sat on the table with their legs swinging. Joyce was in her chair.

Dan said, "I'll take the picture. Which button do I push?"

They lined up—Libbie, Liz and Josh, their arms around each other's waist or shoulders.

"Smile!"

Later, when she downloaded the memory card to her laptop, Libbie saw Dan had gotten Max too, seated at Joyce's feet and near to Adam's dangling legs. Everyone was in the photo except Dan.

Her car was blocking the driveway so she grabbed her keys and drove it onto the grass. Dan said he'd drop Joyce off. Libbie didn't argue. They'd all had a good time, including her, but now she felt deflated. All this sociability was exhausting.

She escorted Joyce from the backyard to the driveway.

"Are you glad you came?" Rhetorical question. Of course, Joyce was. "I'm glad Liz and her family had the chance to meet you."

She nodded as she watched where she was placing her feet. "Sweet kids."

"Liz is great, isn't she?"

"Eh. She's nice enough."

That took me aback. Had Liz said or done something to

226

offend Joyce?

"Everybody loves Liz."

"Well, that's nice for her, I'm sure."

The note in her voice stunned Libbie.

"What's wrong?"

"You're always making up to her. I wasn't going to say it. None of my business. I know how to be a good guest."

Could she be jealous?

"Joyce–"

She interrupted, shaking a finger at Dan's vehicle. He was visible through the windshield, watching them.

"Don't rush me. I'll be along in a minute."

Dan waved at Libbie and shrugged.

Joyce punctuated the moment by ramming her cane into the soft earth. "I got one thing to say to you, Miss Libbie. Hush puppies." She shook her head from side to side. "Hush puppies says it all."

Hush puppies? Was she hungry? What?

"Think, girl. You shared your hush puppies with me."

"You mean that day we met?" She floundered, trying to figure out what was going on. "Liz would've shared her hush puppies too, if she'd been there." Well, that sounded odd.

"Yes, indeed. No doubt at all. That's the point. Liz would've shared 'em, might have given both of them to me."

"Well, then. You see?"

"I do, but you don't. That's why I'm standing here on my worn out legs to help you understand. She'd have shared because it was the thing to do—the polite thing. The correct thing. The civilized thing."

"Okay, I get it. What's wrong with that?"

She hit her chest with a finger. "You shared because you have a kind heart."

A kind heart? She, Libbie, didn't deserve credit. She'd

227

begrudged Joyce that hush puppy. Feeling guilty, Libbie shook her head and uttered an exasperated gasp.

"Listen, girl. You let me nap on your porch."

Without doubt, the day had been too long and stressful for Joyce.

"Let me help you into the car."

She punched the ground again with her cane, this time close to Libbie's foot. She jumped back.

"Hey, are you trying to stab me?"

"Don't change the subject." Joyce coughed. "Your precious cousin would've given me a bed. Would've insisted."

"Yes. Okay. Yes, she probably would've."

"But that wasn't what I wanted. Do you see now? I wanted to nap on the dang porch." Joyce waved her hand at Dan who was getting fidgety. "She's polite. She's so busy crossing her t's and dotting her i's, she cain't see value. She's busy worrying about missing one of them dots or crosses and what that might look like to other people.

"You can want more, but you cain't expect it from those who cain't give it. Think about it." She waved her cane, preparing to move forward.

"And you, Miz Libbie Havens, you see an old, half-witted woman. And I am. That's what I am. But that ain't *all* that I am. Remember that."

She nodded her head with such force she almost toppled over. Libbie grabbed her arm and kept a hand on her until she was safely seated in Dan's SUV, then she closed the door gently. She backed off a few feet and waved as the car backed down the drive.

What the heck had that been about?

Libbie walked to the porch and sat in a rocker. Sunset was a ways off. The horses were in the pasture across the road. They were moving slowly in the deepening shadows, the lengthening shadows that crept out from the boundary of the woods' edge. These were natural shadows, the kind that tucked the pastures in as it was putting them to bed.

The day was done. A good time was had by all, and all had gone home.

The shadows grew along her own tree line too. What of Tommy? Had he watched? If so, what had he thought?

A short time later Dan's SUV drove back into view and pulled into the driveway. Interesting that he came back knowing she'd be here alone. She smiled. Dan saw her on the porch and joined her.

She asked, "Any problem? Joyce got home okay?"

"Sure. Joyce is fine." Dan sat in the other rocker. He leaned forward, with his elbows resting on the arms of the chair. He looked at his fingers, then at the floor. He looked like he was resisting the urge to rub the back of his neck. Despite the betraying mannerisms, his voice was calm and reflective as he said, "Libbie, I've got something I'd like to ask you about." With only the tiniest pause between, he asked, "What happened to your grandmother?"

Dan laid the words out casually, as if they meant little, but Libbie felt the earth quake.

She cleared her throat. "Why…do you ask? Why would you ask about her?"

"Liz mentioned something. You'd gone inside. She seemed…distraught. Josh told her to drop it."

"So, why are you bringing it up now?"

"Liz said she was worried about you. About your safety or…something. It's obvious she cares about you, and I care too. I thought…none of my business…but if there's a problem, I thought you might want to talk about it."

Talk about it? Like it was the stupid weather or

something? She crossed her arms and clenched her jaw while as the sunset grew.

A slight breeze caught a tendril of hair and brushed her cheek.

"Libbie." Dan spoke.

She ignored him. She'd put that very bitter memory away, carefully and neatly. She expected it to stay quietly in the past. Liz should've kept her mouth shut. She'd spoiled this day, but Libbie didn't blame her. She'd been upset about the wrought iron. No, this was Dan's fault. He should know better than to pry, uninvited, into personal, private business.

"You should leave now," she said.

"You can tell me anything. I'm your friend, Libbie."

His voice sounded distant. Yet still, there he stood.

She explained carefully, "I apologize if I wasn't clear. Please go." She needed him to leave. What little composure she had was cracking like an ill-fitting mask. "Now, please."

The steps creaked as he descended. She didn't see him leave because she was watching the ridge. The sunset had peaked. The colors had passed from delicate to gaudy to a faded gray. Gravel crunched. His vehicle was gone.

No, she couldn't tell him. She couldn't form the words. Not so much about what had happened, though that was dreadful enough, but rather because he'd spoken to Liz about it and she knew too well what Liz thought she'd done. It had pulled the wound wide open, ripping the healed flesh along with the bad.

Inside, the cell phone rang. Not tonight. Tonight, she needed to be alone. She went into the house and turned off everything, including her phone.

A length of drapery, fluttered by the breeze, escaped through the open window. It waved and teased her memories.

Libbie missed her cardboard panels.

Chapter Seventeen

When Libbie was a child living in Elizabeth's house, she hid out in her grandfather's unused study. As she grew older and more independent, more combative, she staked her claim and declared it hers. It was on the top floor of Grandmother's brownstone, a long climb up unless one took the elevator. The elevator went to the third floor, so there was still a flight of stairs to be managed.

Her grandfather was dead before she was born. No one came there except the maid to dust and vacuum. Sometimes Libbie curled up in the chair by the armoire and sat and read, sometimes she opened her mind and let the colors reign. Dropping the barriers always eased the feeling of pressure building that encompassed her wherever she went. The carpet was thick and muffling. The windows were tall, almost from floor to ceiling. They opened like double doors on either side of the desk. The windows were covered in blue draperies and fancy ivory lace sheers. There was a narrow ledge of balcony on the outside of each window, not large enough to stand on. The balcony railing was decorative. Libbie was the only person who used the room. She didn't recall anyone checking the integrity of the railings in the faux balconies.

This was her special room, her territory. She'd come here following the last angry words with Grandmother, to shut herself inside, to forget the ugliness and study for exams. Shut herself in. Shut HER out.

Grandmother stepped inside.

The window sheers ruffled, then flared with the breeze.

Libbie was no longer a kid to be bullied. First, boarding school, then college had given her a new perspective. Elizabeth's house wasn't the whole world. There was more out there.

Grandmother was angry because Libbie had been flippant and disrespectful.

They were barely past their latest, greatest blow-up and she figured Grandmother was here to renew the fight. Libbie stood, her fists clenching, as her dear grandmother approached the desk.

"Libbie, enough of this. I've had it with your..."

Grandmother continued talking as she walked past to the windows, but Libbie had stopped listening.

She pushed aside the history textbook and walked with purpose from behind the desk. She came close, to within inches of her. Perhaps the intensity of Libbie's expression unsettled her because Grandmother's eyes grew large and she backed away. She was intimidated and it gave Libbie a heady feeling. There was no premeditation. Grandmother stepped back. The sheers, billowing in on the breeze, wrapped around her legs.

Libbie tripped on the edge of the carpet and stumbled forward, but didn't touch her.

Libbie tripped. Grandmother stepped back in reflex and she tripped. Grandmother, Elizabeth, stumbled backward over the sill. She grabbed for the sheers, grabbed for the draperies, grabbed for Libbie, but found air. When she hit the rail, it gave way immediately.

She fell from the fourth floor to the patio below. It was a brick patio, but even so, if she'd had a little luck she might've hit the bushes and escaped with a broken limb or two. As it was, the upper part of her body hit the iron table and she broke. She was dead before the rescue squad arrived.

Libbie stood in the open window and observed the stillness of the body lying below, partially on the table. She tried to put it together in her head, to force it to make sense. Loud gasps rose from below as Margaret and Liz came into view. Liz screamed. As one, they looked up and saw Libbie in the open window, standing, silent and staring. In shock.

Aunt Margaret kept their stories consistent and stood between the family and the press. She was the "face" of the family. Their adored grandmother had tripped near the window and a dreadful accident had occurred. There was no one to say differently.

Aunt Margaret came to Libbie's room and spoke to her privately. She made it clear there was to be no mention of Libbie's presence in the room at the time Elizabeth fell. There was no need to give anyone cause for conjecture.

"Libbie. This is important. Listen to me carefully. You aren't responsible. It was an accident. Everyone knows you and she had issues, but there's no value in fueling speculation."

She was warmed by Margaret's words, but wary. She'd never been solicitous of Libbie's feelings before.

"Libbie, are you hearing me? I won't have our family name, or Liz's opportunities, tainted by your...your eccentricities. For once, you must exercise self-control and think of other people."

She'd been emotionless, empty even as the shock passed. Now, she felt a vague, familiar stirring. Resentment? Anger?

She asked, "Shouldn't I tell the truth?"

Aunt Margaret went pale, then flushed, then paled again. She smoothed her skirt. "You listen to me. If you've ever listened to anyone, listen to me. If you have any feelings for

Liz, then you will keep this to yourself. All you'll do is hurt her. If you ever had any feelings for Phillip who was kind to you, you won't hurt his daughter. For the sake of this family, I won't tell the police you and Elizabeth were at odds—that she, a grown woman of sobriety and intelligence, just happened to fall through an open window with you there beside her—and you and all of us will be spared embarrassment and inconvenience."

She sat back and smoothed her skirt. "You can go away quietly and everything will be forgotten in time." She finished with a bitter whisper, "Haven't you done enough damage already? She did the best she could for you. Haven't we all? Everyone around you ends up dead or damaged. Think of others for a change."

That was long ago. Libbie had moved on, but it hadn't been easy. Even now, sitting in her home on Cub Creek, alone and in the dark, she felt that suffocating helplessness all over again.

After her grandmother's death, Libbie had stayed in town for the official inquiries. When she could've left, inertia held her in place. Plus, she kept expecting the police to change their minds, haul her down the jail and lock her away.

Grandmother was well-respected in social circles and her death was sufficiently gruesome to gain media attention for a while, but when the police, the flashing lights, the detectives with their questions and hard eyes, all left, and when no new juicy tidbits came out, interest died down.

Locked doors and drawn draperies were her defense. Her prison was her refuge. She contained herself within those walls. Outside, trucks backfired, brakes squealed and traffic beat its own special rhythm, but those things were far removed from her life which was suspended within the shadowed rooms.

She locked herself in the house in the same way that Grandmother had locked her in the bedroom for punishment. She didn't fail to recognize the irony.

Aunt Margaret wanted to wrap up Grandmother's estate and urged strenuous, if discreet actions to remove Libbie from the house. Liz dissuaded her, reminding her of the desirability of avoiding scandal. Liz came often to visit, but when she finally understood Libbie wasn't going to open the door to her or anyone, she knelt at the threshold. She spoke to Libbie through the mail slot as if she knew Libbie was hiding on the other side. On one of her visits, Liz told her Dr. Raymond must be allowed inside or the authorities would intervene.

Dr. Raymond visited every day at first. Why did she let him into the house? She needed rescue. He was a stranger, but his manner was courteous and his voice was soft.

At first she kept him at a distance and pretended to ignore him. Over time, she was drawn in. She didn't mind theoretical discussions.

Dr. Raymond said everyone was emotionally flawed. The nature and degree of the impairment were the most critical factors. The goal of good mental health, according to Dr. Raymond, was to fix what could be fixed and, beyond that, to achieve an acceptable level of functionality. At least, that's what Libbie understood him to say. In short, everyone had issues. Some people were better that others at working around them or hiding them.

Gradually, Libbie opened the draperies, unlocked the doors, and allowed the staff to return to clean the house. Finally, the day came when they were able to begin disassembling the remains of Grandmother's life, and her own, and move forward.

She never was able to put aside the shame and the anger.

Maybe if her grandmother had lived long enough they could have come to terms with each other. Maybe.

Dr. Raymond and she often met over lunch as their relationship became more personal than professional. She hoped his travels had led him to happiness.

As she sat in the dark, the night air rolled in through the open windows bringing a feeling of damp along with it. Libbie considered getting up to close the windows and go to bed, but it seemed a herculean effort and there were too many ghosts whispering in her head tonight.

Would it have been different if her parents had lived? If they'd provided a loving home, as Liz's parents had for her? Maybe. It didn't matter. We are who we are. What was done was done. Regrets and what-ifs meant nothing in real life.

It was dark, inside and out. For most of the night, Libbie sat on the sofa and waited. What was she waiting for? She wasn't sure, but she was willing to settle for dawn.

****

Before five a.m. she rose from the sofa, her joints stiff and creaking. She pulled the throw from the sofa, wrapped it around her shoulders, and walked into the kitchen. She felt deflated and emotionally exhausted.

She made coffee and took it out to the terrace. Being more of a sunset kind of gal, she'd never seen dawn from this place.

The wrought iron was damp with dew. The throw provided some comfort, but she'd left her shoes in the house. Her feet and legs were chilly. She welcomed the cold on her skin because it was normal, or at least indicated the beginning of a return to normalcy.

Normal. What did that mean anyway? She saw this as a wrought iron table—the Bennett's table, now hers. Wrought iron furniture pretty much looked alike, but she'd sensed the leftover happy-family good feelings from its years with the Bennetts. Liz didn't have the benefit of that, but did she have to assume it was THE table? On the other hand, when Liz suggested Libbie take the dining room furniture out of storage and use it, she'd been upset. So, okay, no awards here for consistency.

One point had been proven for certain: never invite family over for a cookout. Hopefully the next time she was tempted, she'd remember. Better to keep visits brief and contact minimal. People couldn't be relied upon. Just about the time a person was starting to feel good about life, they came along and trampled all over you with their big, muddy boots.

The sky began to lighten behind the trees casting them into a relief of dark and darker. Not much color this morning, except very briefly. The sun broke the unseen horizon and peeked through the trees. As the tree line lightened, she saw Tommy standing under the oak near the garage.

She was empty, so empty she could muster no interest as he approached, but sat like a frowsy lump with the rose throw draped around her. She watched him blankly, without thought.

Tommy chose the chair on the opposite side of the table. There was no sound, not from him or caused by him, except for the scrape of wrought iron on brick. He stared past her over her left shoulder, but she suspected he could see her fine. Libbie set her coffee mug, untouched, on the table. It was lukewarm by now. She pushed the mug carefully across the table.

Minutes passed. Tommy continued looking over her shoulder, but she sensed he was aware of the coffee and he wanted it. Tommy's odor was unwashed. Longtime unwashed. Her nose stung. His hair was stringy and stuck out awkwardly from under his baseball cap.

His hands moved slowly, so deftly that if she hadn't been staring, she would've missed seeing the motion. He wrapped his fingers around the mug and brought it to his lips, carefully, warily, and took a tiny sip. He held the mug within inches of his lips while he appeared to consider the advisability of risking another sip. The next was not a sip, but a gulp that ended when the mug was empty.

His hands remained on the table. His fingers loosely cradled the empty mug. She reached out gently, never taking her eyes from his face, and stretched her arm, her fingers extended. The table was wide and it was a reach. When she touched his hand, Tommy didn't change his stare, but she sensed a change in the tension of his body.

The touch lasted no more than a few seconds before he broke into a high, moaning wail. He jumped up and ran, with his awkward, loping trot, across the yard and into the woods behind the garage.

Libbie received nothing in the way of images or colors when she touched Tommy, but the connection was undeniable. Something passed between them. He was like a dry sponge and she thought her desolation might have crossed to him, drawn unintentionally. His cry may have been his dismay. Likely, he'd never come back and that was probably good.

The sun crested the tree line. She rose, too, and stretched, suddenly feeling the freshness of the morning air and hearing the early bird song. It was good to feel alive again.

She'd known she'd recover, but sometimes it was hard to remember when she was lost in that darkness.

Later, with a fresh cup of coffee near at hand, Libbie opened her graphics software and logged into the scrapbooking site.

She played with the saturation and the contrast. She arranged and re-arranged the photos. When she was engaged in creating things, words, ideas, flowed. Like a stutterer who sings flawlessly, the act of creation removed some kind of barrier in her brain. She'd opened the photo of a country road overhung by trees and yet beyond it, in the distance, high rises were visible above the tree line. It made her think of Dorothy's yellow brick road and Alice's Wonderland and the reality that people seemed to make and remake to suit themselves.

All these conflicting motivations and needs confused people like her. It was hard to know where truth ended and camouflage began.

She smiled, happy to feel that feistiness return. Her equilibrium had been re-struck. She didn't know how long it would last, but she'd found that here, in her sweet spot, the meltdowns still happened, but were briefer and passed more quickly than before.

When she pushed back from the desk, she felt the stirrings of hunger. She hadn't eaten since the cookout. The idea of food and the cookout made her think of Max. She hadn't seen him since yesterday. Except for that one three-day period when he'd stayed away, he came home every night regardless of where he spent his days.

She checked the front porch. No Max.

"Max?" she called out, hoping for a response. She checked in the backyard, too. No Max, but through the kitchen window the garage caught her eye. No telling what the deal was with the garage but, definitely, it needed attention. Maybe it needed the attention of a bulldozer.

On impulse, she went out the back door, down the steps, and across to the garage. She lifted the garage door and opened the door on the side. The air inside was heavy and cloying, as usual. It needed a good airing out. Let the wind and rain blow through, should any arrive. There was absolutely nothing in the garage she cared to protect from the elements or from anything else.

With the garage opened, the air pressure felt better, even inside the house. She didn't know why it should, and it made no sense. She went around the house opening the windows. It was a beautiful day and the breeze was sweet.

Libbie sang a tune as she yanked the blue tape from the walls of the dining room. Out with the old and unworkable. It was time for either "tried and true" or "try something new."

Yank and rip, yank and rip—she kept at it until she had a huge ball of painter's tape. She saw the quality of the daylight streaming in through the windows. The French doors and study windows cast shadows and reflections throughout the dining room. The ceiling reflections bent at the corners and ran down the walls.

Libbie went round and round, staring at them.

It was dizzying and electrifying.

Rainbow lights flashed in the reflections, appearing and disappearing before her eyes. She couldn't capture those, but could attempt her own version.

She dragged the step ladder from the corner, snagged a fresh roll of tape, and jumped into the task while the inspiration was fresh and before she could think of reasons why it wouldn't work or would look stupid.

First, Libbie taped the lines of shadow and reflection running from the perimeter of the ceiling to the center where the light fixture would ultimately hang. They arrayed like pie slices, or a pinwheel, off-center and of varying thicknesses that kept the pattern fresh and disguised a century of settling and shifting. She'd already painted the ceiling in a base coat of flat champagne. With the satin finish champagne, she painted the alternating spaces.

As soon as the paint dried, she'd place the tape at right angles, crossing the sections, but staggered with an irregular pattern. The weight of the right angle lines would balance the rhythm. She'd fill in those areas with an eggshell finish.

It was hard to wait. She hated to lose momentum. She eyed the shadows and reflections and tried to fix the pattern in her mind's eye. Patience was called for and hard to come by when she was in this mood. Then it hit her—not eggshell. The right angle lines needed to be a combination of flat and satin for depth and light. It came together for her and she saw the structure clearly. Subtle, reflective, yet sculptured. She forced herself to walk away before she lost the picture in her head.

Patience, she counseled, but standing at the sink, cleaning the brush, she felt restless.

She ran a brush through her hair and checked her face for paint drips, then donned her shoes. Time to take a ride up to Mineral for barbecue and hush puppies.

****

Libbie pressed the accelerator and turned north onto Cub Creek Loop.

Her good mood was restored and she was driving too fast.

She saw the bridge ahead. In her head she heard *slow down*. As she moved her foot toward the brake, the leafy branches overhanging the concrete side rails shivered. A low figure jumped out. Max.

The brake pedal pulsed as she tried to grind it to a stop. The rear wheel hit the dirt and gravel verge. She felt it when the tread and resistance with the road parted.

Lift off—the car took flight. The thick concrete side

barriers of the bridge caved in the side of the car in the instant before the airbags deployed and knocked her out cold.

The airbag deflated. Libbie regained consciousness. She was disoriented. Her vision was blurry and the world was spinning. What had happened? As she reached for the car door handle, it swung open. Someone grabbed her arm. She pushed back.

"Hey, it's okay. It's okay. Easy."

A woman's voice.

"Careful, honey. Libbie? It's Ann, your neighbor. Faith saw it all and called me. You're all bloody. Where does it hurt?"

"Stupid question," She tried to say, but her lower lip was huge and her words sounded like nonsense. She tasted blood.

Libbie squinted and tried to focus. Ann. A man, maybe Allan, was speaking in the background in a muffled tone.

Beyond the car, I saw blue sky and treetops.

"I don't know whether you should stay in the car or not." *Out.*

"Careful, careful. Let me help you."

Ann helped her to maneuver her body. She slid down to the pavement and landed on her knees

"Take it easy," the woman said.

Libbie saw the car had come to a halt with the back end suspended over the slope to the creek. The car didn't fall and roll because it snagged between the side rail of the bridge and a tree.

"Ann, Max."

Her lower lip was uncontrollable. Ann couldn't understand her garbled speech. Libbie looked up at her and the man.

"Max?"

Ann seemed confused. "What, honey? Try to relax."

Noise of sirens and flashing lights in red and blue and yellow filled her senses. The man ran to meet the arriving vehicles. A rescue squad, a police car, and other vehicles lined up along the narrow road. More folks coming to enjoy the spectacle. All she could think was that Alice would never forgive her for killing her dog.

The EMT's moved Ann aside, but blocked Libbie's view. They had suitcases and a stupid wheeled stretcher and if they thought she was going to *stretch* out on that and get strapped in, then they needed to rethink a few things.

A male and female EMT knelt by her and the two men were busy doing something in front of her car, near Max.

"How is he?"

The EMTs pushed, pulled and questioned. "What's your name, ma'am?"

They couldn't understand her. Her fat lip was numb and something was bleeding. Maybe her nose.

"My dog," she mouthed.

"Have you taken any alcohol or medication?"

She shook her head and the world spun in pain.

"Who's the man in the road? Was he with you?"

Almost in tears, maybe in tears, Libbie pushed their groping hands away. "Man?"

"Was there anyone else in the vehicle?"

The questions made no sense. They were gathered around Max, working on him. All she could see were their uniformed backs, but she felt hopeful since they were still trying. Surprised too, that they would put so much effort into saving a pet.

There was a lot of blood on her and she was agitated and confused. Too many strangers. It was all a blur and she couldn't keep up. Her breath came short and her face, her head, and more was suddenly hurting. She slapped at their hands.

They thought she was hysterical. It took every scrap of strength she had to push their hands away and struggle to her feet.

An EMT spoke nearby. "Dan, a neighbor identified her as Libbie Havens. You know her? She hasn't been able to tell us her name. She's extremely agitated. It could be a head injury."

Dan interrupted, "Maybe, but she's naturally that way."

"What?" It sounded like, *Whuff?*

Dan's remark ticked her off, but diffused much of the tension for everyone else at the scene.

"You have to allow the EMT's to help you," Dan said firmly. "You have to go with them to the hospital."

The adrenaline rush was over. Her knees turned mushy. The world revolved like that crazy teacup ride at the fair and black specks danced before her eyes.

They'd rolled a wheeled stretcher over to her.

"Please, Libbie? For me?"

The will to fight was gone. Everything went black as her knees folded.

****

Libbie awoke in the hospital emergency room in Charlottesville as Liz pushed the curtain aside.

Liz rushed over and grabbed her hand. "Dan told me what happened." She brushed Libbie's hair back from her forehead. "You're poor face. Does it hurt?"

Dan spoke. "Nothing that won't heal. You'll be fine in no time."

An orderly wheeled Libbie away long enough for pictures to be taken of her brain, then wheeled her back. Liz and Dan were still there waiting.

Someone moaned loudly a few curtains away.

Dan touched her arm. "It's Tommy."

"Tommy?" Not Max. She closed her eyes and turned her face away.

Liz spoke in a soothing tone and stroked her arm. "Not your fault. You did what you could to avoid him."

It made no sense. It was Max she'd seen. Of course, it was. She couldn't have imagined that. He must've made it past the oncoming car in time, but Tommy hadn't. She hadn't seen Tommy at all. No matter how hard she tried, she couldn't remember seeing him, much less hitting him.

Her doctor was an attractive man with a reasonable sense of humor. The lip was responding quickly to an ice pack, so she was more communicative by the minute. The doctor wanted to admit her to the hospital for observation overnight.

"No, I want to go home."

Agreeing with the doctor, Liz said, "Stay."

Dan said, "Stay."

Dr. Sheldon handed me a mirror.

Ha, ha. Very funny man.

Libbie could hear him moaning and whimpering. He yelped out an unintelligible word.

Not Max. Tommy.

"Is he in pain?" she asked Dr. Sheldon.

"I don't think so. Not much, anyway. But he's frightened and agitated. He's difficult to communicate with."

"I want to see him. I need to speak with him."

Dr. Sheldon was dismissive. "We need to admit you, at least for the night."

"What about Tommy?"

Dan said, "Sounds like his injury isn't serious, but…well, you can hear him."

"He'll be better at home."

"That may be," Dr. Sheldon answered, "but we can't release him in this state."

"Let me visit him. Please. If you do, I'll cooperate. I'll be nice."

Dan nodded at the doctor. Dr. Sheldon pushed around the end of the curtain. After a few minutes of murmured conversation, he returned.

"His mother is with him. She's upset, but she agreed. Are you sure about this?"

"Yes." She was responsible in so many ways for his presence here and his condition. She hoped her ravaged appearance wouldn't frighten him more. What could she do? She didn't know, but she'd surprised herself recently and figured she couldn't make him any worse. It was worth a try.

They brought a wheelchair over and helped her slide into it from the bed. The room spun. She held her breath and the room steadied.

They wheeled her alongside Tommy's bed. Her face was almost even with his. His wrists were cuffed with white ties to the side rails of the bed. His head rolled back and forth slowly. He moaned loudly with each exhale and whimpered each time he breathed in. The sounds were infinitely aggravating. The woman seated in a chair on the other side of the bed was haggard. She didn't speak, but eyed Libbie closely and sniffled. She looked like she'd tasted something bitter and needed to spit. Libbie nodded to acknowledge her presence, but spoke only to Tommy.

"Tommy?" She knew he heard her voice, but he didn't open his eyes. She reached out and placed her fingers around his hand. "Tommy?"

His eyelids fluttered, but remained closed. His head stopped rolling and the moaning halted.

Remembering how she'd sent him the negative burst

that morning...had it been just that morning? This time, she imagined a smile.

She'd never done anything like this before. She hoped it would work.

Libbie visualized a big, bright, white as white can be, smile. She got a little glow herself, feeling the smile. She thought about daisies and kittens and all that sappy crap. Redheaded twins and sticky fingers, too. All in sunshine Sherbet colors. She let them run along her arm like a current.

She saw in Tommy's eyes when the connection clicked. He didn't smile in return, but he relaxed and his eyes opened fully. She believed his anxiety abated. She hoped it would last, at least for a while. Maybe long enough to get him out of this strange and frightening environment.

The doctor, Dan, Liz, that haggard woman across the bed from me—Libbie had forgotten them. They must've made a strange spectacle. She withdrew her hand. Tommy turned his face toward his mother and smiled, if only a little. She reached over and touched his other hand.

They returned to her own curtained area. Dan said nothing. Dr. Sheldon asked what she'd done.

"I reminded him he wasn't alone. That he had a friend."

The police officer came and wanted to ask a few questions about the accident.

"Am I under arrest?"

"What?" Dan shook his head. "No, you nearly killed yourself to avoid hitting someone who suddenly appeared in the road. In the end, your effort paid off. Your car never touched him. He fell, probably startled, and hit his head on the concrete. Lucky for him he has a hard head."

****

The next morning Libbie was sore. Her face had blossomed with airbag bruises, but those didn't hurt much and her lip wasn't as swollen.

"Send me home," she insisted. "I'll hurt no matter where I am, but I'll hurt more comfortably at home." At her sweet spot. Her property on Cub Creek.

Chapter Eighteen

Liz and Josh drove her home. They hovered for a while before accepting she was okay. Josh kept grinning at her. Rather rudely, actually. While Liz made a run to the grocery store, Josh and Libbie had a chat.

"Okay, talk to me," she said. "What's all the grinning about?"

Josh shook his head. "You look awful."

"Thanks so much. I'm glad it amuses you." She was feigning annoyance. She knew Josh found no pleasure in her discomfort.

"No, I've been thinking about you and those EMTs. Tell me, did you plan to take them on one by one, or all at once?"

"Liz has been talking about my business again. Or Dan, maybe, since Liz wasn't actually there at the scene. Truth is, I don't like stretchers. Panic is never pretty."

He turned serious. "Lucky you weren't hurt worse than you were."

When Liz returned from the store, she suggested she'd stay and Josh could go home. Libbie said "No" and was firm.

"I thank you both sincerely for helping me get home, but I'll be fine and you two should go. I'm a little tired and I'd like to rest."

Josh looked at Liz. "I think Libbie wants some time alone."

"Okay, fine. We'll give you a break this afternoon, but I'll be back with supper. I'll be staying here tonight. No argument."

She smiled and regretted it. "Ouch. Okay, no argument."

"Would you like help getting upstairs?"

"No, I think I'd like to sit out on the terrace."

Josh carried her laptop outside and Liz brought a tall glass of iced tea and a bag of cookies. Oatmeal raisin, of course. Liz set Libbie's cell phone close at hand.

"I might get to like this. You two are kind of handy. How do you feel about aprons and dust caps?"

"See you later." Liz waved. She and Josh walked around the house to their car.

Jim dropped by. He strolled around the corner of the house and stood quietly, watching her as she surfed in her open air study. She saw him from the corner of her eye and let him watch for a few moments, thinking he might need an opportunity to adjust to her injured appearance.

He walked carefully across the terrace as if in a sickroom. "Mind if I join you?"

"You're welcome. Always welcome. And, no, it doesn't hurt as bad as it looks." She tried to smile without moving her lower lip too much, not wanting it to hurt again.

"Actually, I saw what's left of your car and, considering its condition, I think you came out of it amazingly well." Jim took a seat at the table.

"I haven't seen the car. Not since…the accident."

"The accident. You were lucky to survive the bridge. You were brave to take a chance like that to avoid hitting Tom."

"I'm not brave. Don't give me credit for what was pure reflex." Libbie shook her head. "I didn't tell anyone this. I don't suppose it matters. It felt like too much effort to sort it out. I never saw Tommy. I was trying to avoid hitting Max."

He chuckled softly. "Maybe it's just as well you didn't

say it, that's if you want to avoid a lot of lectures about not doing something risky to avoid hitting an animal." He shrugged. "In the end, it's all the same, in my mind anyway. That involuntary reflex is the key. The rest of the story is nobody's business but yours."

He changed the subject. "Are you and Dan seeing each other?"

She looked down. "I think so, yes." Her face felt hot.

He touched her hand gently. "If anything changes with that, let me know. If he wasn't my cousin and best friend, I wouldn't be so considerate."

"Sure." How embarrassing. Libbie was pretty sure she was blushing. She tried to think of something clever to say, but was totally at a loss.

He added, "I can be patient when I need to be."

Should she be annoyed that he'd said that? What did he mean, anyway? The remark didn't seem fair to Dan. Was he assuming Dan would change his mind about her? And then what? He'd be there to pick up the leavings?

She frowned and asked sharply, "What exactly do you mean by that?"

"I mean what I said. That I can be patient." He shifted his hand beneath hers and clasped her fingers. He met her eyes. "Don't be slow to ask for help if it's needed, okay?"

She squeezed his fingers gently in return. "Thanks, Jim."

He stopped when he reached the corner of the house and gave a last wave.

Libbie rested until Liz returned with supper. Dan joined them.

He gave her a hard, penetrating look, "Tommy was lucky you swerved to avoid him. Not sure the best choice was to hit the bridge."

"Honestly, Dan, I didn't think. I just turned the wheel." Was that close enough to the truth? "I guess I was lucky too."

Dan picked up her hand and kissed the palm. "Lucky for me."

She was very pleased Dan and she were going to have another chance at a relationship.

"Has anyone seen Max?" she asked.

As if on cue, Max emerged from the woods and settled next to her chair.

It felt like validation of some kind. From a dog. Yeah.

****

Dan and Libbie had a few minutes alone before he left. He took her hand and said, "That question about your grandmother? I'm sorry. It wasn't my place to ask."

She shrugged, but looked away. "What did Liz tell you?"

"It doesn't matter."

He wasn't throwing Liz under the bus. Loyalty was nice. She tried not to mind that it was misdirected.

"It was a terrible tragedy, Dan. She fell from a fourth floor window onto the courtyard below. I was near her when she fell, but Liz saw her... I know how traumatic that must have been." Had she sounded right? Hit the appropriate note of simplicity and sincerity? Would he let it go now?

He kissed her hand and touched her hair. "I'll see you tomorrow."

After he left it occurred to her that, as a cop, he'd surely checked law enforcement records. He must've already known all the details.

She was disappointed. He could've been honest about it.

Maybe all he wanted was to apologize. But what was Liz's excuse?

****

Next morning, Liz and she breakfasted on the terrace. Libbie was okay aside from a few aches and pains. They'd slept in, so it was mid-morning by the time they finished breakfast. They sat at the table enjoying the quiet morning, each with their feet propped in the seat of a chair. Liz seemed to have overcome her negativity about the wrought iron.

"This is a beautiful place, Libbie. It's lovely and I can see why you like it, but I'd be too lonely here."

"Sometimes 'lonely' is actually solitude."

"Solitude is solitude only if someone isn't alone all the time."

"Liz, don't worry about me. I'll be fine."

"Maybe." She scootched down in her chair to rest the back of her head against the top edge. She appeared to be cloud-gazing.

Libbie's eyes were drawn to the garage beneath the wide-spreading branches of the oak. The doors were closed again. Never mind. She had plans for the building. She reached down and scratched between Max's ears.

"He's a nice dog. Do you know what breed he is?"

"Dan called him a Weimaraner." She shrugged. She didn't care. His breed didn't matter. Max was Max.

"I looked it up. They're good hunters and have a strong protective instinct. Not necessarily good with children."

Libbie scratched his head again. "I know a couple of kids he's very fond of."

****

Mary Lloyd knocked on her door a few days later.

Libbie invited her to sit on the porch. Mary's eyes kept stopping on her injuries and then sliding away. Tommy's mother looked like she'd been living rough for a long time. Libbie tried not to stare at the stained dress and the dirt crusted around the woman's ankles. She didn't want to embarrass her, nor contribute to her troubles. Nor did she want to share in them.

Mary stammered, "I'm sorry to…I mean I hope you don't mind... I mean to say I appreciate you are nice to Tommy. After him hanging around and all. I know how he does and it bothers some folks, but mostly he's fine and wouldn't hurt no one."

"He bothers you any, you tell me and I'll do what I can. He's all I got, but sometimes he's too much for me. Cain't do much with him. Cain't keep him in. I do my best, I truly do. Mostly, he's fine and wouldn't bother nobody, I'm sure not."

She left after delivering this pathetic soliloquy. Libbie couldn't recall when she'd been happier to see someone's back, or felt less charitable. Mary left, crossing the backyard and disappearing down the path, heading south.

Tommy didn't have a chance. Never did, was Libbie's guess.

****

Dan agreed to ask around for someone willing to demolish and haul away the garage.

"You sure? It's got some rot around the bottom, but it's solidly built. You can fix it."

"No, I want to start fresh."

He tipped his hat. "Yes, ma'am."

Yes, she liked Dan very much.

Liz and Josh helped her shop for a new vehicle. She felt exposed, roaming the car lots looking like she'd been beaten up. It was nice to have help.

Almost two weeks after the accident at the bridge, Libbie had a new car in her driveway and an appointment with some heavy equipment.

Her bruises had faded and her lip was healed. Liz asked if she could bring the children by for a visit. She said they'd been asking about their Aunt Libbie and now that her appearance was more palatable, Liz thought the timing was good. Libbie suggested she drop them off Friday evening to spend the night. Liz could retrieve them on Saturday afternoon.

In the call history, she saw Aunt Margaret had dialed her cell number repeatedly. If she'd known her aunt was calling, she wouldn't have answered. Still, it could be important. Libbie broke her own rule and dialed the voicemail.

Margaret didn't identify herself. She didn't need to. Her voice was almost hoarse, tense with emotion. "Stay away from Liz. Stay away from my grandchildren."

Some things, some people, never change. She deleted the voicemail.

Dan had a friend of a friend who owned a construction business. The owner was willing for one of his employees to borrow a bulldozer and earn a little extra on the side by knocking down the garage and hauling it off. Dan was planning to meet the man here after work on Friday. The man would do the deed on Saturday.

The kids arrived at suppertime, complete with food. Liz drove off, blowing kisses.

The three ate chicken tenders and fries out on the terrace. Dan joined them mid-meal and soon after there was a loud, grinding vibration as a flatbed hauling a bulldozer rumbled up the driveway.

Audrey sat absolutely still, eyes wide and mouth gaping. Adam was ecstatic.

"No, Adam. Stay here at the table. Don't move," she ordered.

"Aunt Libbie! I'll be careful."

"No. You'll stay right here at this table. Promise me."

It was a sight to see the big yellow monster in her

backyard. They watched the show as the equipment operator maneuvered the machine down the ramp from the flatbed. He parked the bulldozer in the yard beneath the oak. It faced the garage squarely and the intent was unmistakable. It was already late afternoon. The actual demolition was scheduled for the next day.

"Fred Sims, ma'am." He offered his hand. "Dan, how are you? You kids stay off the equipment?"

Fred took a walk around the garage and looked inside too. "Ma'am, you sure you want to destroy this building? It's sound."

"Absolutely sure," she told him. "Contents and all. Knock it down and haul it away."

"Yes, ma'am. If you don't want what's inside, mind if I poke around and see if there's any tools or such I can find a home for?"

"Feel free. I don't want any of the stuff in that building. I don't care what happens to it. I just want it gone."

"Can do, ma'am. I'll haul a dumpster out here tomorrow when I come back."

The boxes were stacked haphazardly in the back corner with a couple of feet of space between them and the wall. Dan helped Fred pull them into the open floor area for better light. He and Fred spent several minutes in serious conversation in the back corner where the boxes had been. It gave her a shiver.

As the late afternoon light diminished, the shadows gathered among the trees at the edge of the woods. The yellowish cast of the light gilded the leaves of the large oak with an eerie glow. The atmosphere promised a storm, but the sky was clear. A chill wrapped itself around her.

Libbie sent the kids into the house with an excuse. "Go inside and wash up. Take the supper dishes with you. I'll be along in a minute."

Dan asked her to step into the garage with him. She didn't want to and hesitated at the open door. He took her the hand and pulled her inside. He pointed down at the area that had been hidden in the dark corner by the sagging boxes.

"Someone's been hanging out here," he said.

"Living here?"

"Just holing up here from time to time, I imagine."

The twisted, filthy rags were arranged almost like a bed.

"What are those little white things?"

Dan put his hand on her shoulder with a reassuring squeeze. "Bones. From small animals."

Speechless, Libbie shook her head. Dan met her gaze. Neither of them wanted to discuss this in front of Fred.

She bit her lip rather than say Tommy's name. What did it mean anyway? That he'd been using the garage as his "home away from home"? For how many years?

Regardless, it was over. She didn't want to think about it and saw no point in discussing it.

"What's this?" Fred plucked something from amid the debris.

Dan didn't recognize it. Libbie did.

"My sweater." She was suddenly so cold her bones ached.

It means nothing—only that Tommy found it and kept it here in the garage.

How often had he crashed here? With her, and the kids too, being a few yards away.

Fred reached down again. He stood and held out his palm to show a few faded, shriveled pink blossoms.

"Are these some kind of flowers?" he asked.

Dan put his arm around her again, but she stepped away from him feeling suddenly panicky as if the air had been sucked from her lungs. She drew the air back in slowly hoping she wasn't making a spectacle of herself.

"You okay?"

Libbie touched his arm and nodded. When she could speak she said, "I will be. This problem is about to be solved."

She walked out of that repulsive garage and into the house.

They played Canasta that evening. Audrey and she partnered against Dan and Adam. They had a lot of laughs.

She refused to think about Tommy. At the end of the evening, she sent Dan home with a kiss and a cozy, whispered promise for a re-match.

Libbie refused to let Tommy and the garage spoil their time together. She was glad that very soon she would be able to permanently put the garage and its contents from her mind and out of her life.

Tomorrow, the bulldozer would erase the garage as if it never existed.

Chapter Nineteen

Once upon a time, Dr. Raymond had told Libbie, "You can try to ignore the truth of what your eyes see and what your brain knows, but it will keep coming back one way or another until you deal with it."

Libbie knew it sometimes came back regardless of being dealt with it.

She dreamed heavily that night. She didn't remember much, but that it went on and on. She woke several times, overwhelmed by a feeling of dread. Her pillow was wet. Tears had run down her cheek and neck. Each time she awoke she looked at Audrey who slept peacefully. Libbie got up to check on Adam and watched until she saw the rise and fall of his chest. She returned to bed, blaming the horrible night on a delayed reaction to the accident combined with the shock of finding Tommy had been using her garage.

What about those bones?

At some point she slept, but when she woke in the morning, she was light-headed and queasy.

Uneasiness kept pushing at her consciousness like a precursor to a violent migraine. She shoved it back. It didn't belong here. This was her home. Her sweet spot. She was taking control of her life and she was doing it well.

Everything was going her way. The relationship with Liz wasn't perfect, but better than it had been in twenty years. The kids liked being here with their Aunt Libbie. And Dan... Well, Dan and she were getting closer all the time. Why did the air around her feel so oppressive? Why did she feel so sluggish and exhausted?

The kids fixed their own cereal. Libbie stood in the steaming shower until the hot water tank was drained. The bathroom window was open and she heard noises in the backyard, like something clanging against metal, but she didn't look outside until she remembered the bulldozer.

She stuck her head out of the window to yell at Adam, but he wasn't in sight. She clutched her robe about her and called down the stairs, "Adam? Audrey?"

"Yes?" Their heads popped around the newel post at the foot of the stairs.

"Stay away from that bulldozer."

"We will. Promise. We're watching TV."

Apparently she hadn't heard them outside, after all. Hearing things, maybe. That thought was worth an ironic chuckle. Anyway, there were no other kids around. Except maybe Tommy, and he didn't qualify as a kid. He had to be well into his twenties. Which reminded her, she needed to discuss Tommy with the kids, especially Adam.

Fred wasn't expected until noon. Libbie finished dressing and went downstairs. She'd tell Adam about Tommy later. At the moment, she wasn't feeling so hot. Hot tea. That might be good. Hot tea and toast. On the terrace.

Liz was due to arrive about lunchtime. Dan would show up sometime early afternoon.

The sun was warm, the breeze was gentle and the morning air was sweet. A few sips of tea, and toast with jam, sat well on her stomach. She leaned her head back against the cool wrought iron of the chair and propped her feet in the chair opposite. Peaceful. All was quiet, including from within the house. She dozed off.

Libbie woke, slowly and begrudgingly, with a sense of

dark suffocation pressing closely about her. The air was bad and a black, oily absence of color pressed against the back of her eyes. A weak alarm sounded in the recesses of her brain. Perhaps it was the smell that warned her, but not soon enough. She heard a quick, delicate snap and opened her eyes. Instinct held her immobile.

Tommy was seated at the table. Libbie could smell his hair, dirty and unkempt. He could not have touched a sliver of soap since his release from the hospital. He wasn't looking over her shoulder this time. He stared directly at her.

She couldn't read his expression. His face was blank. His eyes were dark as if the pupils were fully dilated, and fixed intently. Focused. On her.

His stink was all around. He held a brown rabbit. The fingers of one hand encircled its neck. With the other hand, he ruffled the fur on its side. The rabbit did not, could not, move. Its head hung crookedly.

Her heart contracted painfully as if gripped by a stone fist.

"Aunt Libbie?" Audrey's voice trembled, high and thin.

Her voice brought Libbie upright with a jolt. Tommy jumped back. The dead rabbit hit the terrace with force and skidded roughly across the terrace blocks. Audrey screamed.

"Into the house, Audrey. Now!" Libbie moved to stand between Audrey and Tommy. The screen door banged shut.

Where was Adam? He wasn't in the house. Libbie knew it because his green plastic whistle was hanging around Tommy's neck.

Oh, Adam. Where are you?

"Hello." She controlled her breathing as best she could and tried to sound calm. "You've come to visit." Her tone was tentative. She didn't know what to do.

The merest hint of a smile turned up the corners of his

mouth. The smile didn't extend to his eyes. Because he'd dropped the rabbit, Libbie could see the knife in his hand. It was a small, thin knife. Small. Thin. A few feet separated them.

Fight or flight. Instinct said run. Indecision kept her still. She hoped Audrey was phoning 911. Would she? Libbie wiped her damp palms against her jeans and drew a deep breath.

"Where's Adam?" Her heart was pounding in her chest and in her ears. It was hard to sound firm, yet non-threatening. This was no time for panic. Adam was probably in the woods—maybe healthy, maybe not—but if she left to go find him, then she was leaving Audrey unprotected.

Had Audrey locked the door? Had she called for help? What to do?

Tommy's response was a crooked grin. He moved the knife around as if gesturing. Was his movement random or intended to be threatening? His palms and fingers were lightly scored and slightly bloody, as if he'd been testing the blade's edge. She didn't want to hurt him, but she couldn't allow him to harm the kids. She had to find Adam.

She yelled, "Adam," hoping for a quick response and fought back the fear, the anxiety. She must think clearly. It was her responsibility to make a decision and act upon it. How dangerous was Tommy and his knife?

"No-o," He said in a long, painful, dragged-out syllable. "No-o." He waved the knife in the air with one hand and with the other hand he pointed a finger in the direction of the garage and the bulldozer.

Libbie moved a step closer and put out her hand intending to ask him to put the knife away. He moved more quickly than she expected. Her forearm now had a thin red line, slowly widening. She moved to put the table between them. What should she do?

Something. Do something.

Libbie walked cautiously around the table. He backed a few steps. Decision time. She couldn't choose which child to protect, so one choice remained—stop Tommy. She rushed him.

He was surprised by the suddenness of her move. He backed a few steps more. He put his hand out, the hand holding the knife, but Libbie kept coming. The thrust of her body against his carried them a few feet further until his body slammed to the ground, taking her with it. His head slammed against the bucket edge of the bulldozer.

His body went limp instantly, but his eyes met hers and held them for a long moment before his lids closed.

Libbie rolled away. Somewhere in the collision, her palm had been cut.

There were witnesses.

Liz saw the body blow and the fall. She screamed even louder than when she'd seen Grandmother hit the iron table. Dan yelled something unintelligible and ran to them.

They'd seen the fall, but nothing more. Having just come around the side of the house, they couldn't understand the full situation. They saw the blood on her hand and arm, and Dan took the knife from Tommy's hand, but they didn't understand. The high whine of Audrey's cry was audible from the screened porch.

"Adam," Libbie said. "Adam. We have to find him."

"Adam! Where's Adam?" Liz's cry was ragged.

"Mom? Mom, what's wrong?" He came running around the end of the bulldozer.

He was fresh from the woods, grubby, but obviously fine. When he saw Tommy on the ground, his eyes grew wide and wild. Libbie moved toward him with relief, but when she held out her arms, he cringed. Now wonder. He saw the blood, of course, from her cuts. Would he start screaming too? In the background, she heard Dan calling for the EMT's and the on-duty officer.

Liz pulled Adam's face to her body and held him tightly. Her eyes turned on Libbie in cold accusation.

"Liz, let me explain. Tommy had a knife. He had Adam's whistle."

Adam pushed away from his mother. "I gave it to him. Back at the fort."

"He had a knife." She spoke to Liz's back as Liz turned away. "He had a knife," Libbie repeated. She held out her arm to show her the wounds.

Liz dragged Adam with her as she went inside to comfort Audrey.

Libbie knelt on the ground across from Dan with Tommy between them. With one hand, Dan pressed a handkerchief to the wound on Tommy's head. With his other hand, he sought a pulse.

As she reached toward Dan a drop of her blood landed on his pale cheek.

"Stay back," Dan said.

"Dan, he had a knife. I didn't know what to do." Libbie trembled.

"Not now." His voice was dismissive. Business-like. Impersonal.

She heard the sirens, distant but approaching. She felt time receding, spiraling down. She was cold. Numb.

Aunt Margaret's voice echoed in her head. "Of the people who were close to you, where are they now? How many of them are still alive?"

Libbie shook her head, trying to shake the cruel voice out.

"Dan." His arms should've been around her, comforting her. Tommy's need was immediate, she understood that, but the least bit of encouragement or reassurance would've sustained her.

He met her eyes. His warm, dark eyes were now cool, replaced by the neutral brown of the deputy. Not merely neutral—they were the eyes of a stranger.

Libbie looked down at her bloody hands. The emergency responders would arrive any minute now, crunching gravel and bringing havoc. This was her chance to say the magic words, the words that would restore the special light to Dan's eyes, but she had none. She was mute. Her shirt and jeans were ruined. These stains would never come out.

People come, people go. She still had the property, Cub Creek. She was okay alone. Always had been.

Fingers lightly stroked her shoulder. Adam spoke softly, but with urgency, "Aunt Libbie?"

She looked up, but couldn't make her mouth work.

"Hold out your arm. I'll wrap the towel around it and your hand." Adam was pale, his voice firm.

A vehicle slowed to a stop behind them.

"It's okay, I know first aid from scouts. But we should get out of the way."

He led her to the back stoop and they sat together on the second step while he wrapped her arm in a white hand towel. She cried a little. Adam pretended not to see her tears.

The blood stains were never going to wash out of that towel.

Her wounds were messy, but she refused to go for stitches and they, the EMTs and she, settled for stronger bandaging. Meanwhile the ambulance left with lights and sirens blasting. A broadcast of sorts, that Tommy was still clinging to life.

After the last EMTs departed, the police interviewed them in earnest.

Dan told the police he'd seen the knife in Tommy's hand after she'd tackled him. Libbie was grateful Liz allowed the children to speak with the police officers. Audrey gave an amazingly lucid account of witnessing Tommy twist the rabbit's neck before Libbie sent her into the house to safety. The slice on Libbie's arm and the graze on her palm both argued visibly for the peril, correct or not, she believed they'd faced that morning. She could shed no light on his motivation.

In the back of her mind, unexpressed, was the knowledge that Tommy had been trying to protect the garage. His special place? A dark, dusty corner amid rags and bones? Not Libbie's shame, but still she felt it keenly as if, like her sweater, she'd been tainted by that dank place. Her stomach revolted at the thought.

Dan knew about the garage. He could tell the police if he chose. She couldn't speak of it.

Throughout the questioning, Libbie watched the eyes of the detective and officers. Had they seen her record? Did they know about her? Her past? Had Dan told them she'd already been connected to an untimely death?

The police drove away without her in custody. She could hardly believe it. Dan left at the same time. Perhaps he'd vouched for her. Maybe there were special courtesies extended within the community of law enforcement. Not that Libbie believed she'd done anything wrong, certainly not intentionally, but as before, her unwise actions resulted in dreadful harm and she couldn't erase the memory of Tommy's last, dark stare.

Liz sent the children out onto the front porch to wait for her. It made sense that she needed quiet time with them to help them deal with what had happened. Libbie gave them each a big hug. They'd come through like champs. Liz, herself, seemed to be struggling to control the emotional after-effects. With the departure of the authorities and the lessening of intensity, she might be losing her battle. Libbie was trying to control her own tremors, so she understood that too.

The kids walked out the front door with a half wave. Audrey clutched her whistle to her chest in a tight fist.

Libbie faced Liz in the writing room, wanting to thank her, but those words were never said.

"What happened out there?" Liz asked, her voice low. She dragged her fingers through her no longer perfect hair.

Her attitude confused Libbie. "Well, this morning I..." she stammered.

"No." Liz waved her arms. "Don't repeat all that. I heard what you told the police. Tell me why you attacked Tommy."

Attacked? Okay, one might call it that, but she'd had reason. "I called Adam. He didn't answer. I had to find him to make sure he was okay, but I couldn't leave Audrey unprotected."

"Audrey was safely inside the house. You're the adult, Libbie. Why wouldn't you go inside too, and call the police instead of...instead of...acting so recklessly? Dangerously?"

Liz squeezed her eyes shut and shook her head vigorously.

"Remember, I saw you in the hospital with that boy. You didn't believe he was dangerous then, did you? *I* was certainly worried. I called Dan afterward and he told me all about Tommy and his situation. Dan said he was harmless."

She drew a deep breath and continued, "If you truly believed he had suddenly become dangerous, then your actions were even more bizarre. Suppose you'd been disabled when you went after him? My children would've been left unprotected." She shook her head.

"Libbie, I give you credit for good intentions, at least regarding Audrey and Adam, but I can't be grateful when your response is so out of proportion to the actions of that pitiful young man."

"That's not fair, Liz. You don't understand. Let me tell you what happened."

"No," she interrupted. "I don't care if it's fair or not. It was like watching Grandmother fall to her death all over again. I can't stand it. I can't." She scrubbed the sides of her face with the flats of her hands.

"Oh, Libbie, why do these things always happen around you?"

Liz put her hands over her face and shook her head. When she pulled her hands away she seemed to have reached a decision. She whispered, "Was it the voices? Are the voices back?"

Libbie was stricken mute.

"I thought that was finished years ago." Liz went on, "I thought all that craziness…the voices, the thinking you know and see stuff no one else does, all the emotional problems you had before were because of what happened at Grandmother's house. I thought you'd recovered. Josh convinced me you were okay. I wanted to believe it so much I put my children at risk." She gripped her fingers. Her knuckles turned white.

"I don't blame you, Libbie. You can't help it. It's just how you are, but I should've known better."

Cold settled over Libbie like a dark winter's night. She crossed her arms and turned away.

Liz grabbed her shoulders and spun Libbie roughly around to face her. She asked, "Are you hearing things again? Seeing shadows and things?"

Libbie clenched her fists, but held them close. She wouldn't strike out. She met Liz's stare eyeball for eyeball. With extreme force of will, she held herself immobile until she could breathe, until she could take a deep breath and expel it. When she was able, she lied, "No."

Liz blinked. She deflated abruptly and took several steps backward. "I need to take the children home. I need to speak with them, help them to understand."

She looked somewhere past Libbie as she said, "You put yourself on the line to protect my children as the situation seemed to you to require it. I respect that, but as their mother I can't allow them to be put at risk, to be exposed. I'm sorry. We're going now."

Libbie asked, "When did we ever discuss voices or shadows or anything else?" But she already knew the answer. Hadn't she known what Dr. Raymond was trying to tell her all those years ago? Yes, she knew, but she would've done almost anything to avoid acknowledging his betrayal.

Liz paused in her move toward the door. "Back when it happened with Grandmother, Dr. Raymond told Mother. She warned me...she told me so I'd know. She was trying to help. All she has ever wanted was to help you. She was worrying about you again the other day. She told me so. But you don't want help. Mother was right about that. You don't know the difference between reality and fantasy. She was right about that too." She broke off abruptly, wheeled across the foyer and vanished out the front door.

Libbie let her go. It was done. Over.

She stood at the window watching as Liz approached her car. She motioned to Adam who was standing nearby. They opened their car doors at the same time. As Adam climbed in, Max appeared from nowhere, racing across the yard, and jumped in with him. This time, he found the backseat acceptable.

As Liz's Benz went down the driveway. Libbie saw their faces, Max and Adam's, watching from the rear window. When the car reached the road, it turned south and disappeared.

Seeing their sad faces looking back eased some of the sharper pain. But it was over. She no longer had to worry about dogs or kids.

For the best. Probably.

They left. The police, Dan, Liz, the kids, everybody left. They all left *her*. She didn't belong in their lives.

****

Libbie contacted her attorney. There wasn't much else she could do while it all got sorted out.

The owner of the bulldozer reclaimed his heavy equipment as soon as the police gave permission. He didn't pause to peel the yellow crime scene tape away. The plastic ribbon trailed away from the oak and down along the driveway. One long streamer was stuck to a huge rear tire, dancing along the pavement as he drove away and vanished around the curve.

But the garage still stood.

****

Libbie requested her attorney's assistance with certain arrangements for sowing good will and mending fences—basic damage control. His reports back were optimistic. The "slather the bucks" technique she'd learned from Grandmother was proving effective. She'd heard nothing definite from law enforcement, but all signs indicated no one in a uniform was going to show up with an arrest warrant.

Dan didn't call. Neither did Liz or Josh. There were no visitors and Libbie issued no invitations. When she went outside, she stayed on the terrace. She sat at the wrought iron table and stared at the garage.

She held the little fat guy, Alice's ivory figurine. Libbie scratched at the dirt creased in the carving. She rubbed his pudgy tummy. Alice's gift from her husband.

Had Tommy figured out that Alice was going to sell the property and what that might mean?

Was it Tommy's fear she'd read? Or Alice's?

Had he frightened Alice and caused her to fall? Had he taken the figurine from her pocket as she lay dying? Libbie thought he must have done at least that.

She could do nothing about it or anything. Ever. It made her feel impotent and adrift. Pointless. Tommy was gone. Everyone was gone. They might as well be dead. In a very real way, to her, they were.

She made feeble attempts to resume her life. She cooked an egg. Washed the pan. Gathered clothing for a load of laundry, but forgot to start the machine. Every so often, she found herself pausing, listening and waiting for the phone to ring. After seeing the kid's photos on the wall too many times, she took them down and let the blank spaces speak for themselves. They echoed the void in her heart.

Empty. She was empty. She pressed her hands to the walls. Nothing. No colors. No flashes.

Mostly, she sat and stared at the walls.

Someone knocked on the door. When she heard the departing creak of the porch boards, she peeked out.

Not Dan. Not Jim.

Gladys Bennett. She paused in the driveway before opening her car door.

Libbie touched the doorknob, even wrapped her fingers around it before releasing it and stepping away. Back at the window, peeking around the curtain, she saw Henry was in the driver's seat with the window rolled down. Gladys said something and looked back at the house. Henry nodded and she walked around to the passenger side and climbed in.

She was almost curious and almost disappointed. She thought of Joyce. The Home must have her securely locked in. Unless she was upset about Tommy, too.

She had nothing to offer Joyce anyway. Rather, nothing but grief.

All she had left that she cared about in any way, shape or form was the garage. The need to destroy it grew larger to fill the emptiness. The compelling, overwhelming, mind-chewing need to destroy the garage and its contents oppressed her. It knocked at her brain and wouldn't desist. She tried to understand the obsession, but found no enlightenment, not even in her dreams.

Dreams? Nightmares. Black as pitch. No stars. No moon. The garage was shut up tightly. A red glow wavered around the frame of the side door, shimmering, hinting at the inferno raging inside.

When she awoke she lay in bed and considered the implications.

Fire would destroy the garage.

Chapter Twenty

Later that day, out on the terrace, Libbie inspected the propane tank attached to her gas grill. She ran her fingers across the cast iron hood and checked out the hose below the pan while she considered the possibility.

Silly thought, of course. It would yield such an explosion she'd lose the house, and maybe herself too. She was in a low spot, but she wasn't feeling suicidal.

Mary Lloyd stepped out of the woods. She crossed the yard slowly. That woman had been worn out and ground down before she was born. Libbie was glad the bulldozer was gone and not here for Mary to see.

Libbie stood by the gas grill and waited. Her face had a hard, chiseled aspect and her dress was stained, but when their eyes met, she stood straighter.

"You mind if I sit?" Mary pushed strings of hair behind her ear only to have them fall back across her face.

"Not at all. Please do." Libbie joined her at the table. "May I get you something to drink? Soda or coffee?"

"That's kind of you to offer, but no." Mary cleared her throat a couple of times. "I'm going to Warrenton to stay with my sister."

Mary cleared her throat again with a cough. "She's been after me to come for a long time, but what could I do? Wouldn't have done to take Tommy. Not with his problems. I guess I'll go." Her eyes rested on the bandage on Libbie's arm. "Nice grill. We used to have one some time back. Not nice like that one, though. Had to get rid of it anyhow. Tommy never did understand about fire. It was a problem for him.

"Anyway, she has a cat. My sister, that is. So that would never have worked. Tommy didn't understand pets. He tried to care for 'em. He loved 'em too much. We tried hamsters and different ones, but they got away and he couldn't figure how to keep 'em home, 'til he did, of course, and after that, well, we couldn't keep pets no more at all."

No pets for Tommy. Libbie wondered if she was as pale as she felt?

Mary shook her head. "Both times I let that gray dog loose and chased him off. My boy was crazy about that dog. Hated to disappoint my Tommy, but I couldn't allow him to hurt Miz Carson's dog." She waved her hands. "Not that he would've on purpose, but to make him stay, Tommy might've... The dog came back home, I guess?"

Libbie opened her mouth to ask Mary if she knew "her Tommy" had been crashing in the garage, but where was the value in asking? Except maybe to vent some of her own anger and disgust?

Mary looked at her hard. "When that lawyer of yours came knocking on my door, I didn't know what to think. He didn't tell me much either, but the price he offered for my land and house was more than fair. Now you own my old piece of property, I hope you'll get more joy of it than I ever did."

"Good luck in Warrenton, Mary. I'm sorry about Tommy."

She nodded. "Well, then, that's that. He's better off, I reckon. It'd gotten harder and harder to manage him." Her face brightened as a thought came to her. "It was charcoal. A charcoal grill. The kind you squirt lighter fluid on to ignite the coals." Mary scratched her scalp.

Lighter fluid. The idea began to sink roots into her brain, but there was a problem. In order to acquire it she'd have to leave the property. She didn't want to leave the protection of home. She was afraid that everyone, including strangers, would recognize her guilt. She'd read accusation in their eyes.

Before sunset, Dan came. He didn't knock or ring the doorbell when he arrived, but walked around to the back yard. Maybe he thought he'd find her there. Libbie watched him through the kitchen window. He was wearing his uniform and his tan deputy hat. He stared at the empty space where the bulldozer had been parked and shook his head. When he came back around front, he rang the doorbell.

Even though the drapes were drawn, Libbie stood in a corner away from the windows. She closed her eyes, held her breath and waited to hear the sound of his cruiser's engine starting. All Libbie could see were his cold eyes. A stranger's eyes. She wouldn't risk seeing that icy disgust again.

Jim showed up a few times. He'd done nothing wrong, but he would know by now what had happened. He'd always been kind to her, helped her, but she didn't think he'd envisioned this debacle when he claimed to be patient. She didn't want to see condemnation in Jim's eyes either.

Miller's Grocery surely sold lighter fluid. Libbie made it into the car and settled herself in the driver's seat, but once there, she fumbled with the keys and couldn't bring herself to start the car. Night fell. A damp chill settled over the vehicle, and inside too. The textured vinyl steering wheel cover made an uncomfortable pillow.

Defeated, she dragged herself back into the house. This was similar to what she experienced after Grandmother died, when she was not only a prisoner, but also her own jailer.

This time there was no Liz or Dr. Raymond to rescue her.

Libbie resisted sleep because her defenses were well-built, but couldn't withstand the onslaught of nightmares. She fell asleep despite herself.

From inside the garage, Libbie saw the flickering reddish light framing the door from the outside. A window high on the wall overlooked the dark city street in front of her grandmother's townhouse. Her fingers ached, clutching the window sill. Outside, the night street was damp with a light rain. The rain had raised a layer of oil, like an oil slick on the asphalt, tinted with the white of the street lights and the red of the stoplights. The shadows were illuminated in the midst of the night reflections, blood red and oily. Fiery. But the street was empty. Not even memories remained.

She'd come a long way from the unwanted child in Elizabeth Haven's house, the child who trusted her Uncle Phil and Liz, who'd betrayed her. She'd forgiven Liz long ago. Liz had been a child herself. Libbie had moved forward with her life, hadn't she?

She hadn't gone far. She'd been left behind, trapped, waiting alone in a cold, dark moment that no one was coming back to.

Before dawn, she awoke. Her pillow was damp from the tears she'd cried in her sleep. She was caught in a web of regrets and what-ifs, powerless against them.

She stood in the shower at five a.m. knowing she was lost. She leaned against the ceramic wall tiles, her face in her arms, and cried as the water streamed down her body. This was no journey into a dark place. This time the downward swing was like free-falling off a cliff with no hope of sunrise.

Dripping wet, she pulled her robe on, but couldn't do more than that and ended up back in bed.

Liz was correct. Margaret, Grandmother, and Uncle Phil

had figured it out—she was bad news. Living, walking bad news with a license to hurt.

Libbie had watched Mr. Bennett hook up the propane tank when he delivered the grill. It played in her head like a stage play. It would be easy to untwist the coupling and remove the tank. It would be lightweight after the cookout, but not empty.

Did propane work on the same principle as gas? That a half-empty tank was more dangerous than a full tank because of the accumulated fumes?

It felt theoretical. No more than an interesting question. But it got her back out of bed. She dropped the wet robe on the bed and dressed. Even combed her hair and brushed her teeth thinking about it.

She fixed a cup of coffee and walked outside to the terrace.

The garage door was rolled up and had been since the event with Tommy, a week past. Libbie set the tank on the ground just inside the open door.

She wanted to do it right. *To finally do something, anything right.* To feel something other than the pain inside.

Libbie sat at the wrought iron table contemplating coming events, including her own possible fate, and sipped coffee. She found peace in her decision. Painful memories of Liz, Dan, the kids, all faded into insignificance as she visualized the next steps, steeling herself to cross the threshold of the garage.

The propane tank was already in place. The ignition would be simple. It was easy to imagine. Twist the handle, open the valve. Let the fumes build around the nozzle. Strike the match.

Whoosh.

A small matchbox sat near at hand on the table. She

understood what came next, if it came next, so there was no rush. She could afford to listen to one or two more bird songs. She was in control now. She felt the pressure around her easing up and it felt good.

Short and good was preferable to longevity, if she was forever doomed to repeat...

Jim came around the corner of the house.

He looked well, as usual, and carried a small gift bag.

Leave it to Jim, she thought. Perfect timing. She couldn't repress a tiny smile. She tried to ignore the rough grief stirring uneasily below her calm veneer.

"Are you up to a visitor?" He stopped before reaching the table. "Mind if I join you?"

"Please do." A last visit with Jim? Why not? She'd always enjoyed his company.

He set the yellow gift bag on the table.

"I came by a few times. Your car was here, but you didn't seem to be home. I was worried."

He waited. Libbie kept her mouth shut.

Jim shrugged. "I understand the police are satisfied with the investigation and the witness statements. Looks like it's working out for you."

She hadn't expected him to jump straight into the ugliness. She stared down, fingering the handle of the coffee cup. She didn't want to think about Tommy and everything that had happened. She held her breath and waited for Jim to continue.

"If Tommy had died, it would've been more of a problem. As it is, he's where he should be. I hear it's a good facility. Maybe he'll get treatment that'll help him. Maybe it won't help him." Jim shrugged. "But all other events aside, if he'd stayed as he was, something bad was bound to happen. The countryside isn't as empty as it used to be. Lurking in the woods and in the dark around people's homes... Eventually, someone would've shot him." Jim added, "I heard you're contributing toward his expenses."

She nodded. Her attorney had worked out a number of things, including Tommy's care.

"Libbie, are you going to talk to me? Or should we talk about that propane tank sitting over there in front of the garage?" Jim reached over, pushed aside the matchbox and firmly pulled her hand away from the coffee cup.

His grip was strong and warm.

She found words. "You talked to Dan. He told you..."

"Yes, he feels responsible."

"For what?" She looked beyond Jim, to somewhere over his shoulder.

"For what happened. He tried to help Tommy, but outside of the legal system. If he'd gone to social services years ago, this wouldn't have happened. He's beating himself up over it."

She considered Jim's words, then shook her head.

"That's stupid."

"As stupid as you feeling guilty about what happened."

"Of course I feel guilty. I feel terrible." She was shocked by his attitude.

"Why? Because you tried to protect those children? When you do that—when you take a chance and put yourself on the line—you have to expect to take some hits. It's bold, but risky behavior."

Jim wrapped his fingers around her hand. "Sometimes you have to make your best guess and go with it. Sometimes it works out, sometimes it doesn't. Usually, the result is somewhere in-between."

"Platitudes sound good," Libbie scoffed. "But my family, Liz, the kids, are gone. Even my dog is gone."

He shook his head with a gentle smile on his lips and in his eyes. "You can't blame your cousin and you can't blame Dan."

"Blame them?"

"For letting you down." He wove his fingers through hers. "They are no more perfect that we are. They're a lot alike, did you figure that out? They're about rules. They like order."

Was he right? Liz did like rules. Jim made it sound like a flaw.

"So what's wrong with that? It works for them."

He continued, "It makes them uneasy when their orderly world is disrupted. You, Libbie, are a disrupter. You don't feel compelled to follow the rules. In fact, admit it, you don't even consider the rules most of the time, do you? Not seriously, anyway. That's bound to cause a clash and misunderstanding no matter how much everyone cares about each other. You forget, I've known Dan all my life. He's a great guy, and the same is true for Liz, at least from everything I've seen and heard?"

"Yes, she is. I've always admired her." Rules. Order. The same was true of Grandmother.

"When a person gets pushed beyond their comfort zone, they react badly."

Yeah, she knew about that.

"So you can't blame Liz or Dan and you can't let them define your life. And you can't hold it against them when they can't give you what you think you need."

Libbie tried to push his words away with weak sarcasm. "What I need? Like maybe a little support and acceptance?"

"Or approval?"

She shook inside and spoke to hide it. "Are you a rules person too?"

He grinned. "Sure, if the rules work for me." He released her fingers and sat back. "I have a serious question for you. Are you in love with Dan?"

So much for polite boundaries.

Libbie could only breathe. She closed her eyes and checked in her heart for the answer. She found it, but couldn't find the words to express it. Then a voice whispered sweeter words in her head. She held them close, not yet ready to speak them aloud.

Instead she said, "Did you just break a rule?"

He shook his head. "No, I made a new one."

Her eyes felt wet. She squeezed them shut, determined not to shed tears. When she opened them again, droplets on her lashes picked up the sunlight and sparkled. The yellow of the gift bag folded into that sparkly vision almost like a kaleidoscope.

Jim followed her gaze. "The bag?"

"Did you bring me a gift?"

"Not me. It was on your porch."

"My porch?" she echoed.

He pushed it across the table. "Open it."

Open it? Just like that? How did she get from matches and a propane tank to a yellow gift bag? She couldn't make that leap yet.

She said, "About Dan. I thought I might be falling in love and I was angry with him for rejecting me, for not supporting me when things went bad. Not having my back, I guess."

"And?"

"And." She pressed her fingers against the wrought iron until the edges bit in and hurt. "Maybe I was angry with him, but mostly with myself. He didn't ask me to hide, to shut myself away. That was all on me. And for all the wrong reasons."

She added, "Rules and approval? You may be right. Why couldn't I see it myself?"

Barry Raymond had tried to tell her things and she'd refused to hear. Was she so wrapped up in crap and what-if's and worrying about what she was or wasn't that she couldn't see the truth, no matter how obvious?

Yeah. She thought maybe he'd said something like that.

Libbie picked up the yellow bag. Half-expecting something unpleasant to jump out, she plucked at the white tissue paper and saw the corner of a card tucked in the side. Beneath the paper was one white candle. She took the candle from the bag and set it on the table.

The handwriting on the card was well-formed and feminine. She read aloud, "In the valley of deepest shadows, the light of one candle will show you the way. Just keep moving forward."

"It's from Gladys Bennett. The card says it's from Psalms. I don't know much about that, but I think I know what she's trying to tell me."

Gladys had added 'call me if you'd like to talk.' Libbie thought she might do that. She tucked the card back into the bag.

Keep moving forward and focus on the light?

There Jim was, sitting at the table, his beautiful eyes inviting and bold, and Libbie decided to take a chance.

"I have to tell you something."

He took her hand again. She felt the warmth. She could almost make out a color, but didn't try. She already knew they matched on some unknown level. Neither was more, or less, than the other.

Crazy or not, she said it. "I have to destroy the garage."

"Why?"

Libbie stared in amazement. It was the simplest of questions and she had the answer.

"Because I have to." She shook her head. "The building's rotting. It's been used...inappropriately. It smells like my grandmother's basement. Seeing it makes me think of not being good enough, not being wanted. Unworthy. I have to obliterate it or I'll have no peace."

"Your grandmother's basement?"

"Shall I tell you how she died?"

He nodded never taking his eyes from her face.

"She fell. She fell from the fourth floor balcony. I was inches away. For more than ten years I've been reliving it, wondering if...if I'd tried harder...could I have grabbed her in time?" Libbie looked at her empty hands.

Had she felt the silky fabric of Grandmother's dress slip through her fingers? Or did she imagine that later just to add to her torture?

"We'd had yet another argument. So much anger. I have asked myself over and over...did I hold back because of what had gone on between us?"

Jim brought her hand to his cheek. "I know the answer."

"What is it?"

"You couldn't reach her in time."

"How do you know?"

"Because had it been possible, no matter what had happened between you, you would have saved her. That's who you are."

Her heart cried in her chest. It tried to push through the muscles and flesh. She gasped from the pain and pressed her fist over it.

He asked, "Do you still want to destroy the garage?"

Libbie nodded.

Jim looked at her sideways. He appeared to give her

words careful consideration. Did he think she was crazy?

"It's your property." He shrugged. "Do as you want."

She liked the sound of that very much. Whether she was seeking peace wasn't the point. Jim was right. Her motives were her own business. She was in control of her life. It was her choice to keep control or to relinquish it.

He shook his head. "But not with the propane tank. Definitely not."

"No, I suppose not." She examined her fingers. So he'd understood her intentions with the tank. More strongly, she looked at him and said, "Of course not."

She picked up the box of matches and rattled it. "I could burn it?"

"There are state and local laws about burning out of doors."

Jim's expression and voice were without expression or intonation. Was he joking? She hadn't thought about local ordinances. It hadn't seemed important given other considerations.

He continued, "State law requires the barrel, or in this case, the garage, be at least 300 feet from the woods."

This time she read the laughter in his eyes. She felt a smile growing in her, but she was afraid. She set the matchbox down on the table.

"I wouldn't want to get in trouble with the law again."

"Not for a while anyway," Jim agreed. "Give the authorities a rest. They've earned it."

Jim took her hand again. "Maybe you should get away for a while. See some new sights. Do you like to travel?"

"This is my home. I don't want to leave."

"You can always come back. A trip abroad isn't forever. Home will still be here when you return."

That was an interesting way to phrase it. Travel abroad.

Not forever. Home will be here waiting. She'd heard similar words from Barry Raymond. She'd sent him away rather than risk being hurt.

"Libbie, if you want to destroy the garage, I can loan you a sledgehammer."

A sledgehammer? He was joking again, but the idea of personally pounding the garage to pieces gave her a glow.

She looked at him, recognizing what he was doing. Jim was gently drawing her out of her misery.

"You have friends here. You don't have to manage everything by yourself."

He added, "Why don't we discuss it over lunch? Get out of here for an hour or so. When we get back, I might be interested in taking a few swings myself."

She clasped his hand in return. What would Jim think if he knew how unhealthy it was to be close to her? To care about her? Would that amazing light in his eyes be replaced by shadows?

Aunt Margaret—she'd decided to ignore her a long time ago, hadn't she?

Looking at Jim, the candle on the table between them, Libbie saw what Gladys was talking about. It was that light on the other side of the darkness. She placed the matchbox beside the candle. A much better use for them.

She wasn't ready to check out. There was always light on the other side. She knew that. She'd just forgotten. It took a friend to help her remember.

Guilt and regret would likely return to visit again. Shadows? Dark moods? She refused them, at least for the time being. Her voices—they might not be the norm, but they were pieces of her and she owned them.

You are who you are. And so are they.

It made no more sense to be angry at Liz and Dan for

being who they were, than to blame Grandmother for her lack of empathy and failure to love.

Shouldn't such a realization be personally shattering? Maybe before, but now it just seemed obvious.

Libbie thought she might feel up to facing life again, but this time with a little help from a dear friend. More than a friend.

"I'd be delighted to join you for lunch, but..." She smoothed her hair and brushed at her blouse. "I need to freshen up."

"No rush. I'll wait for you."

She stood. "I wish—I just wish–" She sighed. "I'll miss the kids so much."

"Sure you will." He stood too, and put his arms around her. "But you can't live someone else's life. You have to build your own."

"You make it sound easy."

"It's not that hard. Just make sure you're using the right materials and your plans are sound, then have a little faith."

He nodded toward the garage and tightened his hug, asking "You weren't going to light that tank, were you?"

The matches lay on the table. The tank was in the garage. Hard to ignore all that, or pretend it didn't have meaning, but now, with Jim here, and the air lighter and the sun shining, it seemed so foolish, so unlikely.

She shook her head. "I don't know. Or yes, I was thinking about it, but I don't know if I would've done it. You came along and now I guess I'll never know and I'm glad."

"Everyone has down times, Libbie. Don't judge yourself so harshly."

Her eyes felt wet and her bottom lip threatened to tremble. She shook it off and made a smile happen. Yes, she was in control.

She was almost to the back door when Jim spoke again. "Grab your camera while you're in there."

Libbie turned toward him. "Why?"

"There's some scenic spots around here you might like to shoot. I'll take you there." He grinned. "You've got some empty space left on those walls. Let's fill them up."

"I'll be back in a sec. Wait for me. We have some building to do."

As she stepped inside the house and headed for the bathroom mirror, it occurred to her—she should make some new rules, too.

She stopped short, her hand on the door frame.

A flush of warmth tinted with the soft color of a newly budded spring rose, rushed up her arm. Those sweet words she'd heard in her head while on the terrace came back to her.

Forgive yourself. Forgive Elizabeth.

She owed Dan an apology, for sure, but she didn't think she'd ever offer it, and he'd probably prefer it that way. Dan and Liz, both.

New rules, indeed. Forgive herself. Forgive her grandmother.

She snapped on the light and picked up the hairbrush.

Primping?

Not only new rules, but it was also time to learn some new habits.

****

Libbie came out the back door, purse and camera bag hanging from her shoulders, ready to take a chance, to face again this confusing thing called life. Jim was standing on the terrace speaking with someone.

Correction—*someones*—Josh, Adam and a panting dog.

Max met her halfway up the steps. He jumped, nearly knocking her down, intent on bathing her face. She put her arms around him and stepped backward, fighting for balance.

"Down, boy." But she said it gently and kept her face turned away from her visitors.

Adam approached the steps.

Josh, right behind him, said, "He's your dog, Libbie. He was content to visit for a day, but not to stay."

Max positioned himself on the steps, half-sitting, half-lying across the steps, but staying close to her. She put the purse and bag on the step and bent to scratch his head.

Adam said, "He kept barking at the door, wanting out. He wanted to go home."

"The last time he escaped," Josh added, "I found him several miles away headed in this direction. Max belongs here."

"He does." She repeated, "He belongs here at home, at Cub Creek, with me."

Josh stepped up to where she stood. He approached her tentatively and hugged her, ever so gently. He whispered in her ear, "Thank you for keeping my children safe. I owe you, Libbie, in ways I can never repay."

He stepped back and ruffled Adam's hair. "We'd better get going."

Libbie's eyes were wet. Her eyesight blurred. She nodded, unable to speak. As Josh and Adam reached the corner of the house, Adam smiled sadly and waved.

She descended the last two steps to the terrace. That last image of Josh and Adam...she stared after them imprinting that image in her memory like a still photograph.

From behind, Jim's arms slid around her waist. She sank into them, resting her head back against his chest.

He asked, "You okay?"

She put her hands on his arms, holding him as he held her. "I'm fine. In fact, never better. I mean that."

And she was. She would be okay. Alone, if necessary. Even better with Jim and Max.

Max stayed close. He sat again, this time on her feet.

"Jim? Those empty spaces you mentioned?" She looked down at Max and squeezed Jim's arms. "I think a couple have already been filled."

"It's a good start, but it's just the beginning."

Libbie laughed softly. Max lifted his head and looked at her and she was pretty sure he was smiling. She was, for sure.

****

From a news article clipped from the local weekly paper dated September 8th

Joyce saved it for her:

LOCAL GARAGE EXPLODES - An evening blaze in a detached garage on Cub Creek Loop in Louisa County destroyed the building, but the residence suffered only minor damage. Sgt. Dan Wheeler and Cpl. A. W. Hoskins of the sheriff's office were first responders to the report called in by an unidentified passing motorist who noticed flames in the branches of a large oak over the engulfed garage. It is believed the fire was connected to a loud explosion heard by nearby residents. The Volunteer Fire Department arrived on scene shortly after Officers Wheeler and Hoskins and prevented significant damage to the home. The Emergency Services Coordinator was unable to positively identify the cause of the explosion, but suspected it was related to a propane tank found in the ashes. It is believed the propane tank had been removed from a gas grill on the patio behind the main residence and left in the garage. It is not known who placed the tank in the garage or when. There were no injuries and no one was in residence at the time. A family friend, Mrs. Joyce Inman of Louisa County, reported the garage had recently been in the process of renovation and that the owner, Ms. Libbie Havens, was on vacation with her fiancé, Jim Mitchell, in Sicily at the time of the incident.

THE END

ABOUT THE AUTHOR

Whether writing novels of contemporary romance and suspense or women's fiction with suspense and mystery, Grace Greene always has a strong heroine at the heart of each story.

A Virginia native, Grace has family ties to North Carolina. She writes books set in both locations.

The Emerald Isle books are set in North Carolina where *"It's always a good time for a love story and a trip to the beach."*

Or travel down Virginia Country Roads and *"Take a trip to love, mystery and suspense."*

Grace lives in central Virginia. Stay current with Grace's releases and appearances.

Contact her at www.gracegreene.com.

You'll also find Grace here:

Twitter:
@Grace_Greene

Facebook:
https://www.facebook.com/GraceGreeneBooks

Goodreads:
http://www.goodreads.com/Grace_Greene

Amazon:
http://amazon.com/author/gracegreene

Other Books by Grace Greene

If you enjoyed CUB CREEK, you might enjoy these novels:

BEACH RENTAL   (Emerald Isle #1)

<u>RT Book Reviews</u> – Sept. 2012 - 4.5 stars TOP PICK

No author can even come close to capturing the awe-inspiring essence of the North Carolina coast like Greene. Her debut novel seamlessly combines hope, love and faith, like the female equivalent of Nicholas Sparks. ...you'll hear the gulls overhead and the waves crashing onto shore.

<u>Brief Description</u>:

On the Crystal Coast of North Carolina, in the small town of Emerald Isle...

Juli Cooke, hard-working and getting nowhere fast, marries a dying man, Ben Bradshaw, for a financial settlement, not expecting he will set her on a journey of hope and love. The journey brings her to Luke Winters, a local art dealer, but Luke resents the woman who married his sick friend and warns her not to hurt Ben—and he's watching to make sure she doesn't.

Until Ben dies and the stakes change.

Framed by the timelessness of the Atlantic Ocean and the brilliant blue of the beach sky, Juli struggles against her past, the opposition of Ben's and Luke's families, and even the living reminder of her marriage—to build a future with hope and perhaps to find the love of her life—if she can survive the danger from her past.

BEACH WINDS   *(Emerald Isle #2)*

RT Book Reviews – June. 2014 - 4.5 stars TOP PICK

Greene's follow up to Beach Rental is exquisitely written with lots of emotion. Returning to Emerald Isle is like a warm reunion with an old friend. Readers will be inspired by the captivating story where we get to meet new characters and reconnect with a few familiar faces. The author highlights family relationships which many may find similar to their own, and will have you dreaming of strolling along the shore to rediscover yourself.

Brief Description:

Off-season at Emerald Isle ~ In-season for secrets of the heart

Frannie Denman has been waiting for her life to begin. After several false starts, and a couple of broken hearts, she ends up back with her mother until her elderly uncle gets sick and Frannie goes to Emerald Isle to help manage his affairs.

Frannie isn't a 'beach person,' but decides her uncle's home, *Captain's Walk,* in winter is a great place to hide from her troubles. But Frannie doesn't realize that winter is short in Emerald Isle and the beauty of the ocean and seashore can help heal anyone's heart, especially when her uncle's handyman is the handsome Brian Donovan.

Brian has troubles of his own. He sees himself and Frannie as two damaged people who aren't likely to equal a happy 'whole' but he's intrigued by this woman of contradictions.

Frannie wants to move forward with her life. To do that she needs questions answered. With the right information there's a good chance she'll be able to affect not only a change in her life, but also a change of heart.

KINCAID'S HOPE   *(Virginia Country Roads)*

<u>RT Book Reviews</u> – Aug. 2012 - 4 STARS

A quiet, backwater town is the setting for intrigue, deception and betrayal in this exceptional sophomore offering. Greene's ability to pull the reader into the story and emotionally invest them in the characters makes this book a great read.

<u>Jane Austen "Book Maven"</u> - May 2012 - 5 STARS

This is a unique modern-day romantic suspense novel, with eerie gothic tones—a well-played combination, expertly woven into the storyline.

<u>Brief Description</u>:

Beth Kincaid left her hot temper and unhappy childhood behind and created a life in the city free from untidy emotionalism, but even a tidy life has danger, especially when it falls apart.

In the midst of her personal disasters, Beth is called back to her hometown of Preston, a small town in southwestern Virginia, to settle her guardian's estate. There, she runs smack into the mess she'd left behind a decade earlier: her alcoholic father, the long-ago sweetheart, Michael, and the poor opinion of almost everyone in town.

As she sorts through her guardian's possessions, Beth discovers that the woman who saved her and raised her had secrets, and the truths revealed begin to chip away at her self-imposed control.

Michael is warmly attentive and Stephen, her ex-fiancé, follows her to Preston to win her back, but it is the man she doesn't know who could forever end Beth's chance to build a better, truer life.

A STRANGER IN WYNNEDOWER

(Virginia Country Roads)

<u>Bookworm Book Reviews</u> – January 2013 - 5 STARS

I loved this book! It is Beauty and the Beast meets mystery novel! The story slowly drew me in and then there were so many questions that needed answering, mysteries that needed solving! ...Sit down and relax, because once you start reading this book, you won't be going anywhere for a while! Five stars for a captivating read!

<u>Brief Description:</u>

Love and suspense with a dash of Southern Gothic...

Rachel Sevier, a thirty-two year old inventory specialist, travels to Wynnedower Mansion in Virginia to find her brother who has stopped returning her calls. Instead, she finds Jack Wynne, the mansion's bad-tempered owner. He isn't happy to meet her. When her brother took off without notice, he left Jack in a lurch.

Jack has his own plans. He's tired of being responsible for everyone and everything. He wants to shake those obligations, including the old mansion. The last thing he needs is another complication, but he allows Rachel to stay while she waits for her brother to return.

At Wynnedower, Rachel becomes curious about the house and its owner. If rumors are true, the means to save Wynnedower Mansion from demolition are hidden within its walls, but the other inhabitants of Wynnedower have agendas, too. Not only may Wynnedower's treasure be stolen, but also the life of its arrogant master.

Chapter One

Rachel Sevier stared at the monstrous stone house, and its rows of blank, dirty windows stared back.

She'd driven from Baltimore to Virginia, to this area called Goochland. After leaving the interstate, there'd been a pocket of shiny new construction—a small shopping center and houses—but that snippet of civilization was quickly gone and then she was deep in the woods.

Jeremy had given her directions: drive until the trees crowd in close and the road looks like it's about to end, then keep driving. She had.

Wynnedower Mansion, built of gray stone and mellow wood, looked out of place, as if a giant hand had plucked it from the gently rolling hills of England, dropped it into this clearing, and left it to rot amid honeysuckle vines and Virginia creeper.

Not quite what she'd expected. To her, the word 'mansion' meant something a little more upscale.

Gnats swarmed in the humidity. Rachel shooed them away. Hers was the only car here, and there was no one else, including Jeremy, anywhere in sight.

Several weeks ago, with graduation barely behind him, he'd told her he was taking a job at Wynnedower as a caretaker. He already had a real job in Richmond and was supposed to be preparing for graduate studies, but he wanted to be independent. *It's a great deal, Rachel,* he'd said. *No rent in exchange for part-time caretaking.*

Caretaking? Really? She adored her baby brother, six-foot-two, golden-haired and smart—so different from her own appearance that no one believed they were related until they saw their eyes. There was no mistaking their unusual eye color. But handsome or not, he wasn't trained in security and had no handyman skills. The worst of it was he'd stopped returning her calls two weeks ago, right after he told her he'd met a girl. He'd said it in that special way in which *girl* didn't just mean girl—it meant everything bright and shiny and worth living for.

It was a big sister's job to inject reality and practicality and she'd done her duty. He hadn't appreciated it, and it wasn't the first time they'd disagreed, but he'd never stopped talking to her before.

Finally, she gave in to worry and moved up her visit. Luckily, the change in timing worked for her current job and for the new job she hoped to get, but she needed to find her brother before she could get on with her plans.

She tucked her cell phone and keys into the pockets of her suit jacket and locked her purse in the car.

Scraggly bushes obscured the ground level of the house. A wide stairway bypassed that level and led to the main floor. Rachel paused at the entrance. A broken doorbell dangled by a wire. She settled for knocking.

There was no shade on the porch. She tapped her shoe, tugged at the neck of her blouse and fanned the front of her jacket. She should've waited until after she'd arrived before getting into this suit.

The suit was out of place here. Dressy and expensive, it was not in the budget, but it made a bold statement and was perfect for the event she planned to attend in Richmond that evening. She straightened her skirt, brushed off a speck of lint, and knocked again.

No answer. She tested the knob, barely touching it, yet the door swung slowly inward on silent hinges.

The foyer was the size of her apartment living room, but without a stick of furniture or decoration. Ahead, a wide opening led to an even larger room.

She leaned inside and called out, "Jeremy?"

Her voice traveled through unseen rooms and echoed back emptiness.

Rachel stepped inside and eased the front door closed.

As she crossed the bare wood of the foyer her heels clattered. No one had responded to her call; she was surely alone here. Even so, she removed her shoes and tucked them under her arm.

This room was vast and high-ceilinged. The walls were a mess of half-stripped wallpaper and dingy paint, and none of the work looked recent, but the air was surprisingly, deliciously cool. She paused to soak it in. To her right, a wide staircase climbed halfway to the second floor, did a U-turn and continued upward.

Did she dare? Yes, she'd risk anything for Jeremy.

Dark wood balusters led the way. Upstairs, doors and shadowy alcoves ringed a spacious landing. A hallway continued onward, but she didn't follow it because the only light filtered up by way of the stairs. The doors on the landing each presented the same paneled surface with faceted glass door knobs set into cast iron plates.

She turned the knob of the nearest door. Locked. The door directly across was locked, too. She stooped to peer through the keyhole.

A gruff shout jolted her. "What are you doing?"

He was a tall man, broad and unshaven, with long, unruly black hair. His jeans were rumpled and worn, and marred by paint smears. He wore an unbuttoned, wrinkled cotton shirt over a white t-shirt.

Rachel stumbled back a few steps, then steadied herself. She pointed her spiked heels at him. "Who are you?"

The dark hall deepened the shadows beneath his brows, making his face impossible to read. She felt his eyes take in her shoes, her suit, then drop down to her nearly bare feet.

She felt even shorter than she was.

"You're trespassing. Get out," he said, his voice rough and uncompromising.

"Is Jeremy Sevier here?"

"If you're a jilted girlfriend, that's not my problem. If you're hunting antiques, you're a looter."

"Looter?" Outrage pushed her fear aside. "I'm his sister. Where's Jeremy?"

"Sister? He didn't leave a note. Get out." He turned and walked toward the alcove.

"Wait, tell me what you mean. He left? Why?"

He looked back. "Ask him when you find him."

"You said he didn't leave a note. What did you mean?"

"What I said. He didn't notify the property management company he was leaving, so unless he sends a postcard from wherever, I don't expect to hear from him."

Fear curled up hard and cold in her belly. "How can you be sure he simply left?"

"What?"

"That something didn't happen to him?"

He moved a few, deliberate steps toward her. "If it did, it didn't happen here."

Past her first shock and with her eyes better adjusted to the low light, Rachel realized that his clothing, though shabby, was clean. She detected a whiff of soap. The wild hair that had looked stringy was actually still drying, and the stubble on his face obscured the strong bone structure.

"Are you the owner?"

He made a rude noise. "Owner? Right." He pointed at the stairs. "The door is that way. Leave or I'll call the police. Trespassing is a crime." He walked off, dismissing her.

Rachel waited, breathless, disbelieving his behavior and expecting him to return. Her hands fisted. This man was no help. An impediment, that's all he was. And he'd left, arrogantly assuming she'd follow orders, so he was also foolish.

She went to the stairs, but only descended a few steps, then waited as the sound of his footfalls grew distant. If she moved quickly, she could check the other doors before he returned.

The door opposite the alcove was unlocked. It opened. The brighter light straggling in through the grimy window was a welcome sight.

The corded plaid spread on the bed—she recognized it. She'd purchased one for Jeremy years earlier. He'd taken it with him to college, and this one was bedraggled enough to have been in use for a decade, but it was a common style and proved nothing, really.

A comb, a few pennies and a green dry cleaners' tag littered the top of the dresser. Old paperbacks were stacked in a corner. Nothing identifiable as Jeremy's.

Unlike the floor below, the air up here was musty and hot. Rachel tossed her shoes onto the bed. Through the window, she saw her car below. She pushed up on the window sash. It was out of alignment and budged only one stubborn inch. She gained another inch on the second try but left it at that lest she break a nail. After all, she had plans for the evening, plus the job interview in the morning.

Rachel shrugged off her suit jacket and hung it on the door knob. With the door open and the window up a bit, the fresher air made the heat more bearable. The silk shell stuck to her back. She pulled it away from her damp skin.

She searched the room. The closet was empty except for plastic hangers. In the drawers, she found a few socks with threadbare heels and an old pair of jeans. There were so few personal items. Yet this was where she'd expected to find him and she found it hard to give up that idea. Then she hit jackpot—a sweater she'd given him two Christmases ago.

Relief washed over her. She leaned against the dresser, elbows resting on the scarred wood and her face in her hands. Jeremy hadn't been a kid in a long time, but she'd raised him, bandaged his scrapes and fussed at him to do his homework. As he grew and towered over her, she'd worked to support him. He'd always be her baby brother and he was the only family she had left.

The lack of possessions in the room suggested he'd moved out, at least in part, perhaps in haste. Next, she'd talk to his employer—his real employer, not this guy.

Who was this man, anyway? A handyman? A new caretaker? Had Jeremy already been replaced? She slapped the top of the dresser.

A waft of cooler breeze caught her by surprise and caressed her face. She closed her eyes, relishing the relief brought by the stronger draft—until the door slammed shut.

Continued...   A Stranger in Wynnedower is available in print and eformat via the usual booksellers.

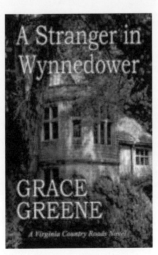

Thank you for purchasing

CUB CREEK.

I hope you enjoyed it!

Other books by Grace Greene

Emerald Isle Novels

Love. Suspense. Inspiration.

BEACH RENTAL
(July 2011)

BEACH WINDS
(November 2013)

Virginia Country Roads Novels

Love. Mystery. Suspense.

CUB CREEK
(April 2014)

A STRANGER
IN WYNNEDOWER
(October 2012)

KINCAID'S HOPE
(January 2012)

Always with a strong heroine at its heart.

www.GraceGreene.com

Made in the USA
San Bernardino, CA
11 June 2014